THE ESTELUSTI TRAIL

Books by Roy V. Gaston

How Can a Man Die Better

PETE HORSE SERIES
Beyond the Goodnight Trail
The Estelusti Trail

Coming Soon!
PETE HORSE SERIES
The Trail of Yellow Wolf

ESTELUSTI TRAIL

Roy V. Gaston

SPEAKING VOLUMES, LLC
NAPLES, FLORIDA
2023

The Estelusti Trail

ISBN 978-1-64540-959-5

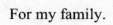
For my family.

Acknowledgments

A huge thank you to my sister Debra Gaston Brigman, without whom my books could never be written.

Chapter One

MURDER OF WILEY THOMPSON
DEC. 28, 1835
FORT KING, NEAR THE WITHLACOOCHEE RIVER, CENTRAL FLORIDA

Wiley Thompson, Indian Agent to the Seminole, paused and lit his cigar. It would be the last of his life. We had come to kill him. Throughout the night eighty warriors crept through the dark Withlacoochee swamps to this saw palmetto thicket in the black shadow of the ancient forest. We were Seminole and Estelusti, what the whites called the Black Seminole.

Thompson stood on a small knoll a hundred paces away. Beside him was Lt. Constantine Smith. The two men were enjoying their customary afternoon stroll down the wagon road outside Fort King. They laughed, sharing a joke. They looked right at us without seeing. I could smell their cigars.

Two hundred yards beyond the men, Erastus Rogers and his clerks labored at the sheds and wagons of the territorial trading post. They bellowed and guffawed and cursed without looking our way. A half-mile away, the gates to Fort King stood open. A small herd of cattle and a couple dozen horses grazed in the pasture.

No one saw Osceola's rifle barrel move just a hair's width, keeping the bead squarely on Thompson's chest. No one saw a sliver of sunlight glint off the scrolled 42-inch barrel that fired a .58 caliber ball. No one saw the hunter and stag engraved silver side-plate on the striped-maple butt of the rifle that had been a gift from Thompson to Osceola just six months ago. It was his apology for laughing while the MacCuaigs raped Osceola's wife.

Willet's hand lightly squeezed mine, but I gave no response. I did not look at her. I wanted to turn and run, but I could not. Not in front of Osceola, or Willet, and especially not my brother John.

Osceola pulled the trigger. The rifle roared, belching flame and smoke. The gun performed better than Thompson's apology. The .58 caliber ball blew a hole through Thompson's chest, lifting him off his feet and dropping him on his back on the damp coquina road.

Like a thunderclap, eighty rifles fired. The trees shook as birds took flight. The bodies of Thompson and Smith jerked as musket balls slammed into them. Bullets peppered the fort's walls. Our whooping, war-painted warriors burst from the trees. Rogers and his men ran for the safety of the trading post's stockade, but the thick-bodied laborers were no match for our sprinters. The soldiers in guard towers ducked out of sight and the gates of the fort slammed shut as the traders went down under an ax and knife swinging frenzy.

Bare chested, Osceola stood over the body of Thompson, howling his triumph like a wolf. Blood streamed down his arm as he pumped a fistful of scalp-skin and hair at the fort. Thompson's scalp belonged to Osceola, to right the egregious wrong. It did not matter who took the scalp of Smith. Half his head had been blown off anyway. One warrior sliced off a dangling flap of hair and skin as another sawed at his remaining ear. More swarmed over Rogers and his men. Willet and I hurried toward the trading post but stayed back from the rampaging mob.

"Go now, Little Sister," Osceola shouted to Willet as we passed, blood streaked across his triumphant face and dripping down his heaving chest. "Hurry to the war camp. Tell Micanopy and Alligator we have succeeded but will toy with these cowardly dogs a while longer. When we tire of shaming them, we will be on our way."

"No, I will leave after I have collected my share of the plunder. Those men wronged me also, and I will take my pay," said Willet. Only Willet dared speak this way to Osceola, the most ferocious fighter among the Seminole. But she did, sometimes like a feisty dog pulling at a pants cuff. Osceola was married to Willet's older sister.

"Very well," said Osceola. "But do not tarry."

We ran for the main storeroom, darting around the warriors who danced and frolicked across the yard, firing their guns in the air, and shouting insults and challenges at the fort. The gates to the fort stayed shut and no soldiers' rifles appeared in the loopholes.

Our warriors could afford to be bold. There was little fear that the soldiers would come out and fight. We had watched the fort for weeks and knew its routines down to the minute, including Thompson's stroll and favorite brand of cigar. We knew most of the garrison had marched out weeks ago, to protect the terrified civilians cowering in Fort Drane. Only sixty of the soldiers inside the walls were fit for duty. The remainder were bedridden due to the diseases of the Florida Swamp.

I would not waste bullets firing nor time dancing, but I felt the same thrill our jubilant warriors did. I felt the lightning bolts of excitement and crashing waves of relief and something like joy. I had felt the same fear creeping through the swamps and the same exhilaration when Osceola's bullet tore through Jesup's heart. We had finally struck back against the Americans after months of waiting in dread and anger and fear, and we now had the mighty American army cowering behind the walls of their fort. Many of our young men had wanted this fight, had yearned and thirsted for it. I did not. I had only followed my brother, who fought because he said our people would be enslaved and erased from the earth otherwise. Still, the thrill was there, but time was precious.

We pushed our way through the celebrating mob at the door. Inside I tripped over a fourth body, that of Robin Rogers, the young nephew of the trader. His slender chest had been blown apart by musket balls and his blond scalp was gone. He had not been a bad boy.

We ran down the dark, narrow, cluttered aisles, shoving our way through warriors who had become happy, chattering boys as they tussled over coveted prizes. We grabbed what we came for and ran blinking back into the sunlight. Outside, chaos reigned. Buildings had been ransacked and storehouses raided, and our men pillaged and tromped through the wreckage.

Warriors danced around in unfamiliar boots and hats, waving their new rifles and pistols. They showed off their other trophies, the bags of coffee beans, sacks of tobacco and silver coins. Barrels of white flour had been smashed open and warriors cavorted through it, throwing handfuls on each other and kicking up a cloud.

The coops, corrals and animal pens and storehouses had been smashed open. Warriors chased the livestock with gleeful abandon. Hooting men hopped alongside flat-eared, hee-hawing, high-kicking mules, trying to strap packsaddles onto the obstinate beasts. Hundreds of frantic laying hens ran around in squawking horror, freed from the darkness of their flimsy sheds only to be chased around by ghostly, flour-dusted phantoms. Snorting hogs and squealing piglets wiggled and wriggled and shot out of the grasp of laughing, diving pursuers.

Only Osceola maintained his rage, taunting the fort with Thompson's bloody scalp as he cursed the cowardly soldiers. John, Yah-hah and Lutcha, two Seminole sub-chiefs, stood watching, bent with laughter and passing a bottle of rum. As we ran past them a blur of white came hurtling at my head. I threw my arms up but was knocked off my feet. A few feet away, a disheveled chicken with an oddly bent neck clucked and flopped weakly in the dirt. The flour-faced boy who'd been chasing the hen looked hungry so I gave the bird a kick. He tossed it in a sack bulging with a few others and took off at a sprint.

***

Gliding down the crooked Withlacoochee River, we sang our victory songs. Our cypress dugouts rode low in the water, loaded down with much more loot than any expected. The entire trading post had been emptied. Our warriors rocked with laughter as they recounted the attack or waved a great trophy. The army had been embarrassed. A great wrong had been avenged. The good spirits were lifted even more by the trading post rum being passed around.

I watched Willet's back. She was the only female warrior taking part in the attack. It was my 15th winter, and the 16th for her. She had been a big, ungainly and awkward looking girl when we were little children. She was tall for a girl, and very dark skinned. Her mother had been a full Negro slave and her father was a full-blooded Red Stick Creek. She had been a shrill and annoying pest. Lately I had noticed she wasn't.

She and her father Mateo had come to live on my family's home island more than a year ago, after their village had been raided and burned. Mateo had once been a great warrior, but now he was very old. Injuries had left him nearly crippled, but he was the best arrow and bow maker among our people. Hunters came from all over Florida to trade for them, but he always saved the best for his daughter.

She did not wear the loose blouse and long skirts of a Seminole woman. Instead, she looked more like a small version of an American backwoodsman. Her hair hung in a long braid, and she wore buckskins. Willet rarely engaged in typical womanly pursuits. She preferred to be out in the forest or beating boys at horse races and archery. I was not sure what I thought about that. Lately, I really wasn't sure of much when I thought about her, but I found myself thinking about her often. Now I was thinking about what this day meant for me and her, and for all our people.

Early last spring Thompson had called all the Seminole chiefs together and told them they had to vacate all our territory in Florida forever. Thompson declared that January 1st, 1836 was the deadline set by the terms of the Treaty of Payne's Landing, signed three years before. He told the chiefs that if they did not comply, President Andrew Jackson would send his mighty army in to remove us.

Micanopy and our Council of Chiefs protested angrily. They told Thompson that only minor chiefs had signed the treaty, and they did not represent the Seminole tribe. Our chiefs said bribes had been paid. The treaty-signers came forward and told Thompson that they had been threatened, coerced, and tricked. Finally, our leaders protested that even if the treaty were valid, we had been told we could stay until 1842, still seven years away. Thompson laughed in their faces and called them dishonest, dishonorable, and bickering old women.

We made ourselves ready. Fishermen and salvage divers from the Bahama Islands smuggled in rifles and gunpowder. Our gardens and fields doubled and tripled in size, and our villages stayed smoky from racks of drying fish and meat. Many councils were held where the men fasted and prayed and smoked their pipes. That summer our people held the longest, most well-attended Dance of the Green Corn that any Seminole could ever remember. The warriors drank the black drink to purify their bodies and put iron in their hearts. Old tribal grudges were put aside. We would stand united against a common enemy.

Our spies in the forts and port towns had watched as hundreds of volunteers assembled at coastal forts, eager for a chance to fight us. They told us when the steamships arrived in Tampa Bay, waiting to take us across the Gulf in chains. We watched from the shadows as more slave trackers prowled the territory, hoping to collect bounties. Three days ago, our spies had told us a column of soldiers had marched out of Fort Brook near Tampa, headed to Fort King.

"I hope Micanopy and Alligator were as successful as we were," I said. There had been a second attack planned for today. Ours was the attack on Wiley Thompson and the trading post. Micanopy would lead the other, against the column marching from Fort Brook.

"I have not so much confidence in Micanopy," she said. "But I do have faith in Alligator and Jumper and the other micos. They will not allow him to falter. We have planned too long and carefully to make mistakes or have lapses in courage."

Micanopy was the hereditary chief of the Seminole, but his authority was mostly symbolic. He had profited nicely from a friendly relationship with the Americans and was not eager to fight them. If not for his sense-maker Abraham advising him to resist, most knew Micanopy would have meekly moved west and continued his comfortable life.

Osceola was different. His hatred of the Americans and their Creek lapdogs burned hotter than fire. For years he had suffered greatly at their hands. Osceola had been elected our war chief after his defiant acts of valor and fiery rhetoric had aroused in us his same hot passion for war. All the chiefs and warriors pledged him their loyalty.

"Perhaps Thompson should not have given Osceola that fancy rifle," I said.

"Osceola would have killed him regardless," said Willet. "Perhaps Thompson should not have scoffed when Chechoter and I were kidnapped, nor laughed as Osceola begged for Chechoter's freedom."

***

The moon was high and bright as we entered the Wahoo Swamp, slipping down the narrow streams. The drums and the orange glow above the trees guided us to the war camp. Shouts and songs reached us as we made the last turn of the winding stream.

Never had I heard such a loud celebration. Four hundred warriors celebrated in the field, and hundreds more had joined the revelry. A pole the height of three men stood between the two largest fires. The pole was carved and painted, and Wiley Thompson's scalp fluttered from the top. A wide hoop hung from the pole just above the heads of the dancers. A hundred scalps, stiff and black with dried blood, dangled from the hoop like bats dangling in a cave.

A circle of old men pounded their drums in the glowing firelight. An admiring orchestra of women and young maidens smiled and made eyes as they played sugar cane flutes and rattled necklaces of silver coins.

A throng of warriors danced around the scalp pole in a frenzy. The whooping dancers stomped and strutted and pranced. They flung their arms and heads back and howled like wolves. They performed grand reenactments of their bravery and prowess, stalking and pouncing with wide sweeping motions of blades and clubs. Prancing and gyrating around the pole they leapt up to touch the scalps.

"Are you not going to dance?" asked Willet.

"I killed no enemy. I have no reason to dance," I said.

"Neither have most of those dancing now," said Willet. "I think some of that is silly. What I have in mind for my retribution is neither fun nor a reason to celebrate."

"You won't be happy when those men are dead?" I asked.

"I don't know," she said. "I have thought much about it. Their deaths will do little to please me. However, I will be happy while they are suffering. For the moment I am more than satisfied with the treasure

I found. Father will be very happy. Your mother also," said Willet. She had collected steel arrowheads, hand axes, small saws, files, and sand-papers for Mateo, but the bulk of the plunder on the blanket was for the women of our island: straw bonnets, bolts of calico cloth, hair ribbons, needles, thread, ivory combs, colorful neck scarves and handkerchiefs and glass beads of every color.

"A treasure indeed. Many found treasure today," I said. The field was cluttered with the spoils of the raids. Stacks of barrels, bulging sacks, bales and crates. Pots, pans, steel knives and hatchets were in piles on the bright new blankets. "Do you want none of the rum?"

"I have seen how stupid people become on rum," she said. "I have no desire to be an idiot. Aren't you having any?"

"I've had the painful head," I said. I admired my grand prize, a 4-draw brass telescope from Shuttleworth of London. I had also grabbed a compass, a bullet mold, and a good rubberized blanket along with a steel-bladed hatchet I needed and a big knife I didn't.

After a bit Osceola walked our way. He wobbled a little. His face glowed with war paint, victory, and alcohol. Thompson's blood had dried on him.

"Little sister, you don't seem pleased by our great victories today," he said to Willet.

"I saw much death and pain. Why should I be pleased? I am deeply saddened at the death of the young Rogers boy," she said. "I do not feel pride or wish celebration over his death. He was a friendly boy."

"It was a great blow to our enemy, the Americans," said Osceola angrily. In the shadow and firelight, his angry face looked fearsome. "That should always be celebrated."

"Rogers played no part in what happened to Chechoter and me," said Willet. "Only his clerks and the MacCuaig filth. Rogers was al-ways fair to me."

"Even worse, then," said Osceola. "A man that does not stand against injustice is no man, but a worm. I have saved him from a life burrowing spinelessly in the ground. Now he merely rots in it."

"I do not mourn him," said Willet. "But MacCuaig is the one I want, the one that must pay. That boy certainly harmed no one. He cared only about his horses."

"They are all our enemies," said Osceola. "He would have grown to plot against us."

"No, they are not, that is a foolish thing to say," said Willet.

"They say it of us," said Osceola, slightly cowed.

"Exactly, so now we are no better?" said Willet. "We do not kill children. That is not our way."

"Our way is whatever we must do to avoid extinction or enslave-ment," snapped Osceola as he turned and walked toward the reveling warriors. "Don't make me regret paying them cows for you."

"Osceola bloats up like a bullfrog when he struts around," I said, after he had walked a safe distance away. "It's funny."

"Better not let him hear you say that," said Willet.

"He knows better than to push me around," I said. "My brother John's alliance to him is too important."

"Your brother John," Willet laughed. "If you want to compare bloated bullfrogs."

"Not unjustly said," I said. "But let's join them anyway."

***

We joined John at the fire. Alligator, chief of a small Seminole village, had just sat down beside him. John was tall, long-limbed and lithe, like our mother. Short, twisted braids sprouted from beneath his calico tur-ban and his skin was dark. He was the best athlete among the Estelusti,

10

and rivaled Osceola and Wild Cat as best among the Seminole. He was a champion wrestler and was always chosen first for stick ball games. John enjoyed some rum from time to time, and he had a big tin cup of it now. Knowing John, it was not his first, nor would it be his last.

"This was a victorious day, but easy victories make warriors careless and overconfident," said Alligator. He had been a gray-haired leader of a simple fishing village before Jackson had sent his soldiers.

"You speak true. The soldiers at Fort King stayed inside their walls. That will not always be the case," said John, who always spoke slowly and considered his words. "Tell me more of your attack on Dade."

"We shadowed the soldiers for three days. Micanopy continued to say he was waiting for Osceola to join us," said Alligator. "He fretted and fussed like an old grandmother. He passed up many excellent locations for ambushes, and we knew soon it would be too late. The soldiers would be too near the fort. Jumper and I argued with him. I told him if his heart was weak, he should leave and go with the women."

"I am surprised Micanopy would sleep without a warm fire and his wives tending to his every need," said John.

"Yes. Staying with the women has become Micanopy's way. For too long he has enjoyed a life of sloth and comfort. It is good Osceola is our war leader, and not Micanopy. He does not have the heart for the war trail," said Alligator.

"But he did today," said John.

"Yes, finally. But even then, as Dade's column approached, Micanopy began to waver. We told him that as chief he must fire the first shot. If he didn't, I said I would shoot the American officer and see that Micanopy was shamed. Finally, he fired. I was shocked, but his bullet struck Dade through his heart. Every Seminole then fired. We killed half the soldiers with that first volley, and most of their officers."

"That is what we must always do. Aim for the officers," said John. "Cut the head off the snake."

"They fired their cannon at us, but we easily avoided it. They cannot move the big barrel fast enough to hit a Seminole, and we shot down the men who tried to load it. New men jumped up to take their place, but we killed them, too."

"The Americans do not know how to fight Seminole in our own land," said John. "It does not matter how powerful you are if you cannot hit your target. I am sure they killed some trees, though."

"Many trees," said Alligator. "They killed so many trees the cannon ran out of balls, and then their muskets did, too. That is when we charged and finished off the last few soldiers. We killed them all, more than a hundred. And we lost only three warriors. It was a horrible scene, but great victory. It had to be done."

"That is a great victory," said John. "But now we have started a war."

"No. They started the war," said Alligator as the drums and whooping went quiet.

Osceola climbed atop a stack of captured crates. He was taller than most Seminole and powerfully muscled, toughened from a life of warfare since childhood. He towered above us now, shirtless, muscular arms outstretched. His body, painted and blood-stained, gleamed in the fire. The warriors rushed to Osceola's pulpit, chanting his name.

"I would thank Mr. Wiley Thompson for such a beautiful rifle that shoots so true," bellowed Osceola to whoops and cheers. "However, it is with great sadness I must report he is unable to attend. He sends his regards as he is otherwise occupied, dancing tonight instead in the pit of demons. He sends his scalp instead."

The warriors whooped and whistled until Osceola motioned for silence.

"Now I tell you this. Our path is now chosen. I will make the white man red with blood. He will blacken in the sun and rain, where the wolf shall smell his bones and buzzards liven upon his flesh! Hooah!"

"Hooah! Hooah!" chanted the crowd, as Osceola howled at the moon.

The celebration continued until the sun rose. By then, after hours of feasting and drinking, the battle reenactments got less fearsome and more clumsy. The dancers staggered and fell, collapsing into each other in drunken piles, laughing at each other's clumsiness.

"It is a good thing that Sharp Knife Jackson's soldiers do not know where we are. This would be a good time to strike," said Willet as two drunk warriors rolled past, laughing as each tried to pin the other to the ground.

***

After two days, most of the warriors had returned to their villages with their share of the plunder. All the whiskey had been consumed that first night. The warriors danced until they had collapsed from exhaustion and intoxication. The next day many suffered severely, their eyes bleary, holding their heads and walking unsteadily.

Only sixty warriors remained, half of them Estelusti. John, Osceola, Alligator, and other leaders huddled in discussion. Osceola was triumphant, buoyant, and eager for more battle. The others were more somber. We all knew the Americans would soon send more soldiers to avenge their dead.

I heard happy shouts of greeting as a small group of men walked into camp. Some were war-painted, but so covered with grime it was hard to tell. Their buckskins and calico shirts were muddy and shredded from the swamps and saw palmetto thickets. Nearly all wore bandages or had visible wounds.

Two men walked in our direction. The smaller man was Wild Cat, who had been John's closest friend since they could walk. He was small and wiry, not much bigger than me, and always bursting with vigor and energy. Wild Cat was the son of King Philip, a prominent Seminole chief whose territory was along the east coast. King Philip had always been friends with the Spaniards whose families lived in St. Augustine for generations. Wild Cat had been raised mingling with the scions of old Spanish wealth. John and Wild Cat had been fierce competitors in sporting events and for girls since childhood. Even with their strong egos, somehow, they had always remained best friends. An insult to one was an insult to both and they were furious and feared fighters.

Wild Cat was a bit of a fancy man and his jaunty arrogance surpassed even Osceola and John. He enjoyed dressing like a dandy in European finery and strutting around the streets and pubs and dance halls of the city. It was said many ladies of the town had enjoyed trysts with Wild Cat, including a few wives and daughters of St. Augustine high society. Even now, dirty, and ragged, he still had a grin and sparkle in his eye. John jumped to his feet and ran to him.

"Hooah," shouted Wild Cat. They squeezed each other with tears of happiness.

"Hooah," shouted John. "I am happy to see you are safe. We heard men were lost and the fighting bloody."

"There were some close calls, but we had much success. I am also happy to see my brother safe," said Wild Cat.

"We had no losses other than Pete being wounded by a ferocious fowl," John laughed. "It was a fierce battle for a moment, but in the end, he was victorious and barely pecked."

"Ha," laughed Wild Cat as they released their embrace. "Young Pete wounded in his first battle. Did you take the scalp?"

"No," I bristled. "It won't be my last battle."

"And the fate of the bird?" said Wild Cat. "No doubt a fine meal. "

"No doubt," I said.

"Pete graciously gave the prize to the boy who was chasing it to begin with," said John.

"You shouldn't be so wasteful in time of war," said Wild Cat.

"I ate half a ham and a tin of English cookies before he ever got that bird plucked and over a fire," I said.

"Very clever. Just like your brother," said Wild Cat.

"He is," said John. "Who is your companion?"

"This is Virgil, my new friend. Our new ally," said Wild Cat. "He hates the MacCuaigs and the MacCuaigs hate him."

Virgil was black as coal and a foot taller than the other men. He had muscles like Samson, the muscle of the men who had labored dawn to dusk every day of their lives on a sugar plantation. His huge hands were scarred up like alligator hide. A flintlock pistol and broad, hooked cane knife were looped to Virgil's rough leather belt. The heavy knife was scratched and chipped, and dry, dark stains ran down the blade.

"Hooah, Virgil. You have come a long way. Here, drink some rum," said John, opening the spigot on the rum keg and filling three tin cups. "This is Alligator, my brother Pete and our friend Willet. Any enemy of the MacCuaigs is a friend of ours. Hooah."

"To many more victories," said Wild Cat and all three took a big gulp of rum.

"Lawd a-mussy. That is some powerful likker," said Virgil, gasping and choking.

"If it's not to your liking," said John.

"Oh, it's to my liking," grinned Virgil, gulping down the rest of the cup. "It is sho' 'nuff to my liking."

"Our plan is working. Florida is in panic," said Wild Cat. "Mosquito County is in flames. We have burned the big houses and sugar mills. We also seized many storehouses of food from the plantations. We have taken many horses and cattle. The Whites are hiding in St. Augustine and hundreds of men have been freed to join our cause. These men are eager for battle!"

"That is outstanding news!" said John, clinking his cup to theirs.

"You are one of the men freed?" John asked Virgil.

"No, I freed myself some months ago," said Virgil.

"Virgil knocked the turds out of some MacCuaigs and now there is a five-hundred-dollar reward on his head," crowed Wild Cat.

"That's Nat Turner money," John said. "They must want you bad."

"With that large reward, it is not safe for him east of the St. Johns. He has been betrayed more than once by people enticed by that gold."

"Hooah. You stay with us as long as you need. No one will find you," said John. "How were you able to escape the MacCuaigs?"

"It's a long story, but I wish I'd busted me a bunch more of them sons-a-bitches," said Virgil, gasping after a big gulp of rum.

"I welcome long stories, my friend," said John, filling everybody's cup. "We have all night and enough rum to float a ship."

"To start, I didn't have no bad life there on the Gentry plantation," said Virgil. "To my good fortune, Massa Edgar Gentry didn't allow much whipping by the overseers. We was treated better than most I've heard of. I had me a fine, beautiful wife, and three fine chilluns and our own little farm plot. I was allowed to hire myself and was saving money in hopes of one day buying my family's freedom. My troubles began last year in the summer of all that sickness. Massa Edgar near died. He had to go north and get out'n this weather."

"White people are not meant for the sickly season. I am confused why they want this land so bad," said Wild Cat.

"Massa's evil-minded brother Barclay took over running the place. Barclay was the opposite of Edgar. He brought in a new overseer boss. Got rid of those who shared Mass' Gentry's mind," said Virgil. "Instead, his new men whipped and kicked and bullied us around for sport."

"Sounds like they were trained by the MacCuaigs."

"I suspect so. A few months passed with us hoping Massa would return. Then Joost Von Bock and Chebona Bula MacCuaig and his gang came through on a slave buying trip. They already had a coffle of more than a hundred," said Virgil.

"Chebona Bula and his brothers are buying as many slaves as they can. They hope to sell to the new Creek plantations in the Indian Territory," said John. "Cherokee, Choctaw, the other civilized tribes, are all clearing land for big cotton plantations. They say the slave trade is going to be thriving out there because cotton is in much demand in the North. They are buying slaves cheap from the planters who are fearful of an uprising."

"Yes, all of us knew what they was doing, but before he went north, Edgar had ordered Barclay not to sell no souls. Barclay stood by that, and Joost was about to ride on by until he spied my Naomi who worked in the house and was always fixed up nice. Joost declares he wants to buy her, as his concubine. At first Barclay would not sell, but finally Joost gave him a price so high he couldn't refuse. Just Naomi. Not the children. Not me."

"Those people are evil right through," said John.

"Naomi and the babies was bawling. I was shouting and cussing. I tried to get at Von Bock, but a bunch of them tackled me and beat me down," said Virgil. "When the other slaves seen what was happening, they started a ruckus. I grabbed a loose shackle and started swinging, leaving at least five of them bone-broke and brain-fractured before they knocked my lights out. Of course, once I woke up dead they whupped me near to death."

"Of course," said John. "Surprised you're not already dead."

"Ain't that the truth?" said Virgil. "I imagine I would be dead if they hadn't wanted to keep me around for entertainment. They bought me just to break me. They intended to geld me, but Laughing Boy decided that if I was intact, I could tolerate a lot more punishment. They gave me plenty of it, and sure enjoyed it as long as I was chained up. They'd whip me until the blood streamed down my legs, let me rest up a couple days, then whip me near dead again. One day I broke out, grabbed a shovel and left another bloody pile of them. I wasn't able to reach my Naomi, though."

"Now you see why the MacCuaigs are after him," said Wild Cat. "They even have a wager of several hundred dollars amongst themselves as to who will get him first. They are out for blood. They have brutal plans for him. They promise they will follow through on gelding him this time."

"We will get your wife," said John. "That I promise you. As for the other, you may get killed fighting beside us, but you will die with everything intact."

"I already made that promise to myself," said Virgil.

"Where are they holding her now?"

"They are holding all the slaves on the Von Bock plantation beyond the St. John's, hundreds of them waiting to be put on ship," said Virgil.

***

Virgil stayed with us when the others went off to discuss strategy. He sipped his rum and stared into the fire, a look of deep sadness on his face. Willet put a blanket over his shoulders and gave him a cup of steaming coffee.

"Don't be worried," said Willet. "We will free your people."

"Thank you, miss," he said. "You speak American better than most Americans."

"I spent several years of my childhood in a Christian mission on the land of the Cherokee," she said. "I was taken there after our village was massacred at the Horseshoe Bend, during the Red Stick War. My mother was mortally wounded and died soon after we were captured. A missionary took claim of me as an infant."

"But you came back to live as an Indian?"

"Yes, I craved it from my first memory," she said. "Thankfully, I was rescued by my father after a few years. He had been lied to and told I died with my mother. I have never known such happiness like my first days of running free through the Cove."

"I know that feeling," he said. "I felt the same when I run off, but for the worry of my family."

"We will get them. We have many brave fighters that will go."

"Yes, I have met several. Still, I am surprised to see a woman warrior," said Virgil. "Especially one raised by missionaries."

"There are many women fighters among us. All Estelusti women know how to fight. Seminole women do too, but not as well as Estelusti. No women fight as well as Estelusti women," she said. "Does your Naomi know how to fight?"

"There wasn't no fighting against what was beating on us," he said. "Not unless you count just not losing her mind, I reckon."

"The MacCuaigs will pay for their crimes one day," said Willet.

"I hope to be there on that day," said Virgil. "What war was that you were talking about, the Horseshoe Bend?"

"The Red Stick War, that is what they call the Creek Civil War. You don't know the wars?"

"They ain't much of a concern to us down there chopping cane," said Virgil. "We got our own worries."

"Yes, I guess you would. But that is the war that created the situation we are now in. That is when Laughing Boy's father first allied with Andrew Jackson and became rich and powerful."

"I've heard plenty about Jackson and know plenty about them vile MacCuaigs and their business, but never knew about no war and them back there. How did that happen?"

"Laughing Boy's father William MacCuaig was patriarch of the largest clan of the Creek. MacCuaig and some other Lower Creek chiefs wanted large plantations with many slaves like the rich Americans. They wanted to establish towns and become civilized," said Willet. "My people, the Red Sticks, opposed becoming servile to Jackson and his gold and the planters. We wanted to live in our traditional way. We had no desire for slaves or owning the land."

"That was enough to cause a war?"

"Yes. It was very bitter. They raided our villages, and we attacked them back. There were many vicious battles. Families were divided. Much gold and many bribes were paid to the MacCuaig traitors to steal our land. William MacCuaig was one of Jackson's generals and led a thousand Lower Creek soldiers, trained and supplied by Jackson. Laughing Boy, the most diabolical of William's sons, has always been his favorite, and second in command. Laughing Boy led his own battalion of the cruelest barbarians. By war's end, my people were either dead, in prison camps, or here in Florida with the Seminole."

"But that wasn't enough for 'em, was it?" said Virgil.

"No, it is never enough for the lusts and greed of the MacCuaigs. After the war, William MacCuaig signed illegal treaties with Andrew Jackson, giving almost all the Creek land to the planters. MacCuaig and his captains split hundreds of thousands of dollars in bribes. MacCuaig was a powerful man but did not speak for the majority of Creek chiefs. Many Creeks protested, some of the chiefs even went to Washington, but MacCuaig's henchmen beat them, burned their homes, even killed them. Eventually the Creek Council assassinated William MacCuaig but the damage was done. The land was gone. The Creek were on their way west with everyone else."

"It's mighty funny how them treaties with the Americans seems to work out," said Virgil. "How is Laughing Boy even considered an Indian? His hair is red as a strawberry and skin as white as a wading bird. And there's so many of them."

"His blood is much more Scottish than Creek. His father's grandfather came from Scotland as a trader more than a hundred years ago. Such mixed breeds control the Creek nation. They are really white and want to live as the whites live. That is why they wear the blue Tam o' Shanter bonnets and clan tartans."

***

Willet no longer spoke of the horrors she had suffered at the hands of the MacCuaigs two years before. On that day she and her sister Chechoter had gone to Rogers' Trading Post to buy coffee and flour. Chebona Bula MacCuaig and a gang of his brothers and cousins were there, harassing peaceful Seminole and Estelusti farmers as they often did.

The MacCuaigs were infamous for kidnapping vulnerable Estelusti and threatening to sell us to the highest bidder, which meant plantation slavery. The soldiers and Indian agents rarely got involved since our Seminole owners did not keep the titleship papers of us that were recognized by American courts. The kidnap victims were seldom actually sold. Instead, the families paid the ransom demanded by the Mac-Cuaigs.

The forts and trading posts were off-limits to their attacks. Before, the MacCuaigs had only snatched isolated Estelusti who were not well known to the Americans. At the settlements, the MacCuaigs bullied and insulted our men and made lewd comments to our women, but the army protected us from physical attacks. Those were the written and unwritten rules up until that day. But Chebona Bula MacCuaig knew exactly who Chechoter and Willet were when he claimed they were runaways and demanded a huge ransom.

Osceola had charged into the fort and tried to kill Laughing Boy, but he was clubbed with rifle butts and stomped. He was slapped into irons and thrown into the stockade. Osceola would not pay the ransom. He had no money even if he had wanted to. He pleaded with Thompson to free his family, but Thompson found the whole incident amusing and refused to intervene. Over the next days the women were subjected to the vilest abuses by the MacCuaigs. Turns on the women were sold to other ruffians that loitered around the fort. The men stood drunkenly in line for hours, leering and cheering. Trapped in the cages, the children witnessed the brutal ruttings.

From his jail cell, Osceola could hear the screams and sobs. After a week, Osceola bowed his head. He groveled and begged. He agreed to pay ten cattle and a prize breeding bull for the release of his family. Osceola was not a wealthy man. He did not own a breeding bull. He had to accept charity, which further humiliated him. Wiley Thompson thought an apology and the gift of a fancy rifle could make up for all that.

Willet's physical injuries took months to heal. Some unseen ones I think not yet had. The abuse had taken her mind and spirit to a dark, distant place for many months. My mother and the women of nearby villages had sat with her day and night, holding her through long episodes of sobbing and soothing. They nursed her, bathed her, read to her, and lined her bed with fresh flowers. It was the same with Chechoter.

Willet regained herself by returning to what she had always enjoyed the most. She immersed herself in the wonders of our forests and swamps. As spring bloomed, she spent many hours alone, sitting in the meadows of wildflowers and sunlight. Then she walked the game trails and paddled the streams, silently and alone. After time, she picked up the tools Mateo had painstakingly crafted for her: the bow, the straightest arrows, the perfectly balanced steel knife, and the weighted war ax. She spent hours prowling through the worst of the swamps, honing her hunting skills. As her prowess grew, she supplied several villages with fresh venison and bear meat. She was praised as a hunter, but I knew she was preparing to kill men.

Chapter Two

BATTLE OF THE WITHLACOOCHEE

It rained and stormed almost continually since the attack. The wind was frigid and the air misty. Willet and I sat cross legged under an arbor of saw palmetto leaves, wrapped in blankets from the trading post. We warmed ourselves by a small fire as the chiefs finalized the attack on the Von Bock plantation. Plans were nearly complete when a messenger arrived in camp from the east.

"What news do you bring?" asked John.

"It is grave," said Hecto, a young Seminole boy. "Call and Clinch come from Fort Drane with eight hundred soldiers. Laughing Boy Mac-Cuaig brings many of his clan."

"Where are they now?"

"Still far away. They march toward the Ouithlocko Crossing, but move slower than a three-legged turtle," said the messenger. "They bring a large train of wagons."

"Do they know of our attack on Fort King? The massacre of Dade's soldiers?"

"No. Not when we left them," said the man. "They would have no way of knowing. They come from many miles in the opposite direction. They have sent no scouts beyond the river."

"That is good then."

"Yes, and we also know this because the soldiers tell us. They speak loudly as they march. It is easy to hear the soldiers' words. Dade's column has not been mentioned. The soldiers are happy and laugh about their big Indian hunt. They boast about the number of scalps they will take and Negroes they will steal."

"They may find it more of a challenge than they expect," said John. "They plan to take Estelusti with the runaways?"

"Yes, everyone. Women and children. All runaways, Estelusti and Seminole will be taken back to the fort and the ships waiting in Tampa Bay. There are death bounties on certain of our fighters, which excited the volunteers very much."

"Virgil, my brother, we must meet this threat," said Wild Cat. "We cannot allow them into the Cove. We cannot allow more of our people to be captured. If we do not stop them here, there will be no point in rescuing your family. The soldiers and Creeks will rampage through our homeland. There will be no safe place. No sanctuary."

Virgil was silent, his shoulders slumped. Anguish filled his face, eyes watery and lips quivering.

"That ain't the news I was hoping to hear," he finally said, very slowly, his voice close to breaking. "I get sick inside thinking of Naomi in that vile place for even one second more. But I understand. I will fight beside you."

"Hooah!" grunted Wild Cat. "We will get her, and soon. But we must strike now, and surprise them before they learn the fate of Dade's column. They are foolish for marching straight into our stronghold, like a fool hare walking into an alligator den."

"Yes, but remember it remains a very big hare," said John.

"Yes, very big. But a big hare is still a hare," said Wild Cat. "The larger he is, the more meat for us. Let us go and prepare a proper greeting for the big hare. Sharpen our blades and prepare the stew pot."

"Hooah!" bellowed John.

"Hooah!" said Virgil, with not so much enthusiasm. Wild Cat shouted for the warriors to gather.

"Estelusti Men! Black men! Hear this!" John shouted. "Clinch and Call march to Ouithlocko Crossing. They have many soldiers. We must meet them! They come under a black flag, the death warrant for Estelusti men. For any black man that has experienced battle and tasted the blood of his oppressor. They want to kill any man here that has tasted freedom. You cannot surrender."

***

The Ouithlocko Crossing was the only crossing within fifty miles that had a bottom solid enough to hold the army's heavy supply wagons. The ford was at the tip of a narrow point of land where the Withlacoochee River turned back sharply on itself.

For decades, even centuries, raiders and traders who moved by land had traveled this route, laden with goods from the trading posts and rich farms in northeast Florida or Georgia. Upon reaching the crossing, they often found themselves in need of a raft to get their goods or plunder across. Over time, all the trees on the peninsula on the other side of the river had been chopped down, clearing it of any cover except a few bushes and old stumps.

The raiders usually timed their forays for this season, when the water would likely be low. However, this time unseasonal heavy rains had caused the banks of the Withlacoochee to overflow. The rain that had started before we left camp three days ago had continued, with constant drizzles wrapped around two roaring, tree-whipping storms. The shallow, tranquil crossing that was normally a couple of wagon-lengths across had swollen to five times that. Broken limbs and logs rode the rushing brown water.

The weather had slowed Call's column much more than our warriors, allowing hundreds more warriors to join us. The column would reach the crossing in the morning, and we had spent our time making barricades and camouflage.

"Have you always lived on that plantation?" I asked Virgil. We had just finished our earthwork of tree limbs and brush, packed tight with mud. Water dripped off our canopy of palm trees and moss-draped pines.

"Not always that one. I was born up in South Carolina. The Big Massa Gentry up there was the father to Barclay and Edgar and a few others. He owned a big rice plantation twice the size of any I've seen in Florida. More than three hundred people worked them fields, and the suffering on a rice plantation is something that's near impossible to fathom. The sickness and dying young, much worser than down here. But I guess Big Massa thought he wasn't causing enough misery in peoples' lives, so when I was about ten, he bought himself that sugar plantation in Florida. Me and a brother and a sister was sent down with a hundred or so more all strung together with rope."

"The rest of your family stayed in Carolina?"

"Far as I know. I never heard no more from 'em."

"Never?"

"Nope. Ain't like we could write letters and such. Anyway, we got here and right off they put us to work, clearing forests and cypress swamps, digging ditches, building dams. That was back-breaking labor, but I was stronger than most, and just dumb enough to work real hard. About ten years ago they made me the boiler's helper. I tried to be the best boiler I could. The boilers, they the most important men on the plantation. The best sugar cookers is precious diamonds. You won't find no good boilers for sale on them St. Augustine blocks. Only top boiler I ever knew of moving to a different plantation was because his drunk massa had gambled him away on a straight to a flush."

"Is that where you got all those scars?"

Virgil's arms and shoulders were splotched with wide, teardrop shaped scars. Every inch of his forearms looked like the burned skin of a hog over a roasting pit. The welted lash stripes across his back were fresher, and they'd been deep.

"The most of them. I never had no whip scars until I seen my first MacCuaig up close though," said Virgil. "Can't help but get burnt in the boiling house. It gets mighty hot up in there, steam rising from huge copper kettle so thick you can't barely see through sometimes."

"I heard it's about the hardest work there is, cooking sugar," I said.

"I reckon that's about true. All day and all night, boiling that cane juice down and down, always thickening and thickening, cane juice turning darker and thicker and sweeter. Ladle by ladle moving the boiling cane juice from kettle to smaller kettle. Then we took it off to cool. If juice was took off too soon it became molasses, and left in the copper too long it would burn," said Virgil, and added with pride: "I just had a talent for it, I guess, knowing just when the time was right, which is why I've been so fortunate."

"That was fortunate?" I said.

"More fortunate than being in fields, fighting the miasmas, the snakes, the rusty blades and the goddamned drunk overseers who ain't above shooting a man for entertainment," he said. "Better than feeding cane stalks into them thousand-pound iron rollers round the clock during harvesting. Them big old rollers will grab a hand or arm like Satan grabs a soul, crush that arm, and onct that happens, nothing you can do but chop it off and patch it with hot tar."

"Fortunate still seems a little strong," said Willet. "But I see what you mean."

"Sure, it was hard work, but the important Negroes get certain privileges. We got a bigger cabin, and we was fed some better, treated a sight better. I done such a good job for Massa Gentry that he allowed me to hire myself out during the off season," said Virgil. "I did some carpentry, some blacksmithing and such. Had me a nice pot of money saved up."

"Our slavery is nothing like that," I said. "We are called slaves of the Seminole Nation, but we were really their allies. We are useful to them. They are useful to us. Until the MacCuaigs came to Florida, the Seminole claim of ownership protected us from being stolen and sold to the plantations. In return, each Estelusti family pays Micanopy or their village chief a portion of what we produce or sell, an amount that is generally considered fair. Our fields are fertile, and our harvests are so large we often give the excess away. That is how it is with most Estelusti and Seminole. As for our family personally, John is paid to act as an interpreter. Like a boiler, his is a privileged position."

"That don't sound bad at all," he said.

"We have been a satisfied people. No Seminole has ever whipped an Estelusti. We are not forced to labor against our will. None of us has ever been threatened with being sold away into chattel slavery. We have equal influence in the council. No one tells us where we can go. No Estelusti has ever been told who he can marry, or who we can associate with. The Seminole do not forbid an Estelusti from reading or being educated. In fact, they encourage it so we can help them understand what the newspapers and legal documents and treaties say. We have always carried guns for hunting and defense and have fought with them against common enemies before."

"I wish some Seminole would put in a claim on me and mine. That's a powerful enticement," said Virgil. "I expect I'd rather give up a slice of my harvest than a whole of my soul. I could come to terms with that real easy. But no one ever asked."

"But now Andrew Jackson wants to put us on Oklahoma land governed by the Creeks, to be subject to Creek law. Creek slavery is the same as what you just escaped, which means working in their fields under a whip," I said. "So, you see, it's not exactly the same fight for us as the Seminole. They will leave this land for another land. It may be worse land, it may be better land, but it will be their land. We would be slaves. If we are sent to Oklahoma, that is the end of the Black Seminole. That's why we are fighting this war. The Seminole fight for land and property. That property is us. We fight for our freedom. For our very lives."

***

"There will be much excitement tomorrow. Much confusion. Many bullets flying," John said to me as we sat under a Palmetto leaf canopy in the rain. "Stay at my side. You will be my messenger to Osceola."

"I don't wish to be a messenger. I wish to fight," I said. "I wish a rifle."

"And I wish my sugar stick was the size of a bull gator tail," said John. "You are more needed as a messenger for now. I must always know what the others are doing, and they must know what I am doing."

"I am old enough to fight," I said. "I can fight as well as any warrior. I was a messenger at Fort King. Someone else can run errands."

"There were no messages to deliver at Fort King. Calm down, this is no insult to you. This war will not end today. Not for many days. Your eagerness for combat will wane well before then. You are the fastest runner among our people."

"There are others who can run fast, if that's all you're looking for," I said angrily.

"That is not all that I'm looking for," John said. "I don't want merely a fleet runner who may trickle down his leg and run home if a bullet passes too close. Our attack will be like a man with many hands. We must always know what the other hand is doing. For this, I need someone that I can rely on. Someone whose eyes I trust to see every-thing, not just one thing. He must have courage. I do not want a weak-ling. A messenger must have the nerve to expose himself to enemy fire and never waver. Does that suit you?"

"It does," I said. "I would rather fight. But I will do as you say. I will not run home, fleetly or otherwise."

"Yes, I know this already," said John. "I have always known this. Now, tomorrow, we will give those soldiers a proper welcome to our home."

***

Shortly after sun-up, Laughing Boy and his men stepped out of the for-est. They came forward carefully, twenty or so of them scanning the trees as they came down the peninsula.

The MacCuaigs tended to large, thick-bodied men. Their hair and beards were more likely to be some shade of red than black. Laughing Boy was taller than the others, long and lean with broad shoulders. Even though red-headed and fair-skinned with freckles, his skin was tanned deep copper. His cheekbones were knobby sharp, and a livid white scar slashed from his left ear to his lip. A white pompom and long plume of white egret feathers decorated his blue bonnet, and a tartan was draped over his shoulder. He wore a broad leather belt dec-orated with beads, quills, and the scalps of dead enemies.

The drizzle continued as General Clinch and his squadron of offic-ers arrived to study the river. Back in the forest the soldiers began chop-ping wood for rafts. After an hour a group of soldiers dragged a battered little fishing boat out of the brush down river.

"Ha, what is this?" John whispered.

"I tremble in fear of that armada," laughed Wild Cat. "That boat has rotted away in the mud for many years."

After a great deal of hammering the soldiers had patched enough holes in the hull to make the boat floatable. Soon the soldiers were shuttling over, eight at a time.

"How many will we allow to cross?" I asked John after ten boatloads of soldiers had crossed, packed into a few yards of wet ground along the bank.

"We will see," he said. "If Call wants to be kind enough to split his forces, we will allow it. That only increases our odds."

As their numbers grew the soldiers attacked the brush with axes and cane knives, widening a trail for the wagons still across the river. Under the evergreen canopy the forest floor stayed dark as night. From those deep shadows we were close enough to touch the soldiers, but instead we observed their labors with amusement. They cursed and complained as they hacked through the razor-edged plants and towering hedges that were braced by webs of vines as tough as bull whips. Eventually, three hundred uniformed soldiers had reached an open, dry field a half-mile from the river. The soldiers stacked arms and made small fires for coffee while they waited for the others to cross.

***

"Osceola says his men are in place," Willet whispered, sliding through the brush.

"Hooah," John whispered. "Tell him we await his signal."

Willet squeezed my hand quickly and slipped away. I carried a heavy canvas bag that held four more pistols and enough powder and shot for a long siege. John and I would be a team. He would do the shooting and I'd do the reloading. More seconds passed as the forest buzzed and chirped and sang. The soldiers were relaxed, oblivious to the danger around them. A few pockets of sentries had been posted around the perimeter, but they were inattentive.

Bare-chested and painted black and yellow, Osceola burst out of the trees. His scream emptied that forest of its birds as he hurtled through the waist-high grass howling in rage and fury. He was on the sentries before they could react, blasting his pistol into one and nearly beheading the other with his ax.

Screeching warriors swarmed out from both sides of the field, over-running the picket lines. From the top of the field our shooters blasted away with reloaders behind them, making a hundred men seem like three hundred.

The officers tried to rally the men with the bugle and flag, but the Major went down with an arrow in his rib cage. Then the bugler went down. The flag bearer was shot, and the flag fell in the grass. The soldiers ran madly toward the river, but the trail was now a gauntlet where our men waited on both sides. Our men sprang out of the bushes and leapt out of the trees, dragging the fleeing soldiers down with axes and clubs.

"To the river, cut them off," John shouted, and we sprinted down a narrow trail. I stayed a step behind him, hearing the vicious fighting in the brush and bugles from across the river.

A trio of MacCuaigs had escaped the gauntlet and charged toward us, rifles raised. John kept running straight at them and launched himself before they could fire. The force of the collision sent all four of them brawling through the brush with clubs and knives swinging. I tried to take aim, but they were too closely entangled.

Finally, the ball of desperate men bounced into a tree and fell apart. John stood with his ax in his hand, facing five Creeks. They were so intent on killing him they had not noticed me.

33

I shot the first one as he stabbed a knife at John's back. When the others spun around, John clubbed one on the head. The third man disappeared through the bushes.

"This way," John whispered, and we slithered away under sprawling briers and berry bushes.

"Where are our men?" I mouthed when we stepped behind a huge oak and reloaded.

"Nearby. Do not worry," he whispered. "Only have few Creek slipped through."

A twig cracked. John put a finger to his lips and scanned the shadows. He caught my eye and motioned with his head. The dry tips of an elderberry bush dipped just an inch. John pointed at a different bush that had just flinched. I caught a glimpse of color beyond the elderberry, too far to be the same man. I nodded and eased the hammer back. John eased into a crouch, one big Howdah pistol in his hand, the other in his belt.

A MacCuaig whipped around a tree. John shot him but another gun roared and then the trees filled with screams and gunshots. It sounded like a hundred Creek had somehow surrounded us and were calling out to each other as they closed in. We scurried around like lizards, with bullets from all directions smacking the trees and shredding the bushes above us. John emptied the big pistols as fast as I could reload them. I heard screams and bodies drop. Sometimes it went suddenly quiet and I heard tiny twigs snap and the soft footsteps of a hunter alone. The sounds of battle drifted one way and another. I went flat when the howls of blood-lusted men in hot pursuit surged closer.

I had no idea where we were. The air above me was deep gray from smoke and drizzle. John stood beside a tree, sighting in with a pistol. I glanced up just as a Creek man leapt out of the shadows ten feet away, aiming straight back at John. They fired at the same instant. John flipped backward and a gush of blood sprayed out of his face like a thick, red rooster comb.

I gasped and reeled but knew to get away. I carried a pistol in my hand, ready for John, and another loaded and still in the bag. I burrowed through the mud and briers, peering for a target. I fired one barrel at a flash of blue, then emptied both pistols at some white plumes floating above a patch of myrtle bush.

When the noise drifted away I crawled back to John. He was draped backward over a log and blood streamed down his forehead from an ugly black hole between his eyes. I pulled him off the log and laid him on his back. I wiped the blood from his unseeing eyes and closed them. Then I cried. I cried until I heard MacCuaigs creeping through the thicket around me. I reached for my pistols and realized that in my grief I had not reloaded. I raised into a crouch, pulling my war club from my belt. The first MacCuaig stepped into the clearing, bayonet first.

"Die MacCuaigs!" Wild Cat bellowed, exploding out of the brush. A dozen Seminoles were step for step with him, firing pistols point-blank into the attackers. Some MacCuaigs dropped dead and the rest sprinted back into the trees. As his men chased the others toward the river, Wild Cat returned shortly and dropped down beside me.

"Are you badly wounded?" I asked him. He was bleeding from several large scrapes, but I saw no deep wounds.

"Not badly," he said. "More bruised than anything. Their blades touched me but not deeply. Your brother?"

"He is there," I pointed, and the tears came again.

Wild Cat crawled over to John's motionless body.

"He is not dead," said Wild Cat. "Hurt badly. But not shot anyway."

"No?" I gasped. "But that wound…"

"That is a bad wound," Wild Cat said. "It looks like the Creek's bullet smashed John's pistol into his face. It split him from chin to scalp, but he lives."

"I can't believe it," I said, and then heard John snore and wheeze a little.

"He will have a bad headache. He may see three of one and not recall his own name or recognize anyone for a few days. Those pistols are as heavy as cannons, but I guess they'll stop a bullet," said Wild Cat. "Still, better a headache than a head you can whistle through."

***

As the sun slowly dropped we rested without speaking, too exhausted from battle. The excitement was gone. My shirt was shredded by thorns and bristles. My skin was shredded, too, and scraped raw where it wasn't scratched. My throat was parched and burning, no matter how much water I drank. My legs quivered, and my shirt was soaked with sweat. My mind quivered more than my legs.

Scattered firing continued down the sides of the peninsula. Our rifles had twice the range of the soldiers' muskets. We raked them with gunfire from three sides. They dug holes for cover instead of trying to cross the river.

John sat on a stump sipping rum and smoking a cigar. Blades had cut him, not berry bushes, and his many cuts were deep. Big pink patches of raw skin as big as my palm were on one shoulder and both knees. His face had swollen until his eyes looked like cracks in a rotting pumpkin. Red slices crisscrossed his scalp, and a wider gash ran from his hairline to the swollen tip of his nose.

"My head feels like it has been chewed by Daddy Long Jaws and shat out his scaly ass," John said. "That heavy gun almost killed me."

"It also saved your life. Maybe I should carry a big pistol like that," said Wild Cat, squinting over his smoldering cigar with concentration. He was reattaching John's forehead skin with needle and thread taken from a dead soldier's kit. I held the flap of skin in place above John's eyebrow while Wild Cat ran the needle through it.

"Hooah," whispered Willet coming through the brush. "I bring a message from Osceola. The soldiers are beaten, but not as badly as we'd hoped. Many were able to reach the riverbank and fort up. However, on the other side of the river, the volunteer soldiers are refusing to cross."

"Refusing to cross?" said John.

"Yes. Our fire is too heavy from here. Also, some of our men crossed upriver and threaten the soldiers from behind. The plan has worked well, but Osceola has been shot."

"Badly?" asked Wild Cat.

"No, only nicked, but he will not be able to use his arm for a while."

"Take me to him," said John.

"No," said Wild Cat. "You are still half-scrambled in your brain. I will fix your face and then I will go to Osceola. I believe we have punched the mighty General Clinch in the face so hard his army looks like your face at the moment. Horrifying, but harmless. He is no worry anymore."

"Osceola believes the same," said Willet. "But he wants to attack. He wants to cross the river and rub them out. Others disagree. You need to speak to him before he orders something unwise."

"Let me tend to my friend, and I will come counsel with him," said Wild Cat. "Tell him to stay put until I can see things for myself. The fighting here has been fierce."

"It will be dark soon," said Willet. "There is nothing further he can do tonight. I will tell him you will come to him soon."

***

"Are you sure you want to do this?" John asked me after Willet left. Wild Cat had gone back to stitching his face. "Has not this battle been enough for you for the moment?"

"I took no part in this battle other than crawl around like a mole with my face in the dirt," I said.

"Yes, and now compare your face to mine," he huffed through his engorged lips.

"I am not needed at home," I said. "You would be going to free the Von Bock slaves if you weren't so badly injured."

"Yes, I would be going. However, I would go knowing there are more armed overseers at the Von Bock place than any ten plantations. I would go knowing it is impossible to free hundreds of people at once and lead them all through the swamps to safety. The pursuit will be furious and deadly. Many will be caught," said John. "I would go knowing there was a good chance I might never return."

"I go knowing these things," I said. "Wild Cat will lead. I will only follow. I will stay close behind him."

"Wild Cat takes too many chances...Ouch!" yelled John as Wild Cat jabbed him with the needle.

"You take many chances, my brother," said Wild Cat to John. "To insult the man that holds a needle an inch from your eye."

"There, you see," said John. "I love Wild Cat. He is my brother. But he takes stupid chances. He threatens me with a tiny needle without noticing I hold a bear-gutting knife inches from his Master John Good-fellow. One slip and he's only plain Jane."

"Humph," said Wild Cat. "You would think a man would be more grateful that I put his face back together. Much more handsome than it ever was before."

"Remember my words before you follow Wild Cat," said John, his swollen face looking like a catfish. "If you get yourself killed doing one of Wild Cat's stunts, Mother will never forgive me and I will never forgive you."

"You have my word that you won't be subjected to her wrath," I said.

"I suspect I shall be, regardless," he said and took a drink.

***

I found some soft moss and made a pillow for John. He put it behind his neck as he leaned against a log, smoking the cigar, sipping rum and cursing the MacCuaigs. Wild Cat and his men were searching the brush around us, looking for threats and trophies.

"These three are mine, these others are yours, I believe," said Wild Cat, returning. He dropped a handful of bloody scalps on the ground.

"They are for the bears and raccoons then," said John. "I don't desire them."

"You wish to take no scalps?" gasped Wild Cat. "After the ferocious manner in which you earned them?"

"Taking scalps is not my way,' said John.

"It is our way," said Wild Cat. "The Seminole way."

"Very well. Let it continue to be your way. It is not mine," said John. "I find no pleasure in it. I would not want it done to me."

"Yet you kill them easy enough," said Wild Cat. "I doubt you want that done to you either."

"They wronged me by coming to this land, enslaving my people. I have answered that wrong, with what is necessary," John said. "Taking scalps isn't necessary."

"It may be done to you regardless," said Wild Cat.

"It may," said John. "That still gives me no desire to do it to others."

***

We found Osceola. His left shoulder was an open bloody mass. Wiley Thompson's blood-stained, bullet-ripped officer's coat was on the ground beside him. The jacket had a new hole where the left epaulette had been.

"I can still fight," said Osceola through gritted teeth. He poked his wound with a finger. "The bullet has passed through and hit no bone. I can continue."

"There is no need," said Wild Cat. "It has been a good day. The soldiers are defeated. There is no need to risk more warriors or waste more bullets."

"We could rub them out, all those on this side of the river," said Osceola.

"We could, but we would lose many men. Too many," said Wild Cat. "We can't afford to lose men in a frontal attack."

"They will be back," said Osceola.

"Certainly. They will be back regardless," said Wild Cat. "But we have bloodied them badly. We did not lose many men. If they try again to cross in the morning, we will be ready."

"Yes, very well," said Osceola. "Let us wait and watch. I think I will not wear this jacket any longer. It attracts lead."

***

Darkness came and the rain stopped. The soldiers began ferrying loads of moaning wounded across in the little boat. From across the river came the banging of many axes and the grinding of heavy saws. Willet and I walked among our people, checking on our friends. We reached a clearing where Osceola and our leaders surrounded six prisoners.

"Please, I beg you to let me go. Our unit goes home today. All our enlistments is up. I won't never come back. I'll tell them others to stay home and not bother you no more," begged a bloodied young volunteer from his knees. His hands were tied behind him. "This ain't what I thought it was."

"What did you think it was? A duck hunt?" demanded Osceola. He was still shirtless, with a bandage over his wound. He loomed over the boy, yellow and black paint ghoulish in the firelight.

"Something like that. I guess I hadn't thought it through," said the boy.

"Did you plan to steal women and children, those that can't fight back?"

"No, nothing like that."

"To run in and grab you some pickaninnies that you can trade for gold?"

"I was just coming for an adventure. Just a sport, is all. I really wasn't thinking of hurting nobody. Not really."

"It is no adventure for us. It is no sport for you to invade us, attack us, force us from our land. To take food from the mouths of our babies. To steal our babies," shouted Osceola.

"That wasn't how it was explained to us," said the boy.

"Now it has been explained," said Osceola. "What do you think of that?"

"I don't know what to think. That was never in my mind," wept the soldier.

"Perhaps we should show we are mighty, but merciful," said Willet to Osceola. "We can expect no mercy and consideration if we show none."

"Leave us, if this troubles you," said Osceola. "I will tolerate no dissent while a battle takes place. From no one, sister, no matter their relation to me. This is not the place. Is that clear?"

"It is clear, brother. I apologize," said Willet and we quickly walked away.

"I just want to go home, peaceful," pleaded the boy as I looked back. Tears streamed down his face.

"Yes, as do we. Only one of us will and it is not a good day to be you," said Osceola, taking the burning spear from the fire. "Here's the adventure you wanted. Your friends across the river can listen."

***

Sometime before dawn I heard scouts returning from across the river.

"What word do you bring?" John asked.

"They will not come again," the spy said. "We could hear the men talking. Mostly they complained and argued. They are cold, wet, exhausted, hungry, and now shot to pieces. They do not want to die here in this swamp and be left for the alligators to feed on. The volunteers are going home. They say their enlistments are up tomorrow. They refuse to cross the river."

"Yes, we were told they only sign up to fight a certain number of days, for the days that get paid," said Osceola. "That is funny way to fight wars."

"Clinch curses Call and accuses the volunteers of cowardice," said the messenger.

"The militia men say this is not the big Indian hunt they signed up for. They said they were promised capturing Negroes would be like picking berries off a bush," said Osceola.

"Ha! They came to beat a dog, instead they encountered a panther," exclaimed Wild Cat. "They have already been well served. There is no disputing that. They did not expect to encounter Hokepis Hejo, my friend Crazy Beast, John Horse. The Great Slayer of MacCuaigs, who killed five enemy alone. His heart is recklessly brave. Hooah! Hooah!"

"Quite an embarrassment for two such renowned dog beaters as Clinch and Call," smiled Osceola. "Hooah!"

***

By mid-morning, Call's volunteer horse soldiers had galloped out of sight, headed to Fort Drane. Gen. Clinch's wagons creaked along that way too, overflowing with wounded men. The soldiers plodded behind, leaving us a treasure of equipment, clothing, food, even rifles. Our losses were very few, only two killed and a handful wounded.

"I will tend to Osceola and John," Willet said as we prepared to leave. "Be careful on your journey. I heard what John said about Wild Cat taking chances. He is correct."

"I prefer the recklessness of Wild Cat to the dangers you face nursing Osceola and my brother," I said. "They will be in pain. They will be complaining they cannot come on the raid. No doubt they will be complaining about rain or sunshine."

"Yes. It is odd that the mighty Osceola would have fought all day despite his wound, but now with someone to cater to him, he is too feeble to pour his own coffee."

"John's that way a little bit also," I said.

"John is much more badly wounded," she said. "That bullet could have killed him. He will have a bad pain in his head for many days."

"Yes," I said. "He is still seeing two and three of everything. His gait is unsteady and he cannot remember some things."

"I'll see to him," she said. "He may be surly and pettish, but nothing like Osceola."

***

"Stay alert. Stay wary. Avoid the villages and don't cross any open farmland," John said. "No one can be trusted right now. Allow no one to see you, even someone you think you know well. There are large bounties on several of the men, not just Virgil, and not just by the Mac-Cuaigs."

"I will be vigilant," I said. "Spies have been watching the plantation for months. They should know of any trickery if there is any afoot."

"Yes, but do not assume that either. Never assume anything to be true until you verify it. Always, but especially in matters of war," said John. "I know these men. They are smart and dependable. But even the smartest men can be fooled."

"I will remember that," I said.

"There is one more thing. As now, I cannot always be there to keep an eye on you. I'm pleased to see your friendship with Virgil in such a short time. I want you to stay by his side. Tighter than with Wild Cat."

"Why is that, brother? Do you think I need a protector? There are other warriors younger than me. I'm not a child."

"We all need protectors," John said. "Some people have the luxury of having one. Virgil is a good man. You complement each other. You know the Cove and he knows the land to the east of the big river. He has the strength and ferocity of five men. And you have the fighting heart of our father and intelligence of our mother. An excellent team for tough times."

"He seems to be a good man," I said.

"Virgil will never be one of those that meekly gives up if things get difficult. Taking a flogging and going back to slavery will not be an option for him. He will be executed," said John. "He has no choice but to fight to the death. It is good to have a man like that with you."

"I see."

"But there is also another side to that," said John. "If he will fight to the death for you, you must also be willing to do the same for him."

"I will not falter," I said.

"I know you will not," said John. "I will pray for your safety and courage until I see you again."

Chapter Three

VON BOCK RAID
JANUARY 1836

The Von Bock plantation was near the town of Jacksonville, far across Florida from the Cove. Much of the land between the two points was open grasslands and pine woods, a vast difference from our sanctuary of dense, watery jungle. Wild Cat set a brisk pace as he led us through the forests and fields and past the abandoned farms and plantations, where all that remained was charred rubble and blackened chimneys.

"We have traveled many miles these past two days. My legs burn like fire," I said as I pulled the ham and hard crackers from Rogers's store out of my pouch. Virgil did the same. We had made a bed of palmetto leaf over a thick cushion of moss and pine needles and were stretched out.

"You ain't lyin'," Virgil said, rubbing his beefy thighs. "I reckon mine hurt about three times what yours hurt, given that mine actually contains muscle and yours is mere twigs."

"Perhaps so," I said. "I would soak my twigs in the stream, but I saw alligator holes nearby. However, if you go first, I will follow. Those big gators would prefer your big hams to my twigs."

"Well, who wouldn't?" said Virgil.

"Do you think you can keep up with an Indian for another day?" I said.

"Don't worry none about me. Compared to chopping sugar cane from dawn to dusk, this here ain't nothing but an amble down a garden path," said Virgil. "That's what they's called, ain't it?'

"I suppose," I said. "Though I've never heard such huffing and cussing coming from any garden path."

"Grab a machete and come with me to the cane fields and we'll see who huffs and puffs," said Virgil.

"I'm not so sure I'd want to be around you swinging that big knife if you're riled," I said. "That's blood on it I figure."

"It is."

"Whose was it?"

"Hard tellin'," Virgil said. "I helped liberate a couple of them other plantations. At times, the fighting got close and hot, and I carved chunks out of a few overseer men. If they ain't dead, they's missing some important pieces."

"No wonder there's a bounty, irritable as you seem to be sometimes," I said.

"Hunger don't help none," he said.

"Here, have the rest of my cracker. Maybe you'll feel better."

"I'll eat a cracker," said Virgil. "The rest of that jam, too, if you ain't gonna finish it."

"You can have it," I said. "I'm almost too tired to eat."

"Boy, I've been missing treats like this," said Virgil, sucking some jam off his fingers and giving a little moan of satisfaction.

"You will grow fat on our island," I said.

"Have you ever ate an otter?" said Virgil. "I think I seen sign of them at that stream we just passed."

"We did once. They are awful greasy and tough."

"I don't mind me a little spot of grease and gristle. That's what I'm used to," said Virgil, licking jam off his finger. "When you've had my lot in life, there really ain't hardly no such thing as bad food. Not when you get down to it."

"Is food all you think on?" I asked Virgil.

"I can think on eating, or I can think on Naomi and my babies in that hellish place," said Virgil. "It's less sadder to think on my growling belly."

"I expect that's true," I said. "We can speak on any dish you want."

Virgil was quiet for a few minutes. I wasn't sure if I'd upset him, or he'd fallen asleep. I was about to doze off when he spoke.

"I wish I had me a mule," said Virgil.

"It would be nice for a while, but the trail we're going, all the river crossings and swamps, a mule couldn't get through," I said.

"I never figured he could. But I was expecting a big hunk of him could make it to my frying pan."

"A mule?"

"Sure, a mule. Mules is good eating. Hardly no different than cow or deer meat, along them lines."

"Isn't it a little tough?"

"Sure, I suppose, if you don't simmer it for a couple days. Kinder stringy. But a hungry mouth ain't never met a tough cut of meat."

"I suppose."

"Properly prepared mules is a delicacy. Every year there was a couple old mules that had worked a plow for 20 years and was about to give out. We was allowed to butcher them when they was two breaths away from collapse. Sometimes there was younger ones that got crippled up somehow, or just refused to take a harness. If they couldn't sell 'em, we'd eat him. Not a thing wrong with it."

"I've never considered frying a mule steak."

"You ain't never spent many days longing to be fed, nor stared all day at the ass end of one of those stubborn beasts."

"Not a one. But truth is, you do not look like you've missed many meals."

"Not after getting to the Gentry's. But back in South Carolina I knew many hungry days. Mass Gentry knows the value of a good hand, especially us in the boiling house. He knows if he's going to work us half to death, he's got to feed us proper. Not near everybody is as lucky as we was."

***

We met the others in the woods a half-mile west of the St. Johns, where campfires could burn with little worry of patrols. Plenty of hot food and coffee was waiting for us. In the light of the fires, I watched the twenty men who would lead us to the plantation. They were all tough-looking, burly men who carried battle-scarred blades like Virgil's. Their bodies carried scars, too. Some were from battle, but most from the cane fields. Many had forearms like Virgil's, the skin burned dead by boiling sugar. Several were one-armed, the other lost to the iron rollers that squeezed the sweet juice out of the cane.

"Do you have any word of my Naomi?" Virgil asked Fredrick and Cyrus, two men who had been on the Gentry plantation before the rebellion. Both had family behind the Von Bock fences. They had been watching the place for months and were able to get messages in and out.

"Safe last I seen her," Cyrus said, sitting across the fire as we ate. "She had to endure some bad suffering for a while but she's back with the others now."

"Von Bock ain't keeping her up there for his personal lusts no more?"

"No, he ain't. He sent Naomi back to the regular pens soon as word come you'd busted loose from Laughing Boy. He was scared you'd get to him somehow," said Fredrick. "Your children were never harmed like Laughing Boy threatened, just scared awful bad."

"That won't spare him any," Virgil said. "Because I will get to him. Somehow."

"I don't expect a soul in Florida figured different," said Oscar. "But she is safe now. She been her normal smiling self again 'cept for worrying about you fierce."

"That's a blessing," said Virgil.

"At first, she was worried when you wasn't back right away. She thought maybe you'd been killed," said Cyrus.

"I got back as soon as I could," Virgil said.

"We know that."

"I intend to inflict every ounce of suffering I can on that man," Virgil said.

"There's plenty that feel that way. He will get it, too, and an eternity in the fiery pit."

"That don't console me none right now."

"No, I reckon it don't. It's just something I told myself some years back when a similar persecution struck me. Just so I did not get hanged for his murder."

***

The Von Bock plantation covered five thousand acres, half of which had once been cane fields. Hundreds of slaves had once toiled in these fields at harvest time and prepared them in between. No work had been done on them towards next year's crop. Now the neglected fields were waist-high with weeds and stank of the decay of cane stubble. Layers of fast-growing weeds and unsown sugarcane had been scythed, left to rot, and scythed again. They soaked with rain and matted, then half-dried until the rains came again. Underneath the thick quilt of moldering weeds the field was infested with rats that came to eat the sweet sugarcane and the snakes that came to eat the rats. The fields were un-cultivated, but sugar was no longer the cash crop of this plantation anyway. Flesh was. People were. The plantation had become an armed complex around a huge holding pen filled with hopeless people awaiting transport to the Indian reservations in the West and sale to a new master. Pine forest surrounded the plantation, with a small river that passed by the sugar works. A small army of overseers roamed the property. They were rough looking men, with pistols and knives stuck in every belt, pocket, and boot.

"How many men defend the prisoners?" Wild Cat asked Oscar. He was a battle-hardened man who had escaped an east coast plantation years ago. Since then he had quietly recruited rebels and prepared them for the moment to strike. He had been leading this band of runaways since the wild, flame-filled early days of the east coast rebellion.

"Seventy, and more keep coming. Most are prison parolees, their temporary freedom purchased by Von Bock. They are to be granted pardons if they can keep our people penned up until they arrive in the new territory," said Oscar. "They are zealous about their jobs."

"Then we will un-zealous them," said Wild Cat. "We will make them wish they were back in their safe prison cell."

"It's not the number of men that worries me. It is the cannon," said Oscar.

"I have no fear of a cannon," said Wild Cat. "They could never hit a Seminole."

"But it will not be aimed at the Seminole. It is aimed at that little box Von Bock set up," Oscar said.

"What box is that?"

"A box of people. The cannon is full of grape shot, aimed directly at a cage of fifty women and little babies. There is no way out for 'em," said Oscar. "Von Bock always keeps a crew at the cannon. First sign of trouble they will yank that lanyard and murder fifty people. The people in that cage will not have a chance. None of them."

"And the gun is always manned?" asked Wild Cat.

"Every second of the day and night. They sleep beside it in tents, and through the night there's always at least a couple of men staying awake, drinking coffee by the fire," said Oscar. "We've watched them practice their drills. They are good at what they do. They like blasting that cannon and scaring those poor people witless."

"If that's the case, I don't see what we can do," said Wild Cat.

"It is very risky, but we think our fastest man can sneak up close and charge the first man to the gun," said Oscar. "There is good cover through the cane field up to about fifty yards from the gun. One very fast man will knock that man away from the pull rope, just to stop that first shot until the rest of us get there."

"We have many fast men among us. Why not rush them in a pack and overpower them?" said Wild Cat. "Then we would know for sure."

"No, too many men could make too much noise, and we would need a large bunch to take out that crew," said Oscar. "The biggest worry is that a bunch of us sprinting down that bumpy road in the dark is more likely to trip over each other fighting for the man going for the gun. It is best to have one man knowing exactly what he must do."

"One man, I don't see how," said Wild Cat.

"We also have a surprise planned. A diversion that should make them hold up for just the one second we need," said Oscar. "Some of your Seminole brothers will be in the woods beyond the mansion. They will light up the sky with arrows of fire which will rain down on the house. We hope that will draw their attention long enough for our man to reach the gun. The timing would have to be exactly right, or all those babies die."

"It is the dogs that concern me more than the men," said Wild Cat, looking at a fierce looking brindle mastiff the size of a yearling calf that trotted alongside a trio of mounted guards. The slit eyes and powerful jaws never relaxed. The handler restrained him with the thick leather ropes used on breeding bulls.

"We will take care of the dogs," said Oscar. "We've been training those hounds for months."

"How so?"

"Abner here knows them well. They are practically his pets," Oscar said. "Tell 'em about it, Ab."

"I grew up on this plantation. My pa trained the Massa's tracking dogs, and I followed after him," said Abner. He was my age, tall and rail thin. He seemed too timid to be part of a raiding party intent on mass violence. "I didn't have no hand in raising them big man-killing dogs, but they ain't kept out at night. The hounds, though, them's my babies."

"That relieves me," said Wild Cat. "The others look more like the lions I saw at the circus."

"Might as well be. They was brought in special from Cuba," Oscar said. "Dogo Cubano. They are wild tempered as panthers, hot-blooded, unpredictable and vicious. The overseers themselves is scared of them and can't control them. Only those Cubans can do it. That's the extra rider in their patrols. Them dogs was bred and trained for only one purpose. To track and kill Negroes."

"And eat 'em, by the looks of those jaws," said Wild Cat.

"Yes, they will. Von Bock sicced 'em loose on a man that tried to escape early on. He dragged the man back and forced us all to watch as he loosed them killers on him. Four of them monsters at once ripped that man apart limb from limb. They rooted through his guts and tore off pieces until there wasn't no more pieces. Them dogs ran around for days burying arms and legs and digging them up. Them overseers got 'em a mighty loud laugh out of that, and it sho' enuff terrified our folks," said Abner.

"Have mercy," said Virgil.

"But like I said, the Cubans are too hot-blooded to be out when the night creatures are scurrying around. They stay chained up tight. It's the other dogs I know. They are pedigreed hunting hounds, bred for treeing raccoons and running deer, not chasing men. They'll track a runaway, but that's not what they was originally trained for. They have a friendly disposition, by nature. I raised them up from the day of their birth and worked and trained them ever' day. I raise fine dogs. They bring some of the highest prices in Florida when Massa went to sell 'em. I know how to get 'em to love me. Those pups will be wanting a treat and a belly rub, not to gnaw on my friends."

"But won't they bark at us, not knowing our smell yet?"

"Not them dogs. Not if I'm within sniffin' distance."

"They come to his call, tame as lambs," said Oscar. "He sneaks in every night, rubs their ears a little, gives them some bacon and a honey biscuit. Keeps them real friendly. The overseers don't have a clue. Too busy lying to each other about women they laid with and field hands they kicked around."

"I'll bet the women they laid with don't brag about it," said Virgil.

"How many dogs do they have out at night?" asked Wild Cat. "They'll all coming running to you?"

"The dogs on the other side of the plantation will be lured away, too, in similar fashion. Those of us taking out the cannon have only the one pair to get past."

"Won't there be men coming for them?"

"Eventually, but not in no great hurry," he said. "We trained them too, whether they realized it or not. They growed accustomed to the dogs chasing varmints at night. Those patty rollers will ride on past us without suspecting a thing."

"And if the ruse doesn't work?"

"It will. I know my dogs," said Abner. "I wish I could take them with us."

"So, not impossible, but extremely risky," smiled Wild Cat, rubbing his chin and pretending to ponder. "Excellent. I will do it."

***

We watched the plantation for three days. The village of slave shacks was deserted. Instead, all the prisoners had been herded into a five-acre stockade on a deserted bean field, covered by a collection of rickety open shelters and ragged tents. A wall of a split rail fence and sharpened stakes kept them in. On one corner a guard tower rose fifty feet in the air, and each corner held a guard box raised ten feet or so off the ground. All the boxes had armed men in them that seemed to be alert.

Wagon roads looped through the property. One road crossed the cane field in front of us and went right up to the cannon, which was always manned. Around the clock men gathered at the fire where an iron kettle and coffee pot always warmed. The men passed their time playing cards and checkers. The sleeping tent held a dozen cots. Different men came and went, but there was always at least two or three at the gun.

"That's the devil's house right there," Virgil said, pointing at the long wall of coquina stone of the sugar works. "The house of pain and misery."

Two smokestacks towered above the wall, and the loading dock of the warehouse was visible. It was piled high with barrels of sugar, molasses and rum.

"Soon it will be ash," said Wild Cat. "We will burn it to the ground."

"That's good," said Virgil. "Destroy it by fire. Those boilers wrecked bodies and souls. It will be like killing a demon. Ain't no worldly way to do it but fire."

"My men on the river have made it unsafe for Von Bock to empty the warehouses from last year. As you can see, many barrels of rum remain," said Oscar. "That rum will fuel the flames that burn the mill. We will show the world how we deal with slavers."

***

"How are you doing?" Wild Cat asked me that night.

"I am well, brother," I said. "I am ready to lead the attack. I will take out the man at the cannon."

"What?" exclaimed Wild Cat. "You heard me tell Oscar I would do that. I am the fastest runner. Only I can get to that cannon without being seen."

"No, my brother. With all respect, you are not nearly as fast as me even when you have two good legs. It is obvious you have injured your ankle. You have been limping badly. You hide it but I see it," I said. "Your ankle could fail you and many people would die."

"You speak to me with a bit more impertinence than you should," said Wild Cat, bristling up.

"I am old enough to speak directly," I said. "There is much at stake here. I only want to give us the best chance of succeeding."

"I will do this, Pete," said Wild Cat. "My ankle will not betray me."

"Speak the truth," I said. "Are you injured?"

"I have never slowed on the trail," he said.

"I know you did not," I said. "But I watched when others did not. When we stopped to rest, I saw you hiding a limp. I saw you with your

56

moccasins off and your ankle was badly swollen. How did you injure it?"

"From the fight at the Withlacoochee," said Wild Cat. "But it will not slow me."

"That is good to know," I said. "I will feel more confident knowing you are a half-step behind me."

"If those men come out of the tent, you will be surrounded. No way out," said Wild Cat.

"That would not be true if your ankle holds up," I said.

"Very well. The timing must be perfect," he said.

"Do not worry about me," I said. "Just keep up."

"Your brother warned me if I allowed you to take needless risk, he would kill me. Torture me and kill me. Feed me alive to the alligators," Wild Cat said. "I don't think he was joking."

"He wasn't," I said. "But this is not needless. It is best. It is the only way."

***

Virgil and I were stretched out under the moon, our last night of peace for a while. We would raid the plantation when the sun went down to-morrow.

"Why is you doing this Pete?" asked Virgil, watching the stars. "Why is you risking your neck to free my Naomi?"

"We're friends, aren't we?"

"Sure," he said. "But not too many friends would risk getting killed just for friendship."

"I don't know," I said, after a long pause. "I hadn't thought about it too much. I am doing it for more than just friendship, I guess."

"That's what I'm getting at. You haven't considered why you're risking getting shot?"

"Well, I mean, I guess, it's the right thing to do, is why I'm doing it," I said. "My brother would be here if he hadn't been so badly injured. John says there are three kinds of people. People that enslave. Those that allow themselves to be enslaved. And those that do not. We will not allow it. That is what I am doing. Not allowing it."

"Sounds right."

"And he says if we believe in something for ourselves, we believe in it for others," I said. "The Estelusti have friends and family among those behind that fence. You fought beside me at the Withlacoochee. I fight beside you. You are trying to get your family free. I am trying to keep my family free. Your fight is our fight, more so than the Seminole fight is ours."

"I reckon so...But I didn't run all the way across Florida looking for a scrap," he said. "I was already right there when that general showed up."

"Maybe I just always wanted to do something big, something gallant and valiant and grand. When I was younger my mother read me many books and told me many tales of bold adventurers and brave warriors. She told me of my ancestors from Africa. From my father's side, the Spaniards had many great adventures. He spoke of the early explorers of Florida, the Conquistadors. Some were likely my ancestors. I always wanted to be like that, I guess. That my destiny would be some great feat or exploit. I dream of those adventures. Do you know what I mean?"

"I reckon a little, but not really. That's one of those things that rarely enters our heads down there in bondage. Never read no books, never been told no books. Never heard no stories about my ancestors being great heroes," Virgil said.

"But they may have been, nonetheless. There were many warrior tribes in Africa."

"Wouldn't that be something? But I've never considered it. Our thoughts centered around having a full belly and not drawing the ire of the overseers. Anything beyond that was fanciful. I wasn't looking for no adventure, no grand battles. Not even no big battles. I only hoped that one day I could get me and my Naomi and our chilluns some place where we could be left in peace."

"Maybe you can have that if we can beat these Americans that will come, maybe if we beat them in such a fashion they'll never return," I said.

"Mostly all I ever heard of any Africans is just tales of woe. Everybody's always saying those glorious things await us in heaven, once we're done with our suffering at the hands of other'n here."

"You don't believe that?"

"Not scarcely, and even if I did, I ain't going to no such lily pure place. I could kill every MacCuaig and kin to them and still die with my heart filled with black hate and cold murder."

"Well, killing MacCauigs isn't murder. This is a holy cause, same as a Knight of the Round Table. Do you know what a knight is?" I said. "They were warriors and adventurers that did good things for their people and vanquished their enemies. Then they lived a life of sport and games surrounded by beautiful women. And the Spaniards, sailing all over the world for months and months, even years, just to see what's out there."

"Sailing all over the world just because that's what you felt like doing? Boy, wouldn't I like to have that kind of freedom," said Virgil. "Cept I rightly don't have no idea what is out there. I wouldn't know which way to point a boat, nor mule team either, for that matter."

"Well, now maybe you can find out," I said. "Maybe we both can. Maybe that is why I am here. Because those adventures are what I have always dreamed of."

"Ain't that something," Virgil said. "I used to dream about getting cold dippers of water without risking the wrath of the overseer."

"Now things are different," I said.

"Just don't seem real yet," he said.

"It is real."

"Maybe," said Virgil. "Maybe it's real. I've had a life where something is only real if Massa say it is. I say red, he say blue, then it's blue. If the supper bell rings at five o'clock and the Massa changes it to six o'clock, well, six it is and that's real. Freedom like this? It's a new thing, is all."

***

Abner led the way as we slithered through the abandoned cane field toward the cannon. His canvas pouch bulged with bacon and hog jowls. Wild Cat was behind him, and I followed Wild Cat. The others followed but stayed well back.

I heard every sound around me, every scrape, every brittle weed bend, every dry leaf crackle. I heard the rats running and chewing. I smelled the musty rot. I watched the ants and beetles and many legged bugs skitter out of my way. I smelled bear grease on some others. I smelled the tobacco smoke and bubbling coffee from our enemy the cannon crew. I was warmed by the smell, even in my terror.

I wanted to jump and run, to sprint as fast as I could, to feel the wind whip past me. Moving so slowly felt like a spiked collar closing around my neck. The longer it took, the more we stopped and waited, stronger came the urge to leap to my feet and run. It became nearly irresistible, and I wasn't sure which direction I'd run, toward the danger or away from it. To save my people or abandon them. But I knew if we didn't act soon, I would run. One way or the other.

Finally, it was time. We would charge the cannon after the next pair of guards passed. I could see them as specks in torchlight hundreds of yards away, coming down the curving road.

Soon Abner gave a short night-bird whistle, and the nearest hounds came loping up, slobbering and friendly. They licked and nuzzled him until he gave them their bacon and sweet biscuits. Their eyes danced with happiness as they gobbled their treats and Abner scratched their ears. When the overseers got closer Abner threw a chunk of pork which the dogs bounded after.

"Get back over here you dumb mutt," growled the man on horseback.

The hounds gulped down the last greasy morsel and rejoined the riders, looking back at us with sad eyes. The guards continued without looking back. We were now within fifty yards of the cannon. The light from the campfire outlined three men in camp chairs. I could hear bits of conversation and laughter.

A tiny light flickered in the pine forest beyond the mansion, then a streak of fire shot high into the sky, almost straight up. Then it plummeted down, toward the roof of the mansion. As the first flaming arrow came down, a hundred more shot up.

"Go!" whispered Wild Cat. "Go, go! Hooah!"

But I was already up and running. The men at the cannon lurched to their feet but turned to watch the rain of comets in the sky. Gunfire and war cries came from the far trees. I ran harder than I ever had in my life. My footsteps sounded as loud as gunshots to me, but the men at the gun were awed by the fire in the sky. They did not hear me until I was right on them. The first man whipped around toward me just as I launched myself. His eyes bugged wide open as I sailed high and came down hard. My club smashed him right above the nose and we went down in a heap.

Wild Cat and his men slammed into the other cannoneers with shrieks of rage. Bodies flew and flipped in the dark. I rolled off the dead man and tried to get up, but another dead man crashed into me and knocked me over. Feet stomped and tromped and kicked as I struggled to my knees. Guns blasted. Another cannoneer fell lifeless in front of me.

I was slammed in the back again, but this time it was a man tackling me. He ground my face in the dirt, and then a powerful arm closed around my throat and a hand dug at my face. I bit the hand as I thrashed and clawed, but he drove into me with his full weight, then lifted up and kneed me hard in the gut.

I moaned and doubled up helplessly but my attacker grunted and released his grip. His body went limp and heavy, and I slid from underneath it. His skull was cleaved in half and leaked red porridge. Virgil yanked his hatchet out and I was squirted in the face with whatever came out of the dead man's head. No cannon had roared. The cannoneers were dead. Oscar was pounding a spike into the vent of the cannon with a mallet.

"It's done," Wild Cat shouted. "To the pens!"

***

"Back away, back away," Virgil roared as bullets flew overhead. Our men attacked the fence with axes and cane knives, splitting the rails and yanking them apart. The people scrambled back as the fence shattered.

Shouting hosannas and hallelujahs, men and women of all ages poured out, carrying bundles and dragging tearful children. We waved them on toward the torch bearers who would lead them down the trails that had been prepared.

"Virgil, Virgil," a woman's voice screamed. Out of the clamoring mob a tiny woman with a baby in her arms ran toward us. Holding tightly to her skirts were two little girls with tears on their cheeks and eyes wide with fear and confusion.

"Naomi, my babies," Virgil blubbered. His tears came down in big drops. He grabbed Naomi and swung her around as she shrieked with joy and held tight to the baby. The girls locked their arms around his huge thighs, squeezing tight.

Virgil put Naomi down with a wet kiss on the cheeks, then picked up the girls. With one in each arm, he danced a little jig. Naomi rearranged the baby, and I grabbed up one of the lumpy burlap bundles she brought out.

"I'm Pete," I hollered at her, trying to make myself heard above all the other shouting and gunfire. "Just follow Oscar right there with the torch."

***

Once into the trees, I was with twenty people who followed Oscar down a trail he had planned for months, clearing it of hazards and memorizing every step in the dark. He carried a lantern with a beam of light no wider than a pencil. The pine forest was flat and open, and we moved easily through the night.

At sunup we finally stopped to rest, a few hundred yards past a stream we hoped washed away our scent. Naomi un-knotted a red kerchief and pulled out some food while Virgil and I pulled down some Spanish moss and made beds for the girls.

Naomi was small, but not at all dainty. Her round face could almost have been considered delicate, perhaps, but her arms and shoulders were sturdy-built and muscular. She removed her straw hat, and a mop of frazzled braids broke free. The girls were little twin miniatures of her, with big baby calf eyes.

"Here, share of the food I brought," she said to me. "It ain't much. We had to hoard it away from the overseers, or they'd know we was fixing to run. They search hard for people hoarding."

"I'm grateful, but I don't want to take what these children need," I said, watching the girls gobble down yams and corncakes, sweetened from a small molasses jug Naomi had hidden away.

"How soon will we cross the river?" she asked.

"Two days, if we encounter no problems," I said. "From here on it will be treacherous footing. Travel will be slow, wading through miles of standing water and land that never really dries. But it will be safer. I know that type of place better than our pursuers."

"Then we have plenty, if there's food waiting there, and Virgil only eats enough for three men."

"There is. And the boat to take us home."

"Then eat this. We got enough."

"Ain't gonna be but a minute and we'll have more food than their bellies can hold, just as soon as we cross the St. Johns," said Virgil. "But I sho' wish we could have got some of them fine hams out of Massa Von Bock's smokehouse, and a barrel of that good bacon."

"I don't know how you'd carry one through here," I said.

"Hungry as I am right now, that wouldn't be a concern," said Virgil. "I'd have already upended it and poured it straight down my gullet, swallered without barely chewing."

"All thousand pounds?"

"Maybe two," said Virgil. "The bears in my belly is growlin'."

"Oh, hush. You been well fed of late, I can see," said Naomi. "We have suffered through some real hunger. It was hard explaining to them hungry kids they couldn't have what I was hiding. That was the worst part."

"That there's all over with now," said Virgil, wrapping his big arms around her.

"Well, it's mighty nice to meet you, Pete," Naomi said. "I reckon this is about as formal introductions as we get."

"A pleasure to meet you too, finally. Virgil doesn't talk about much other than you and these babies," I said, gnawing on a biscuit. "And food."

"I rarely thought of anything else myself," she said.

"I expect not," I said.

"Excuse me for my forwardness," she said. "And I don't reckon you look 'zackly like the Moses they tell of in the Bible, that saved all them folks from the tribulations of Pharaoh. Maybe this swamp ain't the River Jordan. But I could kiss you straight on the lips regardless."

"I don't reckon Virgil would care for that much," I finally stammered after almost choking on my mouthful of biscuit. "As far as the Jordan River, we still have a long way to go yet. But the St. Johns River sure increases our chances of safety."

"Oh, goodness, I am sorry Pete. I didn't mean nothing about them kisses," she said. "I didn't mean to embarrass you. I'm just happy is all. All this here, well, I don't even have the words for all the feelings I'm feeling."

"You can't be kissing on Pete anyway. He's got him a girl. Don't let that pretend bashfulness fool you," said Virgil, a grin on his tired face. "He's like satin with the ladies. He's just private about them matters."

"No matters to be kept private," I said. "Nor satins."

"Sure, Pete. It's your story. You tell it however you want," he said. Then to Naomi, "Pete's people have the little settlement we're going to. Their own private little island. Purty little girl lives there now and she's sweet on Pete."

"Ain't that something," she said.

"You will be safe there. There are others there, also," I said. "Strong people. Men experienced in fighting the Americans and the Creeks."

"The others did not come now?"

"No, they stayed to defend our Cove just in case of trouble. My brother was wounded in the last battle. My mother's man Yancy does not move fast or far anymore. He has old battle wounds of his own," I said. "But he has much experience in war."

"The soldiers won't come to your village?"

"It would be almost impossible. We live on a small island in the wildest part of the Cove, at the edge farthest from any soldiers. We are surrounded by miles and miles of swamp that the slavers avoid because of the snakes and alligators," I said. "But do not worry. Our islands are bright and fertile, not filled with creatures."

"It will be a good place for the children," said Virgil.

"I've never heard sweeter words," said Naomi.

"His mama is a schoolteacher," said Virgil. "They got a little schoolhouse right there on the island."

"Oh, my," said Naomi.

"It is not really a school. She teaches the children to read and write English. History lessons. Other things. She did that years ago when she lived in St. Augustine, before it was illegal to teach slaves to read. My two sisters are the age of your daughters. I am sure my mother would be very happy to have two more students. That is her passion."

"I surely would like my girls to get some learning. They can't read a lick. Nor can I," said Naomi.

"I am sure my mother would be pleased to teach your children. And you, if you want," I said. "For as long as you stay there, or whatever you choose to do."

"Whatever we choose to do. Choosing…ain't that something, darling," said Virgil.

"It sure is, but I reckon we best take a breath and not get over-tickled thinking we can do whatever we choose to do," said Naomi. "You know Von Bock and MacCuaig will be after us, with everything and everybody they have."

"I know it," said Virgil. "But at least tonight we can dream it. Tomorrow we'll keep on making it come true. Now let's get some sleep."

I was exhausted but my mind was still running. I looked at the little girls asleep on the palmetto mats and thought of my sisters, who'd never known a day of hunger or moment of terror in their lives. I thought of the stories my mother and Yancy told about the chains and the ships, and Von Bock's cannon aimed at a pen of little girls like this. I thought about what Willet looked like when she was freed from the MacCuaigs.

"You think this is the end of tribulation, Virgil?" I heard Naomi whisper as I drifted into sleep.

"No, I reckon it ain't," said Virgil. "Jes' different."

***

Day and night we heard the baying of the hounds. Sometimes near, sometimes off in the distance. At times we heard other runaways. We never revealed our presence, worried trackers could be hot on their trail. Once I watched the drama through my telescope as three young fugitives ran desperately through the trees. A pack of howling dogs was just a few hundred yards behind them and gaining fast. The boys reached a stream and dove in. I never saw them again. The dogs reached the bank and yapped and yelped and ran around in circles, sniffing up and down the bank. The furious, red-faced slavers showed up. I couldn't hear what they said, but it was clear how they felt.

We moved at night and stopped at dawn to sleep. Mid-morning of the third day we were resting on a tiny cypress hammock in a wide saw grass prairie. This was a safe place. No one could see us through the walls of titi-bush that covered the banks, and no one could reach us without wading across acres of slow-moving, knee-high water filled with alligators, snakes, and nervous wading birds.

The closest land was a narrow ridge that curved past us more than a mile away. The ridge connected the pine forest we'd just passed through with the palmetto thickets to our south. Once through those thickets we would be at the river.

"I hear dogs," I said.

"Those damn hounds. I told you I feared them worse than men," cursed Wild Cat. "How could they be so close?"

"They could not have followed our trail. I planned too well," said Oscar in disbelief.

"No, it is not your fault. It is just luck," said Wild Cat.

"It was wise to have us come to this hammock to sleep, and not stay on the ridge," I said. "Otherwise, that would be us in chains."

"I did not think they would come in this direction, through so much water. They are very determined," said Oscar.

"Perhaps it is only a couple patty rollers that got lost. I'll go up a tree and have a look," I said. A tall cherry tree in the center of the hammock still held its leaves. I climbed it and got out my spyglass.

Joost Von Bock was on the ridge, on the wide spot that bulged out like a fat frog stuck in a snake's throat. He sat on a horse, casually flicking a riding crop at a row of bloody slaves who knelt a few yards away. Three Robinson brothers stood near Von Bock. The burly, un-washed brothers were part of another large family of slavers, men that hired out as patty rollers and overseers when they were not doing bounty work. I had seen them around the forts, and at the slave auctions in St. Augustine. Further back in the trees were more than a hundred black people chained together with iron collars. Their hands were roped behind them. Most were naked, or nearly so. Their skin was slashed and ripped from fleeing through the swamp, and several were striped bloody from the whip for the same reason.

Laughing dog handlers circled the forlorn people, yanking back on the heavy leather straps as the feverish mastiffs lunged and snapped. My heart sank as slavers started boiling coffee and slicing bacon into skillets. It could spell disaster for us if they stayed long. Our small ham-mock was an excellent place to hide. The trackers had not seen us and would not as long as we stayed put, but they had us trapped. We had no place to hide for at least a mile if we tried to cross that water, and we'd be tromping through muck and underwater perils the whole way. Just as bad, if the MacCuaigs followed that ridge on around, they would be in the thickets that separated us from the St. Johns. We would be cut off.

I climbed back down. The presence of the slavers filled us with fear. The plight of the captured people filled us with sadness. Their fate, and possibly ours, filled some with dread and despair. The children stared wide-eyed and silent. Naomi and the other women kept them calm by feeding them scraps of the little food we had. They jerked but said noth-ing whenever a scream of pain or fear from a slave would drift across the water.

"The children are hungry. We cannot keep them quiet forever. We must leave here," said Wild Cat.

"There is no way to sneak fifteen people across open prairie, especially not in the daylight," said Oscar. "We will have to wait until dark and stay down in the water."

"If we wait until dark and stay low in the water, the alligators will eat the children," I said.

"What if we have to go back the other way?" asked Virgil.

"It would be many wet miles to the next closest men with boats, if they would even still be there," said Oscar. "That would be a treacherous undertaking, especially for the babies."

"One of us could slip through the water and get close to them, and maybe hear their plans," I said. "I will go."

"That would be too risky to go alone," said Wild Cat. "I will go beside you. That way we can watch each other's back for alligators, or any two-legged killers who might prowl around."

"That is good," I said.

"Get everyone ready to run. If it looks like trouble, we will distract them and lead them away. You will have to move fast," Wild Cat told Oscar. "Listen carefully for us."

Wild Cat and I plastered our heads with muddy mats of lily pads and grass, then inched our way through the shallow water. The shallow lake was covered with dying cow lilies and duckweed and scattered with spindly patches of saw grass. Turtles and snakes sunned themselves on the scattered boneyard of bleached logs and rotting limbs that had been washed here by floods. The buttressed bases of the old trees flared out in packed tendrils wide enough to hide a boat, and each tree fielded a legion of knees that grew out of the water looking like rusty, dull knife points. We slithered through the weeds between Cypress knees until we were close enough to hear.

"How many have we captured now?" asked Von Bock.

"More than half, and only had to shoot two. My brother Beathan should be at the river north of us by now, and Clyde is a few miles south with twenty men. But it's a long river."

"Exactly, it's a long river. That's why we need to get moving, right through there," Von Bock said, pointing his riding crop at the hammock where our people hid.

"No, I think we've had enough of chasing these sons-of-bitches through this bleak wilderness. If there's any that haven't reached the river, they are holed up on those stranded hammocks," said Laughing Boy. "There could be a hundred of them lurking in there, just waiting to shoot us to pieces."

"Ridiculous. Those people aren't but a motley lot of ignorant dark-ies and naked savages," said Von Bock.

"Ignorant enough to burn your mansion and blow up your sugar mill and free a thousand slaves. Motley enough to wipe out one army column and whip the hell out of another. This is as far into this swamp as I'm going with these few men. I'm not crippling any more horses either," said Laughing Boy. "I've fought these damned Seminoles and Negroes for thirty years. This is their land. Not yours and not mine. We do not live in the swamps like these mud-burrowing rodents."

"If they are merely rodents, why are you so scared to root them out?"

"These rodents have the bite of an alligator. That is why," said Laughing Boy. "These rodents would happily scavenge my carcass. Yours too."

"Don't be ridiculous. These aren't warriors. They're just a bunch of runaways."

"Runaways with a grudge, you pompous fool," said Laughing Boy. "You're still covered with soot from your burned house."

"Enough of this dithering. Take ten men and go look in that hammock there," Von Bock ordered.

"Bite me bawbag ya ridiculous bampot," guffawed Laughing Boy. "These men here are mostly my kin, not a military outfit. You will not be ordering us to charge an entrenched position."

"You call that clump of brush an entrenched position? When did you go to the military academy?"

"I'd call it a nearly insurmountable entrenched position. I know that much military," said Laughing Boy. "Across all that water? Two or three good men with rifles could kill half of us before we crossed it. From here to the river there are a thousand little fortresses like that. It would be like a fly in a spider web. I have seen this trap before."

"You go, or I'll hire someone who isn't afraid of a handful of raggedy darkies hiding in a briar patch," snapped Von Bock. "Robinson, get ready to search that hammock. You have just been promoted, and your pay tripled."

"That's my money out there, too, Joost. You try to send anyone else after my property, I will kill them. And maybe you too," said Laughing Boy.

"You can try that anytime you want," said Von Bock.

"Careful what you say. No one would question if you never returned from these swamps. Happens to folks all the time," said Laughing Boy. "You command nothing out here. Remember that."

The men in the search party were shifting around. I could see the MacCuaig men had spread out into a wide circle. There were twenty or more of them. The Robinsons were only three and had bunched together nervously.

"I won't stand for a mutiny out here," snapped Von Bock, but his voice was high.

"My men go no further. We have worked hard these past few days, with little sleep or decent food. Now we're going to relax and enjoy ourselves some before we go back home to the wives and the drudgery of home."

"What do you mean?"

"I mean I am done with listening to you. Go on after all the runaways you want," said Laughing Boy. "My men and I have decided this is a nice spot for us to rest and take our amusements."

"There's thousands of dollars running away free through the swamps, and you want your amusements?" said Von Bock. "Just what amusements do you plan to take?"

"Only the ones we need to make our efforts worthwhile, and no more. Joost, the thing is, all you understand is the money end of this arrangement. Chasing slaves is an inhumane vocation one must have a pitch-black soul to engage in," said Laughing Boy loudly. "And those of us that engage in it have come to terms with it, including yourself. We know what we are, what we have become. You should too."

The MacCuaig men laughed or pretended to. It was mostly the chuckle of bullies finding a new weakling. They had their hands on their weapons, as did the Robinsons.

"As you said, I have come to terms with it. What is your point?" demanded Von Bock.

"That it's much different for those of us black-souled wretches that personally engage in the hunt. We do not get our satisfaction looking at bank ledgers. That ain't what gets our blood pumping. Picking out a pretty little high-yellow house girl for some polite and discreet love-making like you do ain't satisfying. You've only had a tiny taste of prowling these snake-infested jungles chasing down desperate runaways. What do you know of death lurking around every bush, when every step you take you feel the breath of the reaper on your neck? Even

73

now you have a company of armed bodyguards around you," said Laughing Boy.

"It's different being out here for weeks at a time, with revenge-minded niggers and murderous goddamn savages just waiting to slit our throats. The turmoil of our overwrought minds and nerves requires a satiation one does not find through normal channels."

"What is your goddamn point?"

"It ignites a certain lust in the men after a few days, the killing and fighting and hiding and fearing. But mostly the surviving."

"You want some whores?"

"Like I said, you would not understand. It ain't the same at all. The boys work up a heat. The dogs work up a heat. I work up a heat. If there is no jackpot, what's the point of the chase?"

"The reward is in the money we get for selling them," said Von Bock.

"Dogs do not understand money. Neither do hard peckers. Once you've done what we've done for a while, there's only one way to end this the right way. We must have certain jollities and entertainments that the good folks safely back in civilization wouldn't understand. Those like you that haven't found their brothers with their throats cut and women defiled," smiled Laughing Boy. "Now, get out of the way you twit, before you end up in the slag pile and left for the gators."

The slaves cried out in horror as Gibb McGillivray and Magnus Murdoch pushed forward two bloodied and beaten male slaves. Wailing and cries for Jesus's mercy erupted when two sobbing young women were dragged through the dirt. The cries of anguish were so much I sank my ears under the water as Wild Cat silently retched.

"Goddammit, you're not wasting a day so you can get drunk, rut on these women and feed the men to the dogs," shouted Von Bock.

"Who says we ain't?"

"I do, and damn sure not with my prime stock you're not," shouted Von Bock. "That's expensive stock you have there. Mine. You are not touching those two. They belong to me, and they will both bring a high price as long as they're not spoiled."

"Well, sometimes it just works out that way," said Laughing Boy. "Now, move aside."

Von Bock took an aggressive step, but Laughing Boy was fast. His big knife was out, stabbing in and out of Von Bock's belly half a dozen times before Von Bock realized he'd been stuck. MacCuaig guns blasted, and the Robinsons were shot to pieces before they could raise their weapons.

Von Bock staggered around in a circle, weeping and groping at his guts that were spilling out and tangling around his feet. Finally, he tripped, and his face slammed the ground. He sobbed and kicked around in a circle until his guts wrapped around him like a mass of bright vines. His slow death seemed to be a source of great amusement to the MacCuaigs, who expressed astonishment the pampered white man took so long to die. As Von Bock choked up his last clot of blood, Laughing Boy yanked his head up and sliced off his scalp. He stuffed the scalp in his bullet bag.

"Injuns got him," Laughing Boy laughed. "Well, we warned that city boy not to come out here to Seminole land."

"I seen the whole thing. Sadly, I couldn't get here in time to save him," laughed Farlan. "There must have been twenty of them, coming at the valiant Von Bock from all sides, howling like demons."

"You don't say? Twenty of them?" grinned Laughing Boy. "Valiant Von Bock. I like that, poor brave fellow."

"That big one they call Virgil was the leader of 'em all," said Greum. "I seen the others up close. I reckon I could put a name to 'em when we catch them. That old bastard Oscar Waller was one, too."

"We'll catch those murderers," laughed Laughing Boy. "We owe Valiant Von Bock that much."

"Can we feed him to the dogs?" asked Liam MacCuaig. "They was going wild while he was flopping around, twisting himself up in his guts."

"No, we must take his mutilated body back to the fort, to show the good folks in the army what these inhuman runaways are capable of," said Laughing Boy. "Now, get these women tied down."

A chorus of sobs, prayers and cries of horror arose as Greum Mac-Cuaig threw the women down on blankets.

"Quit your sniveling," Laughing Boy snarled as more MacCuaigs ripped the clothes off the sobbing girls and pegged their shackled ankles far apart on the ground. Clyde Urquhart staked the naked old men's legs to the ground. The slobbering monster dogs lunged as the Mac-Cuaigs, passed whiskey bottles and threw dice to see who would guard the prisoners and who got first turns on the woman.

Unleashed, the killer dogs sprang on the men. Bones cracked and flesh tore. The MacCuaig men doubled over with laughter as one huge beast ripped off a scrawny arm and charged into the seated crowd of slaves.

"Hell, since we don't have to split shares with Von Bock, bring another one of his up here. Ain't there a Seminole wench in this train?" bellowed Farlan Ogilvie above the sobs of anguish.

We slipped away silently while the MacCuaigs took their amusements. When the sun went down, we hushed the children and risked the alligators. The MacCuaigs were too busy to notice.

***

We reached the St. Johns the following morning. Our friends were waiting with boats and food. As we ate, they told us of those who had already passed through on their way to safety. Everyone hoped their loved ones had crossed elsewhere but we knew many of the waiting boats would not be filled. We rested for a few hours and said our good-byes.

Once across the river I relaxed, if just a little. The St. Johns was almost a mile wide here, and much wider than that in some places. Any mounted or marching pursuers would need a ferry to cross and the closest one was more than a full day away. Even if they crossed, they could never follow us through this maze of shaded streams and impenetrable thickets.

We paddled on for hours as the buzz of insects and thrum of frogs filled the air. Bird calls from near and far drifted through the trees. Unseen creatures plopped and scurried and splashed all around us. Our world was undisturbed by any interlopers.

We steered into a shallow pool, two hundred feet across and barely deep enough to float our canoe. The hot sun overhead warmed the water. Around the banks the air was thick with the smell of rotting vegetation and the decay of half-eaten prey. It was the smell of successful hunts and life flourishing in the swamp. In the winter months, the swamp's hundreds of streams dried and shrank. Some dried completely. From miles around, the fish and frogs made their way to weedy puddles like this one, crowding in tight with no way out. Predators swarmed to the balmy ponds. Egrets and cranes and herons came by the thousands. The birds grew fat on the bountiful fish and the gators grew fat on the birds.

This pond was the realm of Old Spike, who was at least fifty years old and scarred by a hundred battles. The giant gator had ruled this pond for as long as anyone could remember. Over the decades, he had clawed and nosed out and dug through the mud until he'd built a kingdom. Now, in the dry season, he had his own sun-warmed bay fed by small streams that dribbled in from the Withlacoochee.

Many years ago, some unfortunate Indian had found himself in Spike's jaws. The last thing the dying man did was cleave his hatchet blade into Spike's head, slightly off center between his eyes. The blow hadn't been deep enough to do any damage to Spike's iron-hard skull and tiny brain, but half the blade had stayed embedded there ever since. So had his hatred of Indians.

I looked for him now. It was rare, but Spike was known to attack dugouts, if the traveler looked enough like the Indian that had left his blade in Spike's skull. I looked enough like those unfortunates to know I did not want to stay around long enough to arouse him.

Finally, I saw him. Spike lurked behind a curtain of brown weeds near shore, squinting at us with undisguised belligerence. With a few shrugs of his man-length tail, Spike's full length cruised into view. His broad nose turned and slowly plowed through the withered lily pads toward us.

"What kind of beast is that?" Primrose said, pointing at Spike. His lush wig of water plants rode the ax blade like a flower bonnet and covered one eye. Two blackbirds paced down the ridges of his armored back.

"That's Old Spike, the biggest gator in Florida as far as I've heard of," I said. "Virgil, we might want to move a little faster through here. We don't want him to think we plan to loiter."

Spike's tail swung wider. His ugly snout picked up speed and was angled directly amidships of our canoe. I pulled out my pistol and prepared to give Spike both barrels if he got too close, although I had doubts even that could put a dent in Spike's thick skull.

"He scares me," said Primrose.

"Me too," I said. "Stay far away from him, but also remember the Maker of Breath put him here to protect us. The bad men do not want to cross these gators. Any bad man coming in here that doesn't know about Spike will end up his supper. That is our moat. Our safety."

"You remember how he's eying you for a meal should you ever want to traipse off away from our camp," said Virgil.

An osprey that had been hovering above the lake dove, streaking down. He collided violently with the water and plunged under. The submerged hunter's powerful wings beat furiously and whipped up waves. A moment passed, then the bird shot up out of the water with a tremendous cascade.

With majestic strokes the osprey skimmed the pond, working hard to get aloft as the blue-silver glistening fish flopped wildly in his hooks. The bird veered, still only a few inches above the water, circling the lake as he shook the water off his back. He came around straight at us, predator eye staring. He soared at the last second, passing inches over our heads with a gust of wet wind that blew our hair back. The girls yelped in surprise. Their shrieks of laughter startled a deer and two skittish fawns at the water's edge. The deer bounded away, crashing the brush. Ten acres of tree branches shivered, and the water emptied as noisy birds shot squawking into the sky.

"They're so loud," laughed Primrose.

"They watch over us. All that noise warns us of intruders," I said. "We have many such friends here in the Cove."

"Ain't that something," said Virgil.

"Danger always looms in the Cove," I said. "Be cautious but not afraid. Always remember, never linger near the water's edge. You must learn to move silently, always careful not to step on twigs or break any brush. See how just that small noise set the forest into such an uproar? In the Cove there is always someone nearby, even if it is just a sparrow or mouse. Their alarm will cause more alarm. If you are noisy, even if you think you are quiet, you will be given away. Stealth must always be the first thing on your mind from this day on."

Chapter Four

HOME

We left Spike's Pond and entered an even darker labyrinth, countless ribbons of slow-moving water partitioned by braided, overgrown hammocks that were dark as caves. Our natural maze would confound and ensnare any interloper as assuredly as a spider's web would ensnare a fly.

We weaved our way through to a wide inlet filled with old Cypress trees and gnarled knees. The bay was shaded by silver drapes of Spanish moss, and the banks were lined with titi-bush as thick and tall as a castle wall. A stranger could paddle past within twenty feet of it and never suspect that our eyes were always watching.

My family rushed out as I pulled the canoe onto the bank. My two 8-year-old twin sisters, Emma and Maggie leapt on me with such fervor that we fell back in the water with a splash. They romped around on me like a couple of playful otter puppies.

"Enough, enough," I shouted. "I survived a battle, don't drown me now that I'm home."

A strong arm pulled me up. It was Yancy, the Englishman the Indians called Yellow Beard. Until I had met Virgil, Yancy was the thickest-chested man I'd ever met. He was my mother's man and had lived amongst us for several years. He was permanently tanned a deep copper, with a bright yellow and silver beard. A thick braid of the same color hung all the way down his back. The beard covered scars on his face he'd received while trying to pull his wife and child out of the burning rubble of the Negro Fort explosion twenty years before.

Mateo hobbled toward me on his skinny, scarred-up legs. He hugged me and pounded my back so joyously he almost lost his spectacles, a precious gift from a long-ago British ally. Decades before, Mateo had met the famous American, Benjamin Franklin, when Franklin and Benjamin Rush had lived among the tribes. They had come to study the summer swamp sicknesses that killed the whites but rarely bothered the Indians and Negroes.

As he aged, Mateo had been told he bore a strong resemblance to Franklin, who he greatly admired. He was bald on top, but black hair grew long and straight from the back of his scalp. His round belly bulged against his calico hunting shirt and sash. The glasses were always perched on the end of his nose whether he was actually looking through them or not. He used them as he meticulously crafted his arrows and cheated at cards, and sometimes peered over them with meanings clearer than thunderclaps.

"I am glad you are home, brother," John said. He hugged me tight, looking me in the eye. He started to say more but stuttered and stepped away.

My mother squeezed me tighter than I ever remembered as she kissed my cheeks. Relief was on her face, but tiny, new worry lines still lingered. Mother was a tall woman, taller than me and nearly as tall as John. Today, above her long, slender neck her hair was coiled up inside a bright purple, gold and green head wrap. My mother had been raised as a house slave to a wealthy Spanish family, where carefully chosen words and courtliness were demanded and ingrained. However, she was not passive. She was a woman who had fought fiercely for her freedom and protected her family against predatory slave catchers for many years.

"I'm so glad you're back. You've had quite an exciting last few days," said Mother.

"I know you worried," I said. "But I was careful. We did what needed to be done."

"It's a wonderful thing you did, freeing those people," she said. "But I'm not sure how careful you were if you were with Wild Cat the whole time."

"Now I am returned, safe and unharmed," I said.

"You are," she said, and kissed my cheeks again.

"I have brought my new friends. This is Virgil, his wife Naomi, and their daughters Posie and Primrose. The little fellow just waking up is Sam."

"What a beautiful family," said my mother, smiling at the little girls. "You all must be exhausted and about starved."

"Yes, ma'am," said Virgil. "Famished. And wore completely out."

"I imagine so," said Mother. "We have a feast prepared. Come, let's eat."

Willet had stood by, watching anxiously as I greeted the others. Our eyes met and she gave me a smile and some kind of look that she seemed shy about. As we walked toward the cooking fires we touched hands but didn't embrace.

Mother and Susan had indeed prepared a feast. Mouth-watering smells filled the air. Venison turned on a spit over one fire. Over the other low fires, succulent egrets, anhingas and spoonbills roasted. Stew pots bubbled. Bread warmed in the stone oven. We gathered around the tables of the council house, smoothed cypress logs covered with mats of palmetto leaves. The council house had seen a great deal of use in recent months as many visitors came to discuss the looming war.

"Eat," said Mother and we did. For a minute no one spoke as we passed heaping bowls and platters. Lips smacked, juice dripped, and bird bones piled up on the spread-out leaves.

"This here is just about the finest eatin' I've ever had," said Virgil, emphatically pointing with a spoonbill leg bone and chin glistening with grease.

"A splendid meal," said Yancy, dropping a gnawed rib cage on the pile. "Visitors are always a pleasure. We rarely get fed like this."

"That's a wild fabulation that your girth clearly dispels," said Mother. "Though the ale and the rum contribute considerably."

"These water turkeys is deleckable. We was occasionally allowed to shoot us some birds for supper back on the Gentry place," said Virgil. "My Naomi, she's a fine bird cooker herself. Fine cooker of most any-thing."

"Is that right?" mother said to Naomi.

"I try," she said. "With what little we got, like Virgil said. I reckon as long as I have a little bacon grease I can cook about anything."

"She does right smart," said Virgil. "As you can see, I ain't exactly gaunt, even considering my recent months of privation."

"I look forward to tasting your cooking soon, Naomi. I'm able to keep a decent number of different spices here. But right now, after your ordeals, you all just need to get some rest. We can keep the little ones for a few days so you can get reacquainted properly. You would prob-ably appreciate a few nights of privacy. We'll have them sleeping under the stars and frog gigging."

"Well, ain't you talking saucy," said Yancy, as Naomi looked shyly down.

"That's the first you've ever complained about it," she said.

***

"And there went Pete in a tremendulous flinging flying leap. He come down with a crack of that war club, and there wasn't no fear of a cannon blast after that," said Virgil. "One big ol' ka-wham with that hammer, and we was clear."

"I am proud of my brother," said John. "No one else has a brother that attacked a cannon."

"I never seen anyone run faster, and considering he was running straight into danger, not away from it, I reckon he's about the bravest man I ever seen," Virgil said.

"I expected to piss myself," I said.

"Of course you did. Anyone would, and who says otherwise is a fool or a liar," said John. "You acted with great courage."

"Wild Cat was even more terrified than I was," I said. "He thought he would suffer a painful death at your hands if harm should come to me. Especially on his orders, one of those needless risks."

"And he probably would have," said John. "But what you did was not needless. Only a very courageous man would take the fate of those people into his hands as you did."

"Thank you, brother," I said.

"Much more may be asked of you before this is over," said John. "This war could last a very long time. There will be many battles and much hardship."

"I will do my part," I said.

"I know you will," John said. "But the Americans will keep coming. Fortunes are at stake. Just Virgil, Naomi and their children being freed cost the MacCuaigs two thousand dollars in profits, perhaps more. Hundreds of Von Bock slaves remain free. Valuable skilled craftsmen and laborers. That is a king's fortune, hundreds of thousands of dollars. They will want it back."

"I am very proud of both my sons," said my mother. "My youngest is now a man."

"Thank you, Mother. I did not mean to cause you worry," I said.

"It is a mother's burden to worry," said Mother. "You make me swell with pride. Even as I am filled with dread. Few things are ever simple, especially emotions. Even more, mothers' emotions."

***

"Your daughters are more than welcome to come to school with the others," said my mother, watching the romping children. "Every morning we spend a few hours with the books and slates."

"That would be wonderful," said Naomi. "I can't read a lick, and don't know no black people other than you all that can. My girls, I don't know what they'd do, though. Your girls would be way ahead of them."

"Yes, far enough ahead they could help Primrose and Posie get caught up in no time at all, really. Young like that, their minds are still sponges," said Mother. "Also, I'd be honored if you came with your girls. That would be so nice."

"Oh my, I don't know," said Naomi. "I'd dearly like to learn. But there's so many other things need doing."

"And they will be done, all of them. But there is no clock and no overseer out here. There is nothing out here more important than tending to your mind," said mother. "You could be my helper, too. Keeping the children's attention on schoolwork with all these new friends will be a task in itself. I'm sure they'll all be squirming to get out and play."

"Yes'm, I could sure do that," Naomi said. "My girls is well-behaved girls, but this here's a whole new world to them."

"So shall the books be," said mother.

***

"Pete said you was a pirate," said Primrose to Yancy that night after another huge meal of fried fish and roast birds.

"Oh, he did, did he?" said Yancy. "Ain't he a little stinker. I was a Royal Marine."

"What's a Royal Marine?" she asked.

"A fearless adventurer. A loyal stalwart. The bravest of warriors."

"A pirate," I said.

"Privateers, perhaps, but it was for a noble cause," said Yancy.

"Sounds like some exciting tales. I'd like to hear them," Virgil said. "Pete's been telling me there's thousands of stories of exploring adventures I need to hear."

"Yes, but perhaps another time," smiled Mother. "The tales, wondrous and enlightening as they may be, are quite violent. More importantly, apparently they cannot be told without a great deal of the coarsest sort of vulgarity and overly vivid depictions of bloodletting."

"She has a point, if the stories are to be retold faithfully and with proper emphasis. Nothing the children need to hear from an old sea dog's mouth, that's for certain," cackled Yancy with a whoop and a slap on his leg. "I'll think of a few that can be related in a more suitable way."

"I've heard plenty of the stories," I told Primrose. "The stories are exciting. Yancy is a brave man."

"Thank you, lad. It's good to see my adventures are appreciated by some."

"Yes, you have heard too many," said Mother, patting me on the head. "And I pray every night you won't turn out to be an eye-patch wearing swashbuckler."

"Too late, my sweet," said Yancy. "Much too late, but it was always fated."

"Probably so," said Mother.

"Regardless, I'm a pirate no more. No more black flags, hearties and grog for me, not now that my black queen warms my bed chamber," announced Yancy with a hoisted cup. "Now the only flag I fly is for her."

"Stop being vulgar," said mother.

"Why, I've not mentioned a single vulgar act," Yancy said. "Though they are often at the forefront of me thoughts."

"They are always at the forefront of your thoughts," said Mother. "I'm surprised you can ever get anything accomplished, as much as you dwell on it."

"Are you really a queen, Miss Talula?" asked Naomi. "You're sure pretty enough to be one. When you speak you sound like the city ladies that came to visit the Gentries, those in the fancy dresses and all done-up hair."

"Oh," said Mother.

"I'm sorry, I didn't mean no offense like that, like you was like them in no way," gushed Naomi, almost horror on her face. "I just mean the way you talk. Real fancy. I don't mind it. It's pretty. There ain't no mean cut to it like I've heard."

"I was raised to work in a rich family's house," Mother said. "It was demanded of me."

"I did that some, too," said Naomi. "The Gentrys wasn't as exacting. I was just wondering, though. Emma and Maggie told us long ago your family was royalty back in Africa."

"No, not really, not directly, I don't believe. The story I was told was that generations ago, my mother's grandmother Jojo was distantly related to the ruling family. A cousin or something. They were wealthy, but not exactly royalty. She was my ancestor that was kidnapped by slave hunters and brought to America."

"I don't really know a thing about my past like that. My people was sold around too much to keep it straight," said Naomi.

"That is a tragedy," Mother said. The firelight showed the sadness on her face as she spoke. "There are great tragedies in the stories of all people. Mine is that my people, the Fante, had goldmines that were coveted by a much larger empire, the Ashanti. They also were rich, with many more goldmines than we had. The Ashanti had so many goldmines they had large armies that did nothing but capture slaves to labor in them. They raided all the countries around them for slaves. Soon the Ashanti realized the captured people were nearly as valuable to the Europeans as the gold. That is how my grandmother Jojo came to America, captured and sold to Dutch slave traders."

"Even though she was related to the king?"

"Yes, even then. The Ashanti didn't care. They enslaved kings that resisted them. Some they beheaded and fed to the lions," Mother said. "These Dutch slavers realized they had very valuable cargo in the people from Jojo's village, who were skilled and educated. So, instead of the Georgia rice fields, the slavers brought them to the St. Augustine slave market. It was different in Florida back then. It was still a Spanish territory, and the Spaniards did not generally treat their slaves as the Americans did. It wasn't illegal for slaves to read. Educated slaves were sought after and brought high prices. A very wealthy Spanish family purchased Jojo. She was bright and already knew English and Portuguese, so it was not hard for her to learn Spanish. She was trained as a governess for their small children. Soon her duties included the education of the household children. As years passed, she became the head of the household slaves. She married, had children. Had she gone to Georgia or South Carolina, she'd likely have gotten whipped and worse, just for even knowing how to write her name."

"Yes, I know how that is. I seen a girl once, they found out she could read. She had been sending notes to some boy on another plantation. Love notes, silly kid stuff," Naomi said, looking over to make sure the children were asleep. "They made us watch as they stripped her naked and whipped her bloody. They scarred her face so no one would want to write her poems again. They sold her off to Texas or some place, away from her family. I won't say what they cut off that boy so he wouldn't have no interest in love poems no more."

"My story is much different," said Mother. "Generations of women in my family served generations of the Ortiz family as governesses and nannies. Some of the men were horse trainers and coach drivers. I was trained exactly as my grandmothers had been. None of us had it bad, as those things go. Not unpleasant, if you didn't think about it too hard. Compared to a field hand, it was a life of splendor."

"But you still ran away anyway?"

"No. When I was sixteen a handsome young ship captain named Charley Cavallo arrived in St. Augustine. He was a dashing young man, always so full of energy and fire. His father owned a line of ships which my owner did business with. Soon Charley was coming by quite often. We fell madly in love and decided to marry. Such marriages were completely legal and common at the time. We lived peacefully in St. Augustine, and I stayed on as governess to those children. I was still his property."

"Ain't that something," said Naomi.

"It was a nice, comfortable life most of the time. Charley's ships made a little money. But then the United States bought Florida, and everything changed. Slaves by the thousands were brought in to cut cane in the new plantations. The MacCuaig family was already notorious for kidnapping free Blacks and selling them into slavery out of state. Now, acting as Jackson's agents they spread fear of slave uprisings. They committed raids and violence and blamed it on the Seminole and Estelusti, trying to scare the Spanish into selling their land and slaves cheap. Many Estelusti were captured and accused of being runaways. It was a time of great fear."

"Those MacCuaigs are the devil's own spawn," said Naomi.

"The best way to prevent being kidnapped was being owned by another white man, but like many Spaniards, the Ortiz family no longer wanted to live in Florida. They returned to Spain," said Mother. "Charley purchased me. However, because he was an accused and wanted smuggler, the Americans would not recognize my freedom. They branded him a criminal who owed many judgments and declared my children and I were to be taken to pay off those debts. Charley paid Micanopy to claim us as his slaves. That is how we remain, myself and all my children."

"Ain't that something?" said Virgil.

"Charley returned to smuggling, but this time it was smuggling people out, taking fugitives to the Bahamas. That is how he died. Ambushed by the MacCuaigs as he took a load of people to the Bahamas. They shot down his boat and left the survivors to drown in the middle of the ocean. Two young men somehow swam five miles to shore and told people what happened. The Bahamians searched, but no other survivors were found."

"And then you met Mr. Yancy?"

"Yes. I had known him for years. He was a friend of Charley's, back when Charley was smuggling guns and such into the Negro Fort. They shared a few reckless adventures," she said. "When he came back, I got swept off my feet a second time. I guess you could say I've always been attracted to rogues. They're so much more interesting."

"I'm real sorry about your Charley," said Naomi. "But that is a most exciting tale."

"It has been an interesting life. But there's something else we want to talk to you about," said Mother. "We'd like you to make this island your home, if you're willing. You can stay in the cabin as long as you want."

"Our own home? To call our own? Ain't that something Naomi?" said Virgil.

"It's almighty something," said Naomi. "It's an answered prayer, is what it is."

"We are grateful. More than I can say," said Virgil.

"We only stay in the cabin when the hurricanes come this far inland, but that is rare," said Mother.

"Should a hurricane blow in and we have to ride it out, don't mind Talula's snoring like a boar hog. It gets to be endearing and keeps critters away," said Yancy.

"Don't mind Yancy's body," said mother. "I'll bury it before it gets to stinking."

"Now, you all quit fussing, because all this right now is almost overwhelming," said Naomi, smiling through big tears.

"We can help you build another room for the children if you want," said Mother. "As you see fit. We prefer these open chickees, and you will too, once you are here through the warm months."

"I just don't even know how to thank a person for all this," said Virgil.

"No thanks are needed," said John. "We benefit as much as you do. These are very precarious times for the Estelusti. We are glad to have you here, as friends. It also strengthens our self-defense. We welcome you to stay and defend our land."

"Hard saying how long we can stay if they come looking for us," said Virgil.

"At this point, it's hard telling how long any of us can stay," said John. "They'll have to look long and hard to find you here."

***

"Do ships still go to the Bahamas?" Virgil asked Yancy a few days later.

"Some do. It is no easy task since they built the lighthouse. The Americans have ships out, prowling for refugees," I said.

"But it's possible?"

"There will always be some hard-case boat captain willing to take that risk for the right amount of money. The right amount of money would be considerable."

"I have no money," said Virgil. "What I had was stolen by the Mac-Cuaigs."

"It's something you're wanting to do?"

"I sure been thinking on it plenty," said Virgil. "Do they speak American at them places? Or at that Freedom Town Pete told me 'bout?"

"Some do, and some that's barely recognizable. French and Spanish and a butchery of the King's English and dozens of other tongues. There are a thousand African languages, you know? You'd have a hell of a time at first, but people usually is able to get themselves understood."

"And chilluns do good there?"

"Don't have to worry about them getting sold from you," Yancy said. "That's about all I can say for them. Lots of poor folks there. Real poor.'

"But not for sale?"

"Nope. Not for sale."

"Hmm," Virgil said. "What would you do if you was in my place?"

"I'd be studying on it, same as you," Yancy said. "There are places you could go and live peacefully, and there's places you can't. There are many places in the Northern states. Frankly, I'd stay away from Africa. There is much warfare and upheavals. Since you're safe now, and not fleeing through the swamp with bloodhounds on your heels, I'd take the time and weigh all your options. I know a fair amount about many of those places, from first-hand experience. And I keep up on the latest."

"I hope we never have to leave here," said Virgil. "Not if you'll have us. My children and Naomi have never been happier. But I don't reckon we'll be left in peace."

"Should the day come, well, Talula and I have a bit stashed away, and some favors are owed us. The passage would be dangerous, but I still have some chuckaboos in the Merchant Navy, and nearly all the smugglers in the Territory."

"I don't know what to say to that."

"I just ask that you stay a while longer. If all this blows over, there will be no need for you to risk that passage. But, if it starts looking bad, we'll get you out of here."

***

When Virgil and I returned from exploring the Cove, Yancy and John sat at the council table over a chessboard, deep in concentration. A bottle of brandy and an ashtray with smoldering cigars was on the stump beside them, along with a stack of newspapers. That told me Germaine had visited. He was a Bahamian wreck salvager and old smuggling partner of Yancy and my father.

To Yancy, newspapers were invaluable. They were subscriptions from all over, mailed to secret friends of his who passed them to Germaine. It was dangerous to bring the papers here, and Yancy paid Germaine well for the risks he took.

Yancy would study the papers for hours, reading aloud the stories of armies and international affairs and the political games in faraway Washington, D.C. that would decide our fate. The Seminole and Estelusti leaders often visited us, to hear the words on the page and have Yancy divine the meanings.

Virgil and I watched the game for a few minutes. Yancy and John each had a king, a knight, bishop, and two or three pawns. They were evenly matched players and knew each other's tricks well. The games were usually rowdy affairs for the first hour or two, as they drank and played aggressively while pontificating on the events of our world. Once the games got to this point, however, it was quiet, filled with alcohol-influenced concentration. Finally, boxed in, Yancy surrendered.

"Well done, lad," said Yancy, relighting a cigar stub. "I thought I had you early. Careless, I was."

"We need to find new opponents," said John. "That is one thing I miss. The chess saloons in St. Augustine, playing the old fishermen."

"Sure. Watching their daughters net fish in the surf is what you miss," said Yancy.

"I suppose that could be part of it," said John.

"What is in the newspapers today?" I asked Yancy after John walked away.

"Lies, lies, nothing but lies," said Yancy with a string of curses. "All these flat-out fantastic fables meant to inflame the masses."

"Why do you read them papers if they upset you so?" asked Virgil.

"That is a good question. It seems I just have to do it," Yancy said with a morose grin and a head shake. "Mostly to marvel at man's inhumanity to men, and the ease and glee with which it's perpetuated. I should probably find a healthier entertainment."

"But if it's all lies, what is the point?"

"Between the competing falsehoods, outrageous slanders, and inflammatory rhetoric, an awful lot can be gleaned. Given you start with the premise they are all lying," said Yancy.

"I reckon that makes sense to you," said Virgil.

"The lies cancel each other out, and at the bottom of the sludge can sometimes be found a nugget of truth. Like digging through a privy for a lost diamond ring."

"Don't that leave you a stinking mess, digging through them privies?"

"That it does. It is Hell getting the smell off some days."

"Let's get some target practice tomorrow," said Yancy. "We have a wee surplus of lead at the moment, and it would probably be wise to retrieve a few of those rifles I have buried."

"You have guns buried?" asked Virgil.

"Hundreds of them. Twenty years ago, when I was at the Negro Fort, I knew two things. That we were about to be whipped, and that this day would come. Sir Edward Nicolls, my commander, had equipped us with a few thousand rifle muskets, the best infantry rifles in the world. Many more than we had men for, and I did not want them to fall into the hands of Jackson's invaders. The guns are still there, untouched, never fired. A few tons of powder and ball, too."

"And they're still good, buried down there in all this dampness?"

"Slathered in oil, as pristine as if they still sat on the gun maker's shelf. It'll be a bit of a mess getting all the oil off is all."

"I found that shooting at rabbits and turkey with my old shotgun and facing off against a charging MacCuaig man ain't near the same," said Virgil.

"That old fowling piece you have is just as likely to blow up in your face as hit a target. It don't really pack enough punch to be much of a battlefield weapon anyway," said Yancy. "Throw it in the river or leave it for the enemy to put an eye out."

"Shooting folks just ain't my strength."

"There's a trick to it," said Yancy. "Remembering they are trying to kill me has aways been my motivation."

"I'm motivated, but still sometimes feel poorly after. I don't like carrying that burden with me."

"I'm not overly fond of it myself," said Yancy. "But there's times when it is called for. Don't you agree, Pete?"

"Yes," I said. "But it also troubles me that I killed a man. I may have killed more and I saw many horrible things."

"No reason to get the morbs over killing that fellow. He would have killed a lot of people if he'd reached that cannon," said Yancy. "Any man who would do such a thing is the worst, most vile and debased kind of person there is. You saved a lot of lives. Look at it that way, not from the bleak side."

"Yes, I understand that," I said. "It's just…he was staring me right in the eyes as he went down. Never stopped staring, even with his head smashed in. I never expected that. To see it like that, I guess."

"Well, if he was still staring, perhaps he ain't dead at all. Perhaps you will meet him on another battlefield, and there he'll be, pissing and bitching about the headache you gave him," said Yancy. "Then you'll have wished you'd have killed him. Don't leave nothing half done on the field of battle."

"Perhaps. But in my dreams, he is very much dead, and very much unhappy about it. I do not wish to meet him in such a condition," I said.

"Now, chin up, lad. You did well. Pluck to the backbone. The warrior path of courage and duty is not an easy one. You have only acted to protect your family and your people. It was justly and smartly done, and you shouldn't worry yourself about it further. Plume yourself up on this one," said Yancy. "I am proud of you, lad. Indeed I am."

"I'm honored you say so," I said.

"You will see many more horrible things before this is all over, and likely be called on to kill more men. They'll be plenty of time for remorse later, I guarantee you that, once all the guns have quieted and bodies are buried. But now is not the time for it. Thinking on it will only slow you down. Right now, you are on the right side and lives are at stake. That's all you need to have in your mind."

***

"Here you go," Yancy said as he unwrapped a rifle and handed it to Virgil. We were on one of the hidden islands that served as Yancy's armory depots. "A Baker rifle. It has twice the range of the smoothbores the soldiers carry."

"I'll practice up. My aim never failed with this here, though," Virgil said, patting the big cane knife on his side. "It just don't have the range I'd like. I sure been admiring that big pistol Pete has. I ain't never seen no big double barrel pistol like that before. Looks fearsome. What kind of gun is that?"

"It's a Howdah pistol. The nabobs use them when they're hunting tigers on the Indian subcontinent."

"What's a howdie? What's a nabob?" said Virgil. "Nobody told me about no tigers hereabouts in these woods."

"That is in India, way across the oceans, where shooting tigers is the sport of royals. Nabobs are ridiculous twits and pampered ninnies. Princely nobles, mughals, lords, maharajas and that sort of thing. Spoiled sons of wealth and privilege like that Von Bock fellow and his ilk," said Yancy. "Most of them have an illness, an obsession with spending vast amounts of their subjects' money on frivolous entertainments. If you can find me something more frivolous than hunting tigers from a caravan of lumbering elephants, surrounded by a hundred or so tenders and drivers and shotgun guards, well, I'd be curious to see it."

"Never seen an elephant," said Virgil. "They's mighty big, I hear tell."

"Tall as two horses and a nose that flops around like a rope and drags the ground. The howdah is a big box they strap on the back of the elephants. That's where the fearless hunters ride. Problem is, a pissy tiger can spring right up on top of an elephant."

"Is tiger meat good? How do they cook it?'

"No. It's just for trophies. They kill the big cats and then stick their heads up on the wall, with their jaws open and big fangs out."

"Is you making all this up?" said Virgil.

"No, I ain't. That's just how damned silly people with money can get. Money sure don't make nobody smarter, nor braver. This gun Pete holds once belonged to some Rajput lord that died a horrid death from turgidness of the trigger finger and throat pain. That pain being caused by a mouthful of tiger teeth impaled in it."

"Turgidness?" I asked.

"Froze up like a statue," said Yancy. "Now, the mahouts and those lads that run off into the bush with a drum and a long stick, rousting those tigers out and running them close enough for the nabobs to shoot…those boys have furry steel stones the size of coconuts."

"Ain't that something? There sure are peculiar people in this world," said Virgil. "Now, about them tigers hereabouts?"

"No tigers around here. Only panthers. Indian tigers birth kittens the size of your Florida panthers," said Yancy. "They'd clean their teeth with one of those scrawny alley cats."

"I'll avoid the lot of them," said Virgil. "Wouldn't want to be afflicted with that turgidness."

"That's probably best. Now, these pistols are downright frightening and I do have some spares," said Yancy. "Loaded with buckshot these pistols are mighty handy when the enemy is close. It's heavy to carry, though, if you're burdened with other weapons and such."

"I'm a fair hand at toting heavy burdens. I wouldn't mind the extra weight," Virgil said. "I think I'd prefer something like that to a rifle. All the fighting I've done so far has been real up close."

"This pistol would be a good choice."

***

"How'd you come to be here?" Virgil asked Yancy after we'd shot up a few trees. "All the way from England?"

"All the results of a misspent youth, though I had no say in the matter. I grew up in the London slums, born an orphan into a life of crime. Finally, the magistrates gave me the option of a long stretch in the workhouse or joining the Royal Marines. That was in the middle of us Brits fighting Napoleon's legions and I thought it all sounded like a grand adventure. Much grander than the workhouse at any rate."

"And has it been?"

"That it has. Indeed, it has."

"Did you get in the big battles you was seeking?" asked Virgil.

"Not just then. But I had my share later when war broke out against the Americans and my regiment was sent to Florida. We built the fort on Prospect Bluff on the Apalachicola River. The one that came to be known as the Negro Fort."

"You built that?" said Virgil. "I've heard legends about that fort."

"I was there when it was built, but I'll confess I put little labor into it myself. We set up camp there on the river and promised citizenship and freedom to any slave who volunteered to build the fort and fight the Americans. Free Blacks and Estelusti joined us. Slaves fleeing Georgia and South Carolina and fighters from Cuba and Haiti and the Bahamas joined us. All of 'em prepared to fight to the death before returning to slavery. The unit was called the Corps of Colonial Marines and they were trained and armed as well as any army on earth," said Yancy. "And we built a first-rate fort."

"Did you whup 'em?"

"Sadly, no. The war ended in defeat for Great Britain, but because of what transpired in the North, not here, although the Red Sticks were also defeated. The British left Florida. That was my first service with the indomitable Sir Edward Nicolls. The Crown ordered us home, but Sir Edward, a devout man who detested slavery, was not finished. Florida was still Spanish at the time, and Sir Edward wanted to leave some protection against slave hunters. With the help of Charley Cavallo and a few other brave smugglers we were able to stock the fort with 2,500 muskets, six cannons, a vast supply of ammunition and other equipment," said Yancy. "I stayed behind with my new wife, a fine Black Seminole girl named Yona. We had a baby, still on the teat. I worked a farm along the river bottom and taught the novices proper use of their new firearms. More than a thousand people lived on those farms, spread for fifty miles along the river. Fields as bountiful as any I've ever seen, and some of the best beef cattle and horses in Florida. It was at the Negro Fort I first came to be acquainted with Abraham. And first met Osceola, though that wasn't what he was called at the time. He was merely a lad of ten or so."

"Ain't that something."

"Life was grand. However, that many armed darkies right across the river was right unsettling to the planters of Georgia. Andrew Jackson wanted to re-enslave all the Negroes and exterminate the Indians and turn the land into plantations. His problem was that the American public was tired of war after the conflicts with the British. That's where your newspapers come in," said Yancy, his face angry at the memories. "To get the political support Jackson needed in Washington, the publishers filled the pages with blood-soaked reports of Seminole atrocities. Wild, lurid tales of rapacious escaped Negroes and their Indian allies in lustful rampages against the white women of the plantations."

"None of them stories in the newspaper was true?"

"A couple. Not many. There was a little raiding done by some of the young bucks, but that was more youthful exuberance than anything. There was no need to raid anybody. We had plenty. Our field and flocks were abundant beyond belief. If anything, we were being raided. The Creeks committed some raids themselves and blamed the Seminole and rebellious runaways. In the end, their ploys worked. An outraged public demanded justice and an overjoyed Jackson set Clinch and the MacCuaigs upon the fort. Without those outrageous mendacities, Jackson never would have gotten his support he needed."

"Them newspapers did that?"

"May as well as fired the cannon themselves, inflaming the public the way they did. Clinch came up the Apalachicola River with a fleet of gunboats in the dark of night. He heated cannonballs in the ship's furnace while Laughing Boy MacCuaig's men snuck inside the fort. They planted flags to mark the position of the gunpowder magazine, which at the time contained several tons of explosives. At the crack of dawn Clinch's naval artillerymen opened up and scored a direct hit, sending a glowing cannonball straight down the shaft into the gunpowder. The fort was blown to splinters, killing nearly all the three hundred people inside. Bodies and pieces of bodies flung everywhere. The dead included my wife and child. The blast knocked me senseless and tossed me high up into a tree. I guess they thought I was dead, since I was entangled with the parts of half a dozen other people. Or maybe I was too high up in the tree to bother with my scalp, as there was so many for the easy taking down below. But from high where I dangled, I had a bird's eye view of all their horrors, the scalping and murdering and other atrocities by MacCuaig's Creeks," said Yancy. "So you see, I have as much hate for them MacCuaigs and Clinch as you do. Maybe even worse. At least you still got your woman and children."

"I guess it don't get no worse," Virgil said quietly.

"It took a long time, but I healed up while being hid out by friends in the Everglades. I stalked Laughing Boy for months but never could get to him, as he was always too closely guarded. But I did take the scalps of a number of his cousins," Yancy said. "Finally, they put a large bounty on me. The American army declared I was a spy and that I should be hung. Half the country was searching for me, and the other half hoping to get a chance to snitch. Charley put me on a fishing boat and took me to the Andros Islands. I held up there for a while."

"You was lucky to have a friend like that," said Virgil.

"Yes, he risked his life for me. That was the most dangerous voyage I ever went on, but he took it, scooting right past two patrol boats," said Yancy. "While hiding out, the rage for vengeance boiled inside me until finally I decided to take pay in blood from any involved in the slave trade. I hopped from one British ship to the next until I reached the West Africa Squadron, stationed in Sierra Leone. I was reunited with my old Commander Nicolls, which was a joy. The Royal Marines new mission was the perfect spot for me. Great Britain had outlawed their international slave trade fifteen years earlier and the Royal Navy ruled the seas. We had the fastest ships on the sea, and the best gunned."

"And you went over there to stop it?"

"We went over there to stop it happening to those Africans friendly to the Crown. Committed by those that wasn't. But we stopped a good bit of it, regardless."

"What was it like out there on the oceans in them big warships?" asked Virgil. "I've seen some of them and wisht I could jump on one and sail away."

"There's no feeling like sailing the ocean, nor excitement known to man that compares to that which rushes through you when you're with sails full and closing on an enemy slaver," said Yancy. "The blood lust takes over the whole ship when the pursuit gets hot. Everybody steeling our hearts for the fight to come, readying our sabers and pistols. Many of our men had once been chained in the bellies of those ships them- selves, and they'd be kneeling on prayer rugs or pacing or murmuring prayers or making war chants in a dozen different languages. We were like fighting dogs, straining at the leash. I was the same frothing beast as any of 'em. I demanded revenge for my wife and little one. That is all I thought about. I suppose all any of us thought about. Vengeance and retribution."

"Did you have to fight your way on board?"

"Aye, sometimes we did," said Yancy. "We couldn't shoot solid shot into 'em, or we'd kill the cargo. We would blast away the masts with chain shot, making the ships dead in the water. Most surrendered meekly, knowing they had nowhere to go. But sometimes the slavers would give us a fight, if they were facing a hanging. There were a good many hellacious brawls that left the deck bloody and slick with slaver gut. Chum in the water. The sharks were all abolitionists those days," said Yancy. "But I seen horrid sights. Five hundred slaves down below in chains, full of sickness. Dead ones still tied to live ones. As many of one as the other."

"I reckon them slavers tried their best to avoid you," said Virgil.

"They did. But our ships was fast and our power absolute, or nearly so," said Yancy. "We confiscated the ships that carried slaves. We also seized ships headed to Africa that carried the tools of bondage, chains and collars and shackles. I inflicted a great deal of punishment and killed dozens for every friend and loved one I ever lost. However, and this may come as a shock to you, that bloodthirsty environment wasn't the best way for getting over my family's murder. Quite satisfying when I was slaying the demons, but witnessing the suffering wore on me. And then, of course, all the booze in between voyages."

"Well, you done a mighty good thing, as bad as it wore on you."

"Maybe it mattered to a few, anyway," Yancy said. "Vengeful, murderous wretch that I'd become, I kept at it for another fifteen years, although it wasn't all as altruistic as that. There became a selfish motive as well. From the captured ships, each marine and sailor was allowed a cut of the plunder we confiscated. I became quite wealthy that way. Gold and ivory. Jewels and emeralds, and ores, even wild animal skins. That's just how it was. Do not muzzle the ox."

"And you took what you wanted?"

"It's not like we was stealing from the church collection plate," said Yancy.

"What did they do with the people you rescued off the ships?"

"Some joined the Squadron, where they would be entitled to a share of the plunder. Many wanted revenge, and many wanted to collect enough booty to buy land, or their people back. Sometimes it worked out, sometimes it didn't. It was a powerful incentive, either way. It's quite a sight to see the look on the slavers' faces when they realized they was about to be swarmed by armed Africans, whose very children could well be in the hold below."

"I hope to see that fear on Laughing Boy's face one day," said Virgil. "That's exactly what I want."

"Now I'd buy a ticket to that, lad, I surely would," laughed Yancy.

"Then I'd jump in a ship and sail around the world to where there ain't nobody trying to throw a chain around my neck, if there is such a place."

"There's plenty. Some of the people we liberated from the ships we took to Freetown on the west Africa coast, which is a British colony, made up of nothing but freed slaves. Much like the Bahamas. Some of those we freed went back to their homes in the interior, but many stayed there in Freetown, where no slavers could enter. It became quite a thriving city."

"That's what John wants to do with our people," I said.

"Take them to Africa?"

"No. Not Africa. Possibly way out west somewhere. But not a colony of anyone else. Just our own," I said.

"That is sure something to think on," Virgil said.

***

We spent the rest of the day blasting away at trees and cleaning the grease off twenty-five rifles and ten pistols we'd keep ready for battle. Yancy made a small raft and floated a barrel of gunpowder home behind us. My arm was sore from the kick of the guns, and eyes burned from the smoke of the powder.

"After all that adventuring, how did you end up back here In Florida?" Virgil asked Yancy as we floated along.

"I finally left the Marines but still carried a lot of demons in my head. I vagabonded from port to port, brawling and drinking, working from time to time as a merchant marine. I didn't need the money but did need the hard labor. Maybe even the hard labor of the hoosegow since I got myself twisted up with the local law more than a few times. I even did a stint in the stocks in Tavoy. And I was lucky it wasn't worse after I got caught up with a Konbaung heiress. She was getting her adventuring by doing the roger with a rogue from the sea, but it was me that paid the heavy price for it," said Yancy. "That rum can get a man in all kinds of trouble. Those jails are no place to be, so I wised up about that."

"But you still drink rum," Virgil said.

"Sure. I wised up, like I said. I could put down the rum and avoid the jails. Or simply go where there ain't no jails and continue to enjoy my bumboo. I chose the latter. Like I said, wised up. Ain't been to jail since. No hard labor for me," said Yancy. "Us lads from the Limehouse are wily that way. Without the influence of extraneous vices and vulgar brutes and rude buffoons with their foul-mouthed heathenry always looking to try a man's mettle, I no longer get pugnacious. Only need-lessly verbose and fantastic. Prone to crudity and aggrandizement, or so they say. They may have a point. I think they themselves embellish."

"You came all the way here just not to go to jail?"

"That would be stretching it a tad. I came to see my old chuckaboo, Charley, not knowing he'd already passed on. I came for a visit and became a tenant for life. But, I mean, who could imagine a better life than here? The only thing missing in this wondrous jungle paradise is suitable entertainment of a grown-up nature. A good billiards saloon, mostly. And a good boxing arena. But we have this balmy weather. And the women, well, I've been all over the world and there ain't no more beautiful women on God's Earth. Them tall, lathy Gullah gals with a little Spaniard and injun in them. A fella could just sit in the shade with a cool drink and watch them walk by all day long."

"I wouldn't know," said Virgil. "I only got eyes for my Naomi."

"A wise way to be lad, a wise way to be," said Yancy. "You'll save yourself much heartache later on that way."

"You didn't think coming back here might put you in harm's way again?"

"I considered it. I knew war was brewing again between the Estelusti and the Americans. I always considered I might get another shot at some MacCuaigs and maybe an American officer or two. I guess I'll always choose to go where the stout-hearted lads and free-spirited lasses go. I've always had a place in my heart for them at odds with the world. The Marines. My flash house lads, the folks at the Negro Fort. These people here. That is my family. Always has been," said Yancy. "And anyway, ain't life with a wee bit of danger and risk just sweeter and more precious?"

"I'm learning that," said Virgil.

Chapter Five

GAINES CAMPAIGN FEBRUARY 1836

My sisters and Virgil's daughters danced along in a line, splashing across the knee-deep water. Willet was leading them as they dragged a net, making a commotion to hurry the fish downstream into more nets and traps we had stretched across the stream. We'd spent the day at various pools, filling our baskets with fish to dry over low fires. The pool was shallow and clear, but Virgil and I stood ready with double barrel guns should any curious alligators cruise up.

"What's that smell, Pete?" Virgil asked. "Don't smell like cooking smells."

I sniffed the air. It wasn't a smell I'd smelled before, but it was definitely the smell of something burning. Not wood. Not meat or soup.

"No, it doesn't," I said. "I'll have a look."

I hurried up a tree. There were wisps of greenish smoke coming from a small cooking fire Mother tended near the water. Several men were sitting with John and Yancy in the council house.

"What is it?" Virgil said.

"Mother's burning something in a pot that makes odd smoke. Naomi is with her, chopping what looks like her medicine roots and herbs," I said. "Some Estelusti fighters have come."

"Should we leave?"

"No, we were sent to gather fish, so we'd best gather fish," I said. "Whatever it is, they won't leave without us."

"Is there a problem?" Willet shouted.

"We have visitors," I shouted back, climbing down the tree. "Let's finish up so we can get back and find out what's happened."

We pulled our dugouts up near my mother and Naomi toiling at the foul-smelling fire. The men were still engaged in conversation in the Council House.

"Medicine," Mother said to the quizzical look on my face. "This is the second kettle. Gaines is coming."

***

"Hooah!" grunted John as we slid under the palm leaf shelter where Wild Cat and the others sat. It was drizzling and misting as it had for three days. "What is the news of the column? Why have they not tried to cross the river?"

"Hooah. They have been too busy marching and begging for food," grinned Wild cat.

"Begging for food?"

"Foolish, foolish man, this General Gaines," said Wild Cat. "At night, we are able to sneak close to their camps and hear the soldiers complain. They speak carelessly. He brought a thousand men and their horses all the way from New Orleans, assuming food would be at Fort Brooke. It was not. They barely had enough for themselves. Of course, Fort King had none. Gaines went on to Fort Drane, but General Scott had already sent orders to General Clinch, forbidding him from supplying Gaines. Scott claims everything is for his own soldiers. He is also coming soon."

"Do they want to defeat us or each other?"

"Each other, I think," said Wild Cat. "Clinch gave Gaines enough supplies to return to the coast. Instead, Gaines ignored his orders and marches for the Ouithlocko crossing."

"What does all this mean?" Wild Cat asked Yancy. "I don't understand the ways of this American army."

"Glory seekers. Gaines wanted to get here first and snatch the next general's star away from Scott. There might be two wars in Florida soon," said Yancy. "Winfield Scott is the general that really has control of Florida. Gaines has command of the western states and the Indian territories, with some latitude onto Florida's west coast. Scott has the eastern command, which includes ninety percent of Florida. They both want the parades and promotion that would come with defeating the Seminole."

"There is only one horse in their parades?"

"You could look at it that way. You see, those two have hated each other for twenty years, since the War of 1812. Gaines was infuriated that Scott was promoted to Brigadier general at the tender age of 27, taking the promotion Gaines felt should have been his," said Yancy. "It's been a bitter and public feud, a real pissing contest with some national headlines."

"So, our destruction is a pissing contest?" said John.

"It could be seen as that," said Yancy. "Yes, quite easily it could."

"The only pissing is being done by the soldiers," said Wild Cat. "They pissed like scared bunnies when they found Dade's dead soldiers. Burying all those skeletons distressed them a great deal."

"They know they are really digging their own graves," said John.

"Many feel they have been duped, I think," said Wild Cat. "They had been told we would not fight."

***

Once again, the weather favored us. Three days of hard rain had flooded the streams and low ground. The army slogged along and built a road as it went. They cleared stumps, patched washouts, and built bridges. Still the wagons bogged in the mire. Wheels and axles broke.

Overworked mules dropped dead. Gangs of mud-slathered men heaved and towed and pushed the wagons through the churned-up ooze. They pushed more than they marched.

"Gaines should just push the wagons into the water and try to float them as slow as they are going," said Virgil.

"The cavalrymen want to fight, not push wagons out of the mud," Wild Cat said as we watched another company of mounted volunteers trot right past another bogged wagon. "They won't degrade themselves by engaging in labor meant for slaves."

"Pride goes before the fall," said John.

***

The following day three wagons fell far behind. Between them they had one broken axle, two broken wheels, and a team of half-dead mules. As dusk neared, fifteen soldiers dragged and heaved the wagons into a small, dry knoll.

"That is all the escort they leave for the wagons?" I asked John.

"Yes. I think we can be thankful the horse soldiers ride so far ahead to avoid the work," said John.

The early night hours passed quietly. The soldiers and teamsters tended the mules and cooked supper and boiled coffee. We waited. There was no rush. Up the road, our men moved into place, ready to block any rescue attempt.

At midnight thick clouds covered the moon. Our best warriors slithered through the wet grass toward the unwary sentries. Osceola hooted like an owl and our men pounced. The guards died silently, and the soldiers sleeping around the wagons never woke up. We emptied the wagons without speaking.

"Burn the wagons! Let them know we are here! Let them see the Withlacoochee belongs to the Seminole. Let them tremble. Let them quake!" shouted Osceola, as his torch flared.

"Hooah! Hooah! Hooah!" chanted our warriors.

Osceola threw the first torch, and others quickly followed. The lamp oil in the wagons, blasted out a big fire ball fifty feet in the air. As the flames consumed the wagons our warriors whooped and fired their guns in the air. No soldiers came to investigate that night.

***

At dawn a company of cavalry returned to the black ash of the wagons. I hid behind a thick oak limb that grew across the road. The officers stopped right below me. They remained mounted after seeing the carefully arranged bodies we had left them.

"Dear God, these murdering filthy heathens," swore the uniformed officer. "Lieutenant, send a patrol out and find their trail. Looks to me like the savages have taken the mules right back down the road. They should be easy to follow."

"Not if them mules was made of pure gold and pissed whiskey," cackled the silver-haired, buckskin wearing man next to him. "I guarantee you they got us surrounded right this minute. Probably outnumbered ten to one. Look around. They could have ambushed us any time in the last few days. They chose this spot for a reason. It is bare of cover. They can close off that trail between us and the rest of the column with a handful of riflemen. If that happens, we'll be as dead and desecrated as these poor fellows here."

"I'll not let this abomination stand," snarled the captain.

"Better one abomination than two or a bushel," said the grizzled militia man. "Didn't they teach you nothing at West Point? Like which is bigger, ten or one? Or how to recognize an ambush?"

"There's no reason to be insulting, but perhaps you're right," said the captain, peering around. "Well, we at least need to bury them."

"Burying your soldiers is getting boresome and redundant," said the backwoodsman. "Before the Academy sends the next bunch of bright-eyed tacticians down here, I wish they'd have you all attend a few young soldier funerals. West Point needs to teach you youngsters a class in burying and the causes of it. Which is generally naive and short-sighted perspectives such as yours, that don't understand the causes of it."

"You wouldn't want respectfully buried?" said the officer.

"I wouldn't want killed, respectfully or otherwise, is the point. The longer we sit here, the likelier that becomes," said the backwoodsman. "The Dade party stayed unburied for two months. Once they was put to rest, it didn't make them a sliver less dead."

"You shouldn't speak disrespectfully of dead military men that way."

"The opinions of dead men don't lose me any sleep, and I'm quite sure mine ain't disturbed theirs. The thought of joining them, however, can be quite disquieting," said the backwoodsman. "Be damned quick about it if you're going to dig holes, or dig enough holes for all of us. We will all be rotting here in a ditch if we don't get clear of here soon."

"Sergeant," shouted the officer. "Get these men shovels and dig some graves."

The soldiers scooped out a shallow trench, dragged the bodies in and threw a few inches of mud on them.

"Those graves aren't deep enough. Alligators and bears will get those men," said the captain.

"You could bury them six feet down and they likely wouldn't stay buried long. Scavengers in these swamps have outstanding noses, especially for carrion," said the bearded man. "Now, it's time for us to get on. Staying here might be seen as a challenge."

"We'll leave when I say," said the captain.

"You can leave whenever you want," said the volunteer. "Me and my boys are leaving now."

"I'll have you shot for disobeying an order in the face of the enemy," said the officer.

"In the face of remarkable and stubborn stupidity, you mean. You wouldn't live long enough to enforce it. My men will shoot you to pieces if the Indians don't," said the man. "We are fighters, not grave diggers. If you wanted graves dug, you should have brought you some strong-backed field hands."

"There were none to be had," said the officer.

"Exactly. It is them who watch from the trees, which is why we need to be moving on."

***

By the time Gaines and his plodding army arrived at the crossing more than a thousand Seminole and Estelusti had gathered in the shadowed thickets on the south bank. The officers rode up and down the bank of the same sharp river-bend that proved to be the downfall of Clinch and Call. They were clearly irritated at their predicament. Behind them the soldiers lounged, pitching tents and boiling coffee.

"Apparently Gaines didn't believe Clinch, if he was even warned of their aborted crossing here," said Yancy.

"The soldier generals don't talk to each other?"

"Not when they're feuding, and generals are almost always feuding," said Yancy. "That's just how most generals are, in every army on Earth. It's their nature."

"So why attempt a crossing now? The water could be down tomorrow."

"Stubbornness again. My guess is he believes Scott is already on his way here," Yancy said. "Gaines can't have that. They will not wait. They will try to cross today."

Finally, a tall lieutenant entered the water, with a chain of men hooking arms behind him. He probed the depth with a long pole and struggled for balance against the fast water. The lieutenant was chest-deep with twenty men in the water behind him when our marksman fired.

The lieutenant spun around, and his arm ripped free of the surprised man behind him. More rifles roared. Geysers of water erupted all around the floundering soldiers as they scrambled for the far bank. Half were down, wounded or lifeless, caught in the water weeds or swept away in the current.

Bugles blared across the river. Hundreds of soldiers who had just been drinking coffee stampeded to the point and fired wildly into the brush and trees over our heads. They'd responded exactly as we'd hoped, and our bullets raked them from three sides as they stood exposed, completely in the open. Within seconds they had fled for the safety of the trees far down the peninsula.

The last of the soldiers reached the forest and our rifles went quiet. The smoke cleared and our triumphant war cries filled the air. The field was littered with dead and wounded. Dead soldiers bobbed in the river. An hour passed. Then two. An orderly line of soldiers marched into the clearing and fired several volleys in our direction. After our men with Baker rifles killed two more of their officers they stayed in the trees.

They rolled out their cannon and blasted it a few times, but we scooted back into the thickets and were laughing at their slowness by the time they got it fired. Some trees were killed on our side of the river, but the cannoneers fell to our bullets from the flanks. After that, Gaines kept his far back in the tree line. As darkness settled in the swamp, we heard the echo of axes striking trees.

"Come," said John. "Let's go to Osceola now. The river is falling. We must plan our next move. They may try to cross."

We picked our way down the trail that followed the riverbank, checking on the men we knew. We had suffered few injuries.

"Hooah," said John, sitting down in the circle of chiefs around a fire. He took a slug from a bottle of rum that was passed to him. "The axes tell me the soldiers plan to stay. What are your plans?"

"We need spies to swim the river," said Osceola, looking at me. "Those who know the soldier language."

"I will go," said John.

"No," said Osceola. "I need you here, to lead your men if we need to fight. To plan tomorrow's battle."

"I will go," I said.

"That is good, Pete Horse," said Osceola. "You would make a fine spy. Are you a strong swimmer? The current is still swift."

"He can swim like an otter. I just hope the big gators have not returned," John laughed, clapping my shoulder.

"You are not filling me with courage," I said.

"Do not fear, Little Brother. The sounds of battle has surely scared away even the biggest bull. The bodies are fresh, and the water is cold and running fast. The smell has not yet spread. They will not return tonight. Tomorrow the smell will be too much for them to resist. But tonight, you are safe."

"I hope you are right, brother," I said. "But I have seen the brain of an alligator. It is smaller than a nut. Old Grandfather Long Jaws may be lurking, too stupid to know guns from thunder. Gambling my life on the intelligence of an old alligator may be poor odds."

"No. Even the dumbest gator knows the sound of the gun," said John. "But tomorrow will be a very bad day for a swim."

I took a deep breath, steeled myself one last time and slipped under the cold water. I came up next to a lifeless soldier bobbing in the weeds along the far bank. He'd been shot in the forehead, and an empty-eyed fish skeleton was tangled in the weeds around his throat.

Two soldiers walked toward me, carrying a small lamp in the pitch-blackness. As they poked through the weeds with a stick I slid backwards and stayed low. The men reached the dead boy I'd bumped into. He had been their friend. They said kind things about him and his family as they dragged his body out of the mud.

Like a short-legged alligator I slid through the dead lily pads and flattened weed-beds. The weeds thinned out and I slithered up the bank. Groups of soldiers were roaming the forest with axes and torches.

I found a little rabbit path and crept closer, staying in the deep brush and away from the ax-men. The soldiers were building a head-high fortress of chinked logs laid lengthwise and connected like a rail fence. The gaps were loosely packed with brush and mud. There were many dark corners I could squeeze into without being spotted by a sentry.

I slithered through the brush until I was tight against the wall, peeking through the crevices between the logs. Ten feet away a coffee pot and small kettle hung over a small campfire. The soldiers were squeezed in tight behind the rough walls and there were hundreds of such fires.

Time passed. The sentries never came close, and I was able to gain a familiarity with the disgruntled Tennessee volunteers at the closest fire as they drank coffee and gnawed on thick crackers and chunks of bacon.

A man named Adams seemed to be in charge. He was a big, greasy, rough-looking man with a heavy beard, mean eyes and gravelly deep voice. The others seemed to defer to him.

Two brothers, Marv and Myron, were bossy and loud but not as intimidating as Adams. Simon was gaunt, with long, stringy hair that might have been blond. Francis was round-faced, soft and whimpering constantly. Thaddeus was older and quiet, and seemed amused by the non-stop complaints of the others. There were a couple others who just sat and listened, too. None of the men were happy about their predicament, that much was obvious.

"I reckon we should try to get some sleep," said Adams, after the men had finished a lengthy discussion on who back home raised the best horses.

"Who can sleep with them hooting out there across the river," asked Francis.

"Nothing to be concerned with as long as they stay on that side of the river," growled Adams.

"I don't like this one bit," said Francis. "I ain't wanting to end up like Dade's men, kilt, scalpt, and left to rot out in this miserable jungle."

"That ain't likely to happen," Marv said. "We got more than ten times the soldiers Dade had."

"Maybe there's ten times as many Indians, too," said Francis. "Did you ever think of that, genius?"

"There ain't that many Indians in all Florida," said Marv.

"They sure had plenty enough to shoot hell out of us in the river. They had ample enough to capture some of our precious supply wagons and skin them boys," said Thaddeus. "Clearly enough to keep us penned up here."

"I don't care how many there are, they won't rush this fortification. It's solid," said Adams. "Nobody will charge a thousand rifles."

"I was a damned fool to join this expedition. A fool to believe Gaines was some great Indian killer," said Myron. "That damned Gaines, marching off without our supplies."

"It ain't gonna do any good you complaining about it now," said Thaddeus.

"It's Scott's fault more than Gaines. There was supplies at Fort Drane, but he wouldn't give them up," said Marv.

"Those were Scott's supplies he had shipped in, waiting for his army," said Adams. "What was he supposed to do? Then what's his men supposed to eat in the godforsaken wilderness? Beavers and rattlesnakes?"

"Beavers ain't bad eatin'," said Thaddeus.

"The supply train from Fort Brooke should be on the way," said Marv.

"If it was coming, it would have already been here by now. It's likely on its way to some Indian village," said Adams. "You think they're going to trap a thousand of us here, but allow a wagon train and a hundred soldiers to pass?"

"We'll starve," whined Francis. "Won't matter how many guns we got, if we're starved too dead to shoot them."

"Quit your bellyaching," snarled Adams. "So we're stuck here for a few days. I've been in worse spots. Now be quiet so I can sleep. Them savages across the river can keep up their bird calls all night. Won't bother me none, but your incessant whining about it surely does."

***

"What do the soldiers say?" John asked when I returned. I sat close to a warm fire, with a heavy blanket over my shoulders and a big tin cup of coffee steaming in my hands. We had more fires than we had men. Instead of trying to hide from Gaines, we wanted him to think we were many more than we were.

"They will not attempt to cross tomorrow," I said. "They have little food left and will wait for General Clinch to arrive with more supplies. That is what the soldiers believe. Some of them anyway. Some think we have already attacked Clinch and taken all the supplies. All of them are very unhappy with General Gaines for bringing them here."

"He does not retreat? He supposes to build a fort?" said Osceola.

"Yes," I said.

"Let them work," said John. "They build a coffin, not a fort."

"They have many wounded since yesterday. They cannot move quickly," I said. "They are hungry and unhappy. They see Indians behind every tree branch. Every owl and bat they think is a warrior coming for them."

"Perhaps the soldiers should eat that gold they thought they would receive for our enslavement," said John.

***

For the final part of our plan, three hundred of our men went upriver and crossed in boats. I went with them. We crept through the forest and converged on the road Gaines had marched down the day before. As long as the river stayed high, we had Gaines and his thousand men completely surrounded.

The sun came up. The forest floor was a field of fresh tree stumps, trimmed limbs and piled brush. All morning we waited in silence.

When the patrols ventured out, we retreated. The scouts poked around in the thickets close to the fort but never strayed far from it.

At midday, a patrol of forty soldiers and Creek scouts came out of the fort and marched more than a mile down the road. We let them pass, stalking them the entire way but staying far back from their prowling eyes.

We attacked just as the patrol was within sight of the fort. Our men charged out of the trees from both sides of the road, hitting the patrol in a shrieking wave, overrunning them instantly. Some of the patrol made it to safety, but most did not. We dragged them down like wolves as they sprinted desperately for the fort and hacked them to pieces as their comrades watched from behind the wall.

A relief force charged out but heavy fire from our riflemen quickly forced them back. The soldiers tried again with their cannons by firing shrapnel into the thickets. The cannons were slow. Once again, we moved to the side and easily shot down their artillerymen.

We made no assaults against the fort, but our marksmen responded to any glimpse of uniform with a bullet. During the night our warriors taunted and harassed them by chanting or screeching like swamp creatures. An occasional flaming arrow would fly through the night sky and scatter the sleeping soldiers or panic the horses. We were three hundred and they were a thousand, but it would take at least ten times that many of them to force us from these swampy woods.

***

"The dogs have stopped barking," said John on the fifth morning.

"Yes?" I asked.

"That means they are in the cook pots. Perhaps they will not be so eager to return for another Indian hunt," said John.

"I'm told soldiers don't care for the taste of dog," said Wild Cat.

I went back up the tree. The camp routine continued behind the wall. They kept their heads below the top log, playing cards or sleeping. Surgeons in bloody aprons came and went from the only tent. In one corner a long canvas sheet stretched across the ground. The feet of a dozen dead soldiers protruded from beneath, and a line of graves had been dug near the river. Dead horses were piled in another corner. Several showed obvious signs of being butchered. Crows and buzzards squabbled as they tore at the horse carcasses. I had never smelled anything like it, and I'd walked up on dead whales rotting on the beach before.

***

Three nights later I again crept close to the soldier's wall. After an hour of listening to their complaining, I caught Adams, the big burly man, staring at me through the tiny crack between the logs.

"Don't move. Don't say a word," Adams whispered a warning. The others froze. Adams' eyes bored into mine. Adams slowly pulled his pistol from his belt, cocked and aimed it. I stared into the deep black hole of the barrel. He fired. Dirt and wood chips flew into my face and an odd black shadow flipped in the light of the fire.

"Cottonmouth," said Adams. "A fat son-of-a-bitch, too."

"Good lord," wailed Francis. "Is there a plague that ain't upon us?"

"Oh, don't be so dramatic, Francis. He's dead," said Adams.

"That's right, Francis," said Marv. "There's only a million more slithering out there through the dark. Hardly enough to concern a man."

Sentries were hollering behind me. Adams and Marv shouted back and swung the snake around the fire. It was longer than the men swinging it. For a dollar Adams sold the dead snake to Titus MacCuaig, who planned to grill it.

"I reckon we better start keeping snake watch as well as Injun watch," said Myron when the commotion settled down.

"Don't talk no more about it. Snakes scare the water out of me," said Francis.

"Swamp rats and other critters come to feed on that putrid hill of dead horses. The snakes naturally follow," said Marv. "Every flesh feeder and rotten meat eater in the swamp will be crawling all over that stinking pile. The goddamn gators will build ladders and come over these walls to get at that smell eventually. I can hear them out there, slithering around."

"That ain't what I want to be thinking about. Why in the hell did I ever come here?" said Francis.

"Same as any of us," said Thaddeus. "The pay and the adventure. The pay best be what they promised, because the adventure sure ain't fulfilled the billing."

"Ain't gonna be the pay we thought it was, that's for sure," said Adams. "I don't expect we'll be collecting bounties for any captured nigras. So plentiful it would be like plucking fruit from trees...them liars."

"They's in the trees, all right. I see them and the damned Indians perched up there all damned day, like flocks of vultures, just staring down waiting for us to croak," said Marv. "Just watching. And waiting until we're dead or too weak to fight. It's unnerving."

"Ain't that relief column ever going to get here?" said Francis. "It's scandalous that a column of a thousand men needs to be relieved against a bunch of redskin rabble."

"If I'd know what such fools lead our army, I'd still be back home fornicating Sally," said Myron.

"But since you ain't, the whole town is back home fornicating Sally," said Marv.

"That ain't funny," said Myron. "If I wasn't so weak with hunger, I'd wallop you one for that. Another crack like that and I'll shoot you, though. I got strength enough for that."

"Save your anger for the Seminoles. And for Gaines, for lying and getting us in this predicament," said Adams. "I am mighty glum about our hopes of getting out of here."

"There's a thousand of us," said Francis. "Good lord a mighty, we should be able to shoot our way out of anything. There ain't but a thousand Indian warriors in all of Florida."

"Well, every damn one of them has us surrounded, and there ain't a thousand of us anymore. You see that pile of men under the blanket, plus them already under the mud?" said Marv. "We're shot to hell and the sickness is taking people in this filth."

"We could shoot, but we can't eat bullets," said Myron.

"You ain't lying," said Adams. "And I don't relish the idea of walking out of here. The army best reimburse me the cost of my horse, as guaranteed."

"Indians shooting our horses like that," said Aubrey. "That's low of them."

"Most of the horses fell over from hunger, not bullets," said Marv.

"I sure hated to eat Ol' Buck," said Francis.

"You ate enough of him," said Adams. "By rights, they should only reimburse you half."

"Your horse is looking peaked itself," said Francis. "I'll just wait and take a steak out of him while it's still warm."

"I see you around my horse, I'll gut you," said Adams.

"Ain't funny," said Myron, as one of our warriors let out with a long, haunting wail.

"Man, I hate them bird calls," said Francis. "Or whatever beasts that is."

"It ain't no beast, dummy. That's Indians," said Marv.

"I know its Indians, idjit," said Francis as another long chorus of haunting howls came through the trees. "But they're making bird calls. If I hate Seminoles, it only makes sense I'd hate their damn woo-woo calls, too."

"You two quit bickering. We got plenty enough to worry about with these military geniuses we got," said Thaddeus.

"I sure hope none of them get shot in the back before we reach the fort," said Adams.

"You don't reckon the Indians will follow us, do you?" said Francis.

"I didn't mean by Indians," said Adams. "And that's another big issue right there. Those damned Creek guides led us right into this trap. Be a shame if my gun went off and blowed a hole in one."

***

There was a war council the next night.

"They are sick and weak," said Osceola. "We need to strike now and wipe them out."

"They are not that sick and weak. They still have more men than us," said Alligator. "We would lose many men. They are strong behind that wall. We have no element of surprise. "

"A charge would give them the advantage. That cannon can never hurt us unless we charge it. Then it would destroy us," said Yancy.

"I don't think we would lose that many men," said Osceola, bright eyes and eager face showing his battle lust. "If we sneak close enough in the dark, we would have surprise on our side. We could sweep over them like a wave in the night."

"We would still lose many of our brothers," said John.

"The ground is too soggy to sustain fire, or I would burn them out," said Osceola. "Force them to charge our rifles."

"I say just be patient," said Yancy. "Hungry soldiers make for dead officers. Being forced to eat their own dogs and horses must be real insulting to these Tennesseans. Right about now, some of those soldiers would kill Gaines before us. They're probably just about ready to throw down their guns, hand over Gaines, plead for mercy and walk out of here. I've seen it happen. Revolt or starve."

"We can continue the siege until the Americans starve to death. We are not suffering. We can last here for many days," said Alligator.

"No. Clinch will come eventually. They will not starve or revolt before that happens," said Osceola. "We should have attacked that first night, before they could fort up."

"We had no way of knowing what they were doing," said John. "It could have been a trap to split our army. You chose correctly to wait until day light."

"Even if we rub out Gaines's forces it would only rouse American determination to annihilate the Seminole," said Abraham. "Since they are in such a poor bargaining position, why not at least try to bring about a resolution? If we show them mercy, perhaps they will see we are reasonable, civilized people and not savages. Perhaps they would see that a civilized solution could be reached."

"Civilized for who?" said Osceola. "They would never honor it. If we kill a thousand soldiers, they will fear us and leave us alone."

"We wiped them out two months ago and they return with ten times that many soldiers," said John. "The other column comes soon. I say we let those survivors return and tell the other soldiers of the great suffering here in the lair of the Seminole."

"Our spies from the north tell us that General Clinch is asking the white father to quit this war," said Coa Hadjo. "A council with the general might be wise."

"Perhaps that is best," said John.

"Will you come to the parley?" Osceola asked Yancy. "I want to make sure our words to Gaines are not twisted."

"I best not this time. I would probably just be a distraction to the proceedings," said Yancy.

"How so?"

"My cutting his throat might dampen things," said Yancy. "I've not forgiven any of the officers that killed my wife at the Negro Fort. That includes Gaines. Trust me when I say I can't say for certain I won't do anything rash."

"Abraham comes, and he was also at the fort."

"Abraham can do as he wishes."

"Very well," said John. "It is good to know yourself."

***

In the afternoon John and I walked toward the Army camp. John carried a large white flag and planted it fifty feet from the wall. A hundred rifles were aimed over the wall at us. We had riflemen in half the trees.

Captain Ethan Allen Hitchcock led a squad of filthy, bedraggled soldiers out to meet us. Hitchcock was different than most of the officers stationed in Florida. He had always been courteous and respectful to the Estelusti. His usually spotless uniform was torn and muddy and a stained bandage had replaced his left sleeve. Hitchcock's constant companion, a muscular black dog, was not at his side now.

"We request a parley with General Gaines," said John.

"State your offer," said Captain Hitchcock.

"I will speak to his face," said John. "I do not want my words made backwards."

"I'm afraid you can't dictate that," said Hitchcock. "General Gaines authorized me to speak for him."

"Apparently, I can dictate that. I speak to Gaines only or I don't speak. If I don't speak, your men die. Our riflemen await your answer," said John. He raised the flag and three of our best riflemen put bullets at Hitchcock's feet. Soldiers shouldered their rifles, but Hitchcock ordered them down.

"How did your dog taste?" John asked. "Ticonderoga was his name, was it not? Do you speak for him also?"

Hitchcock's eyes flashed fury and his hand went for his sword. The grizzled sergeant and two men grabbed him.

"We'll fetch him," said the sergeant after Hitchcock relaxed.

"Hitchcock is not a bad man," I said as the Americans walked away.

"The time for soft hearts is after the bullets stop, my brother," John said. "We can parley, but we cannot be swayed by old friendships. They no longer exist."

We waited, staring back at the soldiers who stared over the wall at us. There were angry voices and a commotion of bodies. The log gate opened, and General Gaines limped toward us, stomping angrily through the pain. His hawk face had a big scrape and bruise on the left side.

"What is your name, you impudent prick?" Gaines demanded of John.

"I am John Horse."

"I see. The ferocious Estelusti warrior. I hear they call you Hokepis Hejo, the Crazy Beast. They say you killed a slew of Laughing Boy's kin. He's a little upset about that," said Gaines.

"I hoped he would be," said John. "If he sends more, he will have fewer brothers."

"I'll pass that on."

"Who's this?" Gaines pointed to me.

"My brother," he said. "Pete Horse."

"Young for a parley, isn't he?"

"He's old enough for you to kill him, so he's old enough to see your face."

"I see."

"Maybe you do, maybe you don't," said John. "A cub needs to learn early how to recognize a snake."

"I don't much care for that remark," said Gaines.

"I did not say you were a snake," said John with a smile. "Only how to recognize one, should one reveal itself."

"What is it you want?"

"We want to parley, like I said," said John. "We could kill you all or starve you. But we want peace."

***

We met the following afternoon on a cleared patch just outside the festering soldier camp. The sun came out hot. The air smelled like an alligator den full of rotten eggs and rancid meat. Blue flies as big as bats dove at our heads. Laughing Boy and the MacCuaigs stayed behind the log wall, glaring at us with murder in their eyes. Five hundred Seminole and Estelusti warriors watched from the woods behind us.

I sat just behind John and a dozen other chiefs facing Gaines and his officers. Ogletree, a Creek interpreter, sat beside Gaines. He told Osceola to state his proposal. Osceola responded with a long string of angry words in Muscogee.

"What does he say?" said Gaines.

"He says John Horse speaks for him," said Ogletree. "John Horse knows the heart and mind of the chiefs that want to parley. He says if it were his choice, he would kill you now and bathe in your blood. But for now, he will accede to the will of the others. For now."

"That's a fine way to start peace negotiations," growled Gaines. "More bullshit like that and we'll just get to shooting. You wish to parley only because you know General Clinch is coming."

"Ha," said John. "We know more than you do. We have spies in the forts. General Scott is already in Fort Drane. No food is coming for your hungry men. Scott says you disobeyed orders by coming here, and that you have already consumed supplies meant for his men. All the remaining supplies go to Scott's Army. All the reinforcements, too."

I knew that was not the whole truth, but close enough. If Clinch's column had left promptly, it would have arrived five days ago.

"That no good insufferable, pompous, scheming, son of a bitch," snarled Gaines.

"Yes," said John. "I believe those were his words, too."

"I don't believe you," said Gaines.

"That those were his words?"

"No, I believe that," said Gaines. "But that he would issue such an order."

"Be that as it may, your men must be tired of eating spoiled horse meat. Are you not tired of eating your dogs and sleeping in your shit? Have not enough of your young men sickened and died?" said John. "We are weary of fighting. We want to be home with our wives."

Gaines fumed. His face was full of red, murderous rage. Hitchcock, sitting beside him, reached over and gripped Gaines' arm. After wordlessly working his jaw for a few seconds, Gaines finally spoke.

"We are tired of your resistance. The planters and farmers are tired of your raiding, of stealing their cattle and their slaves," said Gaines.

"We stole no slaves because people cannot be owned. However, yes, we have your cattle. Those your soldiers brought anyway," laughed John. "They are delicious. Some coffee, too. It's up to your standards since it came off your wagons. It's been quite difficult to keep my men from drinking it all. You should decide soon. We will have a cup."

Gaines glowered at John and Osceola. The soldiers glowered at Gaines.

"You're an insolent bastard, you know that?" snapped Gaines.

"You're not the first to say it. I don't believe it, but, then again, I suppose an insolent bastard never would," said John. "Now, your men must not want the coffee and beef. That must not be their bellies I hear rumbling."

"Speak your piece," snapped Gaines.

"The Great Master of Breath decreed these lands are ours! No one has a right to remove us! We were on these lands from the beginning," Osceola loudly shouted in clear English.

"Do not start with all that high sounding nonsense. I'll shoot you myself and take a scalping for it. I am weary and have no patience for such pretension. You were not even born here, you are not even a Seminole," shouted Gaines. "Just get to the point. I am a practical, military man. Legal boundaries and lawful treaties are what I respect and enforce. Spare me the religious mumbo jumbo and spurious ancestral assertions. Just talk facts."

"It is hardly nonsense. We have rights, human rights, same as you. As a sovereign people same as any Spaniard man, or English man, the right to defend themselves, to defend their land from invaders," said Osceola. "This land is ours. You have no claim to it."

"The Treaty of Payne's Landing says we do," Gaines said. "Your chiefs agreed to this move. They signed the treaty. It is time to honor your word."

"Who told you those chiefs spoke for me? Or any of our people? No one man, or seven men, speak for us. Many did not sign it. I did not. Micanopy did not. My father, King Philip, did not," said Wild Cat. "Those that accepted gold to sign the paper have been shunned by our people. They never spoke for anyone anyway. Those seven men did not have the authority to make decisions for all our people."

"Our government doesn't see it that way. You sent representatives. They signed," said Gaines. "As honorable men, you must honor those terms."

"Well, our government sees it differently," said Alligator. Those that did sign it now claim they were tricked and threatened. Maybe they were. We believe some were bribed."

"Preposterous," snapped Gaines.

"Were you there?" John said.

"I was not," said Gaines.

"Then you cannot say," said Wild Cat.

"Abraham was there. He was a witness for the Seminole."

"I only signed my mark as a witness to two men. I can only say they signed," said Abraham. "I cannot say whether any or none were threatened or duped or bribed. But they now say they were. Who am I to say they were not?"

"I signed," said Jumper. "But I did not agree to be ruled by Creeks, or have my black brothers put back in chains. Those are lies."

"I also signed," said Sam Jones. "But my wife is Estelusti. I was told my wife and children would be put to work on a Creek plantation if I did not sign. The others that signed were also threatened in this way."

"The treaty seems to say whatever the Americans want it to say," said John.

"That you misunderstood the treaty is not my concern," said Gaines. "Men that are here have seen the reservation. There is good water and fertile ground. Many have returned with the message that it is not bad land. There are forests to hunt game and plains full of buffalo. You can grow large fields of crops, ten, a hundred times the size of those little plots you plow up now."

"It could be the most fertile and abundant land in all of creation," said Alligator. "That is not the point. It is not the land we chose. It is Creek land. It is not our land. This is our land. That is the point."

"Why would I want a large field? I do not want a large field, to work ten or a hundred times harder for something I do not need?" said Wild Cat. "I do not want to spend all my time working in a field, no matter how large it is. What kind of life is that? Or do you expect us to enslave our brothers to work it?"

"Perhaps it is not good land?" said Wild Cat. "Good or bad land, we do not want it. We have good land here. Stop trying to take what is ours and replace it with something we don't want, and which is not yours to give anyway."

"It is ours to give," said Gaines.

"Stolen from other Indians," said John.

"If the land is yours to give, give it to your children and leave us be," snapped Osceola. "If it is so fine, why don't you give it to those that want our land? Tell the planters to move there. Then we would all be happy."

"Good land or bad land, it is too late for this debate. By the terms of the treaty, the land now belongs to the United States. You are now trespassers. But I came to kill no one, only to enforce the treaty that was signed by your chiefs," said Gaines. "Once you comply, there will be peace and goodwill."

"We've heard that before, from your lips," snarled Osceola. "Even now our compliant red brothers, the Cherokee and Choctaw, die by the hundreds on what even your newspapers call the Trail of Tears. That is what you Americans said before you blew up the Negro fort. That is what you and Andrew Jackson claimed when you destroyed all our villages along the Apalachicola. That is what you said at the Moultrie Creek treaty, so we took less for peace and goodwill. You come with the gun to bring peace. Every time. Now you come again. You will kill us until we are no more. All our black people will be enslaved by you, sold to some rich man. One man does not need 5,000 acres. No one needs so much land he must have hundreds of slaves to work it for him, just so he can laze about all day in the shade and count his money."

"You waste my time with old arguments. You requested this parley. Let's get to it," said Gaines. "What is it you want? What is it you offer?"

"We offer your men their lives," said Osceola. "We have you surrounded. We can show mercy, or we can curse this land with your blood and bones."

"You would lose many braves if you tried to attack us," said Gaines. "Don't be a fabulist."

"Who is the fabulist? Didn't you just bury the bones of a hundred men on your way here, and another fifty since you have been here? We see the graves from the treetops," snapped Osceola. "Your Major Dade apparently also thought us fabulists."

"Murdered in a dishonorable ambush," said Gaines.

"Dead is dead. If we just wait, you will all starve and be just as dead. Or you will die trying to fight your way back to Fort Brooke. Those are your choices. Perhaps your men will revolt, and hang you from that tree," said Osceola. "Clinch does not come. Vow to leave us alone, and we will allow you to walk away. From this day forward, we will stay below the Withlacoochee, if you promise to stay above it."

"I cannot make that promise. I am without authority to make such a binding agreement," said Gaines. "But I think your proposal makes sense. I will recommend it to my superiors. I came to make peace with the Seminole. I came to peacefully get you to the boats in the harbor before General Scott gets here to make war. I have fought the Seminole before. I have always treated you honorably."

"I do not think you brought cannons as a gesture of goodwill. The attack on the Negro Fort was honorable? The death of those women and children?" shouted Osceola. "I was there. And you did not come with honor now. You will agree to anything to save your miserable lives. You will slink out of here like whipped dogs, but you will come again to kill us, pretending to be lions."

"I promise nothing other than that I will present your case. I will recommend it," said Gaines. "I will tell them you showed great mercy and acted as gentlemen, wise ambassadors and diplomats. I will tell the President you understand the situation and have a sincere wish for peace. That you are not savages. That you wish to live as friends."

"We do not want to be friends. Only to be left alone," said John. "We are men just as you are. With all the same rights which your laws admit do not come from paper, but from the Maker of Breath. Just as yours do. Just tell him that."

"Whatever suits you," said Gaines.

The first gunshots came within seconds.

***

"Clinch comes, with many men!" a breathless warrior screamed as he sprinted out of the trees, holding his bleeding side.

"What the hell, Colonel, what the hell?" screamed Gaines at the colonel beside him. The colonel looked as surprised and confused as everyone else.

"Liar," screamed Osceola at Gaines and lunged toward him. John and Wild Cat grabbed Osceola and dragged him with us as we ran for the thicket.

"No, it is not so," shouted Gaines. "I did not do this!"

"It's Clinch's scouts, sir," shouted an officer. "They think we're under attack."

"Get out there, stop them," screamed Gaines. "Cease fire! Cease fire you idiots! We had ceased fire. We were treating!"

"Gaines lied," panted Osceola as we slid behind some bushes. "It was a trick, a lie. I am shamed I believed him."

"That is not so," said Wild Cat. "We allowed no messengers to pass. Clinch has no way of knowing we were talking peace. And Gaines had no way of knowing Clinch was that close."

"It doesn't matter," said John. "We know Scott comes soon with the entire army. This peace would have been meaningless. Scott despises Gaines. He would never honor such a peace. We must prepare, not argue."

We stayed across the river and watched. Clinch's men had brought rations for the starving soldiers. Injuries and sickness were treated. Gaines sent several messengers to the river's edge, to plead with Osceola to renew negotiations. The pleas were ignored. The next day, Clinch kept a steady stream of patrols pounding the brush.

On the third day the column headed toward Fort Brooke. The soldiers were strung out for miles, staggering along. Five hundred horses had died. Many of the others were too weak to carry riders and were released into the forest. The wagons were full of casualties. The soldiers cursed us but cursed Gaines more. Our sharpshooters made them even more miserable as they trudged along in the open ground. Dead men were dragged into the weeds and abandoned.

Chapter Six

SCOTT CAMPAIGN
MARCH 1836

Four days later Germaine arrived in camp from Jacksonville, where he'd been working on the docks. Germaine had relatives in every sea town in Florida, and they had watched every move as General Winfield Scott assembled his army.

"Scott brings five thousand soldiers in three columns. He personally rides with the largest column of two thousand coming from Fort Drane," Germaine said. "Another column comes east from Fort Brooke, and the other west from St. Augustine."

"And you are certain?" asked John.

"Completely. It is hardly a secret," Germaine said. "Scott himself announced his strategies in the Jacksonville Public square. He pranced through the city on a splendid white horse, and his soldiers strutted along behind, starched and polished, with a marching band banging and tooting. He hung ribbons and streamers all over the courthouse balcony and gave a thundering speech. He says he will squeeze the life out of the Seminole like a snake. He promises that within a fortnight, every Indian in Florida will have sailed out of Tampa harbor, bound for the west. He told the crowd to prepare for the grandest celebration Florida has ever seen."

"Exactly as I'd expect Scott to act. He's a showman. That blowhard loves an audience, that's for certain," snorted Yancy. "It may be better for us that Gaines was ordered back to the Texas border."

"Why is that?" asked Wild Cat.

"He's the one I always expected would come after us. Gaines made a poor showing at the Withlacoochee, but he's been fighting Indians in similar terrain for a long time," said Yancy. "I have studied Scott. I've read his histories and battle accounts from previous campaigns. He is no swamp fighter. Scott will be lucky if he sees one Seminole in his promised fortnight."

"You know much about him," said Germaine.

"Yes, I do. Always know your enemy. I learned that at an early age," said Yancy. "Scott thoroughly trounced my countrymen up near Canada and I harbor him no ill will for that. What chafes my jolly bobs is all the bloviating he did afterward, strutting through Washington like the triumphant return of Richard the Lion Heart. The news rags comparing him to Napoleon is nonsensical hero-making. Napoleon commanded six-hundred-thousand men and crossed continents. Scott led a brigade at the Battle of The Chippawa. It is not the same accomplishment. He ain't the first general to win a battle."

"He leads more than a brigade now," said John.

"Indeed, he does, but he'd probably be better off with fewer men down here in the swamps, not more."

"They always leave with fewer than they came with, if that helps," said John.

"Apt observation," said Yancy. "Though not one the generals would likely take as a constructive didactic."

"So why do you believe this is better for us?"

"Because I know military men. Generals stick with what has worked before. They'll stick with what hasn't worked before, too. They'll stick with whatever they damn well feel like sticking with. Generals are stubborn. Scott probably takes that a notch above. He won't change the very tactics that got him promoted to brigadier general at the tender age of twenty-nine. That's the promotion that set off his feud with Gaines, so now he'll want to prove what a smart boy he is. He'll come prepared to fight chess-pieces battles, with formations moving in nice straight lines with flags high and fluttering. He'll try to force us into a position where he can use massed volleys and entrenched positions. He will bring lots of artillery which he'll want to place on the high ground and besiege us, but there ain't no hills in Florida," said Yancy. "Large bodies of cavalry can't move through here. We have no supply lines to cut, but we can cut his easily. His chess board has no front, back or squares."

"Perhaps you underestimate him, Yellow Beard," said Germaine.

"Possible, of course, but I doubt it. He spent years in Europe studying their large professional armies and hobnobbing with their patrician warlords. He returned and wrote the manual for tactics and drill for the entire American Army. He would consider it beneath him to deviate from his own manual, especially for a handful of unsophisticated Indians and runaway slaves."

"What you say makes sense," said John. "But still, we must be ready."

"Of course. But bringing all those heavy wagons and a cattle herd tells me he doesn't understand what he's facing," said Yancy. "He hasn't learned a thing from the misfortune that befell Call and Gaines."

"He brings a herd of cattle to chase Seminole and Estelusti through the Cove of the Withlacoochee?" laughed John.

"Yes," said Germaine, shaking his head with a grin. "Scott boasts his men will feast in the land of the enemy, not starve like Gaines' men."

"Perhaps they will. Or perhaps the beef will roast over the fires of our hungry warriors," said John.

"That would please our men."

"It would please me as well," John said.

"He seems like an unserious man."

"True, but it's been a while since I've seen a parade. I might fancy that," said Yancy. "Let's go greet him."

"You are coming with us, Grandfather? We have far to travel," John said to Yancy. "We'll be moving fast, and considering your advanced age and infirmities…"

"Oh, bah with your advanced age and infirmities," said Yancy. "I can sit in a canoe as well as any man. You got a boat, don't you?"

"Plenty of boats. Don't fret, we'll get you there, papa," said John.

The rainy season had come early, and the road was soft and full of puddles. For three days Scott's heavy wagons churned the road into mire and moved less than six miles. Finally, Scott decided to build his own road. Platoons of men with machetes and axes chopped through the swampy thickets. Engineers used the downed trees to build bridges and pontoons.

"I'm suspicious," John said as we watched the soldiers labor. "I see no MacCuaigs."

"They are all with the other columns. Scott refused to employ them, as he believes they intentionally led Gaines into a trap," said Wild Cat.

"Why would he believe that?"

"Who knows? These American generals suspect their own shadows of sedition and treachery. Instead, Scott brought Delaware and Shawnee, who have never seen land such as this," said Wild Cat.

After two weeks the columns finally converged in a large prairie, still several miles east of the Cove. We silently encircled the field as the last weary soldiers dragged into camp, thoroughly beaten by the hostile swamps and skin-ripping thickets.

The camp was a noisy racket. Hundreds of axes chopped trees and split firewood. Mallets and sledges drove tent spikes for thousands of soldier tents. Toward dusk, we heard the sound of horns and drums.

"Let's have a look-see. We may see a parade yet," said Yancy.

We crept through the thicket to a point where we could see the entire camp. I had never seen anything so huge and noisy. Tents for ten thousand men covered acres of grass field and freshly cleared pine forest. In the dim light of dusk, I could see the large, square officers' tents on a raised knoll about seventy yards away.

Long tables draped in white tablecloths were arranged for a banquet, set with China plates, flower vases, wine bottles and twelve-wick candle towers. Sides of beef turned over fires. Under a canvas canopy, cooks tended pots and grills. Officers in dress uniforms mingled around the long tables. White jacketed waiters stood behind long counters of liquor bottles or carried silver trays of long-stemmed glasses through the crowd. Beside the largest tent a forty-member symphony orchestra was seated on camp chairs, in four rows of ten, with instruments at the ready. Their red jackets sparkled with gold braids and tassels.

"Thar She Blows!" snorted Yancy as Scott emerged from the big tent, strutting past the two sentries who snapped to attention. He wore a wide bicorne hat trimmed with gold braid, a towering white egret plume and a gold eagle centerpiece as big as an apple. Two rows of glittering gold buttons ran down his chest and gaudy gold epaulets the size of jellyfish bedecked his shoulders. A long saber with an ivory grip was in a scabbard on his hip and a red sash was wrapped around his gut.

Scott waved his hat and the band jumped into a rousing tune. The peppy conductor whipped his baton and bounced on his toes. Drummers drummed. Horns and tubas tootled and blared. The officers saluted and cheered as the mountainous general swaggered across the clearing.

"Don't that tub of guts look right resplenders?" said Yancy. "Be a shame if some horny hawk lands on his head for a quick shag."

There was a rustling in the brush behind us.

"He mocks us with music," snarled Osceola, nostrils flaring and eyes narrowed in anger as he slid down beside Yancy.

"I'll handle it," said Yancy. "I come prepared for one thing or another."

As Scott mingled with his officers, Yancy cut a notch in the log we hid behind. He slipped the barrel of his Baker rifle into the cut and flipped up the folding sight. Brushing his beard out of the way he put the gun to his shoulder and squinted down the sight. The peppy bandmaster bounced on his toes and whipped his baton around. The band played with gusto as Scott took his position at the head of the table. He raised his wineglass and toasted his officers. They hurrahed and returned the toast.

"Fire in the hole," Yancy whispered and squeezed the trigger. The rifle blasted and Scott's hoisted goblet exploded in his hand. He lurched backward, tripped over a chair and his full weight slammed down on the table. The table snapped in half and flipped up on both sides. More tables crashed over as more of our rifles blasted. The candleholders spun in flaming loops. China plates and saucers flew, crashed and rolled through the grass. Cockades and gold tassels flashed as the officers and musicians dove behind the overturned tables or ran for the tents. Shattered fruit bowls sent apples and oranges and pears bouncing. Scott galloped toward his tent like a bear on all fours, with a line of junior officers lumbering along behind him. Yancy put another shot into the dirt to speed them up. The burning candles met spilled liquor and the tablecloths caught fire.

"Bloody marvelous," cackled Yancy as our riflemen blasted away. "His arse looks like four hams in a one ham sack."

A troop of soldiers rushed forward and fired a volley at us. A hundred hidden Seminole riflemen riddled the soldiers with bullets, and they retreated. We reloaded and waited. Now four or five hundred soldiers had formed up. As they prepared to charge, we fired heavy volleys until they scattered.

Finally, the enraged officers had assembled three regiments of infantry with bayonets fixed. We blasted one more volley of three hundred guns into them. By the time they had picked themselves up out of the dirt and charged our position we were half a mile away.

I found a thick-leafed tree and climbed up for a look. As Scott's regiments chased our shadows, more of their soldiers had been formed up on this end of the huge campsite. Scott raged and waved his fist as he stomped the fire-blackened circle in his camp. He bellowed and called us cowards who refused to come out. He roared at his staff and called them cowards, too. His bushy unkempt white hair was wine stained and glittered with bits of glass. His magnificent uniform was torn and befouled. His hat was as bent as a shipwreck. The cloud-white egret plume had snapped, and the gold eagle centerpiece had mud in its eye.

We were ready for the soldiers who were bumbling and stumbling around in the dark forest. We had laid traps. We shot and ran, over and over, drawing them further into the swamps where we easily evaded the noisy, slow-moving soldiers. They charged where we had been, but never where we were. Scott roared and thundered until the camp was nearly emptied of soldiers. Our torch-waving warriors kept running. In the darkness of the trees beyond the thousands of campfires I saw a new flame. It grew and then split up and into dozens of specks of light, like fireflies swooping across the field. The fireflies were moving fast and firing guns. There were hundreds of them, and they were surrounding Scott's cattle herd.

Wild Cat's painted, torch-waving horde charged out of the trees at a dead run. The few soldiers who had been guarding the herd threw down their guns and ran for safety. Scott screamed like he'd been burned in the face when he realized what was happening. Thousands of terrorized cows stampeded through the abandoned camp, dragging tents, toppling campfires and smashing over wagons. Scott roared at his officers to protect the herd, but they were all out chasing ghosts in the bushes south of camp.

***

At sunup I was stretched out beside Yancy, underneath a palmetto bush just out of range of the army muskets. Across the field, muddy, ragged soldiers repaired the trampled tents and campsites. Burial details were at work. The hospital tents were back up and busy. The moonlit charge into the swamp had done little damage to us, but many of Scott's soldiers were limping and gathered around the trampled but repaired medical tent. A collection of trampled tubas and trumpets was piled where the band had been seated. A grisly pile of crippled cows was being butchered. We would be butchering our share, too, of the hundreds we had successfully rounded up. We'd left many more bogged down and broken-legged, but nothing went to waste in the swamp. The alligators would feast again.

Clinch was supervising the camp repair as Scott, in new pants but the same muddy, smoke-smudged, grass-stained dress tunic, stomped around in a fury.

"You could have killed Scott easy," I said.

"I could have," he said.

"Why didn't you?"

"Damned if I know, lad. I very much wanted to, but at the last moment, I couldn't bring myself to do it. I despise him, but I always consider long ranged killing to be ungallant except in exceptional cases," said Yancy. "I want to look in his eyes and make some final remarks.

I'd like to take a rusty bayonet to his entrails but doubt I'll have the luxury of that much time. I want him to know just who done him. In fact, I'd expect the same courtesy."

"Someone else might shoot him if you don't," I said.

"That would be fine. Hopefully, they'll be a worse shot than me and he will suffer longer. Beyond that, I just suddenly had an overwhelming urge to embarrass the man. To some, that's a worse pain than death. I've killed many a man, and I guess I decided the giggles I'd get from watching him piss himself would be worth much more than one more body on the stack. And I was not disappointed, lad, I was not. I've not seen such comedy in the best of theater houses."

"That's what you were thinking when you were aiming that rifle?" I said.

"A good bit of it, yes. What should I be thinking when considering taking a man's life?" he said. "That he has a wife that loves him and three beautiful babies at home? That he donates to the orphan's fund?"

"I suppose not."

"And generals like Clinch or Scott, especially that bloviating Scott, would be a delicious martyr the gazettes would use to inflame the public against us. I can see the headline: "Gallant Heroic General Murdered by Savages in Cowardly Ambush." Nowhere in there would it mention he shat himself. Twenty-thousand more soldiers would be in Florida in a week, and another twenty the week after. But now that I've spared his life, that son of a bitch will remember Yancy Yarbrough. Perhaps he'll mention my name at his victory parade when he returns home and cleans up."

"He knows it was you?"

"He will now. I ain't finished with him. Watch this."

Yancy slid the Baker out. He scooped the mushrooms out of the rotten log in front of us and slid the rifle barrel into the soft wood. Scott's aides had pieced together his tent.

Scott sat under the awning of his tent. A map was spread out on the table and several officers were gathered around. There was none of the good cheer of the night before.

The bent-up bicorne hat was on an empty chair beside him. The gold eagle crest on the crown had been cleaned. Yancy fired and the hat flipped in the air. The officers under the awning dove for cover.

"Hey, you fat tub of guts," shouted Yancy as he leapt to his feet. "A gift from the lads of the 100th A Foot."

He dove back into the brush, rolling and giggling as bullets clipped tree branches far above us.

***

I was delivering a message to Osceola when I found Willet resting under a tree. I could see the pain on her face, but saw no blood leaking through her shirt.

"Are you hit?" I asked her.

"Yes, in the side. A broken rib, I think," she groaned. "No blood. It must have caught a ricochet, or a ball almost out of power. I am not seriously injured."

"You better let me have a look," I said. She lifted her shirt to show me her wound, a purple bruise the size of a fist, ringed bright red. I saw her breasts. My eyes pulled there and held for just a moment.

"My wound is down here," she said, grinning slightly.

"Sorry," I said, my face burning with embarrassment.

"I wish you wouldn't be," she said. "You have seen me naked plenty of times before. I have seen you too."

"We were children then. It's different now," I said.

"Is it? In what way?"

"Don't pester me with silly questions," I said. "We need to wrap your ribs tightly before you get in the boat to return home."

"I'm not going home," she said as a challenge.

"On this you'll be overruled, even by Osceola," I said. "You might be hurt bad inside. There will be no more fighting now, only waiting. You need to go home and heal."

I wrapped a spare shirt tightly around her middle.

"Is that too tight?" I asked. "Can you breathe?"

"I can," she said, taking a few painful breaths.

"Are you sure it's not too tight?"

"No, it is fine. Come closer." she said. When I did, she sat up and gave me a kiss.

"Ow, that hurts," she said, leaning back quickly.

"Then why did you kiss me?" I said.

"I swooned. I was not thinking clearly," she pouted a little.

"Clearly not," I said.

"Despite your rudeness and trickery to send me away, I will worry about you."

"I am not sending you away. You are injured. The war will not be over tomorrow. You will have many chances to fight," I said.

"I will be fine. Pain is nothing. I am a warrior, same as anybody," she said.

"From what I just saw under your shirt, not exactly the same," I said.

"You noticed," she said.

"I did," I said. "Probably nothing I should be pondering in the midst of battle."

"Probably not," she grinned.

Chapter Seven

DRANE PLANTATION APRIL 1836

Scott's grand campaign was over after another week of tromping through the swamps. He accomplished nothing but getting his men shot, sickened by the swamp, and horrified by the swarms of deadly snakes drawn to the camp. If the soldiers saw us at all, it was only after we'd fired from the tall branches, or our backs after we had lured them into another watery trap. Scott continued his tantrums, blasting his big cannons at us but only splintering more trees. When Scott marched back to Fort Drane, his band was not playing. We returned home tired, scratched and bruised up, but well-fed on Scott's beef and otherwise unharmed.

"I worried about you," said Willet.

"There was little excitement after you left," I said. "And I also thought of you. How are your ribs?"

"Badly bruised," she said. "By the time we reached home my back was on fire. I thought I would pass out with each breath. The first two days home I relied on Yancy's laudanum and your mother's tender care to get by."

"But it is better?"

"Yes, better," she said and then paused for a long moment. "So, this kissing thing. What did you think of it?"

"What kind of question is that?"

"An honest one."

"I enjoyed it," I said. "I can see why people write stories about it. I thought of it often when I was away."

"Is that so?" she said. "You should not be thinking of kissing when you are on a dangerous raid."

"I suppose not, but I did nonetheless."

"But you enjoyed it?"

"I did. I had not done that before. Did you enjoy it?" I said. "Did I perform as expected?"

"You did."

"That's good to know," I said.

***

Mother and Yancy were sitting at the council table smoking cigars and reading through a fresh stack of newspapers. A round, brown brandy with a French label on the table looked about half-empty. Germaine usually brought a treat or two with the newspapers and other necessities.

"What's the occasion?" I asked.

"All manner of joyous events. A war has broken out in Texas and it sure is looking ugly, or beautiful, depending," said Yancy. "Soon we may no longer be the biggest concern of the American government."

"Where's Texas?" asked Virgil.

"Mexico. West. It borders the territory where they want to send us. Texas is in revolt against their government, which currently is the Mexicans," said Yancy. "They want to be their own nation."

"A revolt like ours? That kind of revolution?"

"About exactly, but vastly different. At least from the viewpoint of the United States Government," said Yancy. "Still, it could be of great benefit to us."

"If they're way out west, how will it help us?"

"Just about all Texians were once Americans, and they still have many important and powerful friends in the American government, including Andrew Jackson, who seems to be kin to half of Texas. It's being reported that two-hundred and fifty Texians were massacred at a place called the Alamo. Four hundred Texians were executed after they'd surrendered at Goliad," said Yancy. "That has caused quite an uproar amongst the American public. They are demanding Mexico be punished, and that would be a blessing for us if it occurred. Gaines is there now, just waiting for word to attack. If he hadn't blundered around down here, he'd probably already be halfway to Mexico City."

"They would take their army from here to fight the Mexicans?"

"If it came to that, they'd about have to. Knowing Santa Ana, he will take the opportunity to attack the States if he's not stopped," said Yancy. "The Americans have a puny army compared to Mexico anyway, and the Texians have none at all to speak of. Volunteers more than likely related to the ones down here. They should call that place Western Tennessee, not Texas."

"What is the other good news?"

"For once the rags all seem to agree on one thing: That Scott and Gaines are jesters, bumblers," said Yancy. "It's near unanimous that never in the history of this country has so much bloviating gas-baggery been bloviated. That this chapter is a huge stain and embarrassment on the American army. That it is shameful that a bunch of primitives could so thoroughly whip their best generals. And they're infuriated that so much money was spent to kill so few redskins and capture so few Negroes."

"Ain't that something?" said Virgil.

"In Tampa and St. Augustine, they've taken to hanging Scott in effigy and burning the body."

"What's that mean, effigy?" asked Virgil.

"Hanging dummies of them," I said. "And setting them on fire."

"Ain't that something?" said Virgil.

"Many in the north, the abolitionists and pacifists and advocates of the Seminole, applaud their ineptitude," said Yancy. "There's dummies hanging from lamp posts up there, too."

"That's in our favor, then, ain't it?" said Virgil.

"It is. And the feud between Gaines and Scott has become a very public scandal. They've taken to insulting each other in the gazettes as glory seekers and scoundrels. They accuse each other of sabotage. They've both been called before boards of inquiry for serious allegations of official misconduct."

"They should not have come to the Cove," said John.

"In retrospect, it seems that way, don't it?" said Yancy. "It's a real mess. Jackson favors Gaines, of course, his old friend and battle mate. He can't stand Scott, but he can't fire the hero of the Chippewa either. Trying to fire him, loudmouth that he is, with all his powerful connections, would be much more of a fiasco than Jackson needs right now. Also, since Gaines wasn't supposed to be here anyway."

"Will they be punished?"

"If they are, there will likely be no official record of it. Instead, before it's over, one or both will be made a hero. I've seen this before, when things get bungled so badly. Pin so many medals on their chests that allegations of incompetence would be seen as seditious," said Yancy. "That's how the Queen does it anyway. Knight a cad for failure and slather him in glory beyond reproach. How dare you accuse a knight? That sort of thing."

"I see no honor in what they do," I said.

"Yes, well, the British military is full of such men. The East India Company especially. Nepotism and blue nosed inbreeders. Buffoons, chumps, and negligent murderers of epic proportion raised in rank due to family tradition. The Abercrombies and Howes and such," said Yancy. "Nicolls was a bloviating swaggerer himself, but no fiercer warrior ever pissed on a tree. Sometimes a situation calls for a bloviating swaggerer, as long as he's got the iron to back up the swagger. And the good sense to know when to back off."

"And those are their generals of generals?" Wild Cat asked.

"Generals of generals, perhaps, but not General of the Cove," said John.

"In Georgia and Alabama, more Creek are rebelling against the forced move West," said Yancy. "Jackson has seized the property of the Creek that fought the Red Stick, and also even the land of some of them chasing us now."

"The MacCuaigs?"

"No, the land of the subchiefs and soldiers. They have revolted and attacked the town of Roanoke and slaughtered a bunch of people."

"And the American army now fights them?" asked John.

"When has Andrew Jackson ever passed up a chance to kill Indians and steal their land?" Yancy said. "That's where Scott is now. Clinch has retired to Georgia."

"They will leave us alone?" asked Wild Cat.

"No. Nothing like that. Since the Federal army is tied up with the Creeks, Governor-General Call is trying to raise an army of volunteers."

"Call?" John scoffed. "We embarrassed him once. He comes for more? He will pay for that arrogance."

"Apparently so. At least he wants people to think he is, so they'll calm down. He says he will raise enough volunteers to rid Florida of the Seminole and Estelusti once and for all, just as the others bragged," said Yancy. "It's all bluff and bluster. It will take large bounties and very high pay to entice enough men. No one wants to come to this land in the rainy season and fight an invisible enemy."

"Hooah," said Wild Cat. "He can't bring an army through here in the sickly season. Half the soldiers would end up in ambulances within a week."

"I believe so too," said Yancy. "Jackson's War Department is funding Call, but I don't think he'll find many takers. He won't move until fall, no matter what nonsense he spouts."

***

Willet grunted and drove my face into the sand. She had both arms hooked under my armpits and hands locked behind my neck. Fighting exhaustion, I shot my legs out and bucked up. We rolled and grappled until we were face to face, gasping for air and blowing sand in each other's mouths. We'd been at it all morning. As we did every few days, we had been honing our fighting and grappling skills. Over the years, Yancy had taught us kicks, holds, joint-beakers, flips, throws and eye gouges he'd learned in ports and barrooms all around the world.

"Alrighty then, I guess that's enough for today," said Yancy. "It's getting warm out here anyway. Time for a little shade and refreshment."

"I suppose so," panted Willet. "I told the girls I would help them with their archery skills today. They will be fine hunters soon."

"Can I ask you a question, without any jokes?" I asked Yancy after Willet gathered her things and was headed back to our island.

"Sure, lad, of course you can," he said. "Worried about something?"

"Not worried, exactly," I said. "I am not sure. What do you think of Willet?"

"I think she's a darling. A diamond of the first water," Yancy said. "A combination of beauty and pugnacity like I've rarely seen in a woman. Smart, too. What do you think of her?"

"I'm not sure," I said. "All those things you said. And a little more. Lately when I wrestle her, I am not sure what I should do. I did not want to wrestle too hard and hurt her. It was not always that way. I would not want her to think me weak but losing to her would be even worse. I find the whole thing very disconcerting. Do you understand what I am saying?"

"I'm pretty sure I understand what you're trying to say, but you should probably just concentrate on trying to win and not getting hurt yourself," he said. "You have some feelings for her, do you? The kind that ends up with marriage and babies?"

"The baby making part probably more than marriage, but yes, those feelings."

"You act like you shouldn't."

"Well, I'm not sure I should," I said. "She is nearly a sister living here. And what if I said something to her, and she did not feel the same."

"She is hardly a sister. You may have known her since you were ankle-biters, but she's been here barely a year. And I will tell you what. I cannot imagine a better way to get acquainted with a romantic prospect. Side by side you have been through extraordinary and trying circumstances. You've seen every speck of what she's made of. And her of you. You've both spoken your minds without all of the normal lies that usually come with a gentleman trying to squire a lady, or vice versa," he said. "I've seen so many lads get in them whirlwind in-port romances and get hitched, only to find out they've wed the sister of Satan, and she has a large family."

"I do not know much about the courting thing. Not much, about, you know, laying with a woman."

"Few do. They just lie about it, and it almost always works itself out," he said. "She is a swell lass, she truly is. I've seen the way she looks at you sometimes and speaks of you."

"Speaks of me? What does she say?"

"It's not like she sits around blathering love sonnets about you; for that we can all be thankful. It's not actually what she says. More in the way she says it. If you've had a successful hunt, or just done something interesting. And plenty that really ain't all that interesting to anyone but her. And if a lass speaks of you glowingly when us others are bored to tears, you're safe to assume that she shares your feelings."

***

JULY 1836

Virgil and I leaned against an old log. A pile of orange peels was between us. We had cane poles in our hands and cork bobbers in the quiet stream in front of us. Behind us the girls squealed happily as they chased each other through the bushes. Not even the birds were disturbed by their happy chatter.

"Shhhh," Virgil whispered.

"What?" I said, reaching for my pistol. I looked around. Nothing disturbed the chirp and snick and buzz of the Cove. The giggles never paused, and I saw the blur of happy faces and bright ribbons on bouncing pig tails.

"The only thing I hear is the girls laughing," I said.

"Zackly. Laughing like they ain't got a care. Laughing with their whole bodies. Laughing without one eye looking over your shoulder for who's listening. A rare sound in our previous life. You know what I mean?"

We had enjoyed three months of peace. Only a few soldiers manned the forts and no large armies tried to enter our sanctuary.

Virgil's bobber disappeared under the water, and he gave a quick yank. He let the fish fight its fight for a minute and then pulled it in, adding it to his heavy stringer.

"I've never seen anyone hook as many fish as you," I said. "I prefer the nets. It is a lot easier and doesn't take up so much time."

"Time took up fishing ain't time poorly took up," said Virgil. "As for them cages, I never seen somebody so lazy. Just putting them fish traps down and let them dumb fish swim in."

"You're not exactly sweating and breathing hard there with that pole stuck in the ground beside you. And I'd say your fish are dumber than mine. They swim right up and bite a hook that's right there in front of their eyes."

"Well, I suppose you have a point there, but still, there's a strategy to it."

"Sure, there's whole books written on it. They're just real skinny books, pictures of men sleeping beside ponds, mostly."

"A man with a line in the water is peaceful fella."

***

I had been asleep under a shade tree near the water when voices woke me up. I started to make my presence known when I heard Naomi sob and my mother console her. I decided to just let them be.

"What is it, Naomi?" I heard Mother say. "Is that a tear on your cheek?"

"It's the silliest thing," sniffled Naomi.

"It probably isn't silly at all," said Mother. "Tell me what's bothering you."

"My feelings is all messed up. Sometimes I get this tugging inside, telling me ain't none of this is real. That it'll get took from us at any minute. And look. All we been blessed with and me crying. Silly crying about losing what I should be rejoicing. Silly, like I said."

"That's not silly at all," said Mother. "You have been through a horrible ordeal. You've lived a life no one should ever have to endure. I'm sure it doesn't seem real, or lasting."

"I just really ain't used to being alone in my thoughts. When you're a slave, what's the point of even having thoughts? What was there to look forward to? There's little pleasure in pondering the bleak future of life in bondage. But now I am overwhelmed with the fear of going back. Of my children going back. Now that I've had a little touch of living free, the fear of my children losing this hurts me deep in my heart," said Naomi. "Ain't it silly?"

"Not at all. Once your eyes are opened you cannot unsee. It will all take time. As you said, you are experiencing thoughts and feelings you never had before, or kept down way too deep to understand," said Mother. "Now you are being full human. That is the greatest act of rebellion. They can never fully enslave you again once you have the knowledge."

"I sure don't mean to seem ungrateful. Inside, I sing a great song of joy. A silent great song of joy," said Naomi. "But I want to bust out in song. A song so loud every bird in them trees will fly off in wonder at my song."

"You do not need to keep anything inside here. Not songs, not tears, not thoughts. We are alone and safe. Your songs of joy do not have to be silent. There is no overseer to jump on you for being happy," Mother said. "I sing. The children sing. The birds sing. We all sing around here.

It is an easy place to sing. You do not need to be shy about it. I sing, and I have no talent for it."

"I expect that last part's not true," said Naomi.

"Yancy says I have a fine voice for begging bacon," giggled my mother.

"Well, now, if he said that I'll clobber him with a tree limb."

"He said it, but if you clobber him, clobber him for being indelicate, not untruthful."

"We'll sing some songs tonight," said Naomi.

"Yes, now miracles come."

***

I sat beside John on a thick mat of palmetto leaves in the council house. Osceola, Wild Cat and other Seminole chiefs were there. The rainy season sickness had struck the Americans worse than ever, and our spies reported the forts were being abandoned because too few soldiers were fit for duty. While it was weak and undermanned, we would attack Fort Drane, located on the 3,000-acre sugar plantation belonging to General Clinch. After Clinch retired, the mansion had become the officers' quarters.

"A relief column comes from the east," said Wild Cat.

"How many soldiers?" said John.

"Barely a hundred. Only enough to bring wagons to remove all the sick soldiers," said Wild Cat. "They have more sick soldiers in Florida than ones who can stand a post."

"Governor Call's Florida Militia doesn't come?" said John.

"No. He cannot raise enough volunteers. Men join to fight the Creek in Georgia. They go to Texas to fight the Mexicans. They do not want to fight the Seminole."

"They are no longer eager for a big Indian hunt?"

"It would seem not. Call has doubled the pay for volunteers and increased the bounties on captured Negroes," said Yancy. "The newspapers are putting recruitment pitches beside the listing of bounties on escaped slaves. The dollar figures are in big print. Virgil's name is there, near the top. $1,500 alive. $500 dead."

"Have you told him that?"

"I doubt it would come as a surprise," he said. "I wouldn't mention it around Naomi, though."

"We should attack the column and wipe them out," said Osceola. "That is an insult, thinking a hundred men can pass through unscathed. Afterward, we can surround the fort and watch the sickness kill them."

"Yes, we could attack the column, but that could cost us many warriors. Surrounding the fort would be entertaining, but before enough soldiers could die, a much larger column would come and we would walk away with nothing," said John. "There is another way. That fort and plantation are full of plunder. In the spring, many wagons stocked it to feed hundreds more soldiers than have ever been inside. There is enough to supply our people with food and gun powder and bullets for a year. We can take it without a fight."

"How so?" asked Osceola.

"We just let them walk out," said John. "Their wagons will be filled with sick soldiers. They cannot take the supplies in the fort with them. Not crates of rifles. Nor kegs of gunpowder. Nor potatoes, for that matter. Let them come and remove the sick but leave the rest for us."

"They will burn what they cannot carry out in the wagons," said Osceola. "They won't let it fall into our hands."

"Perhaps they will try," said John. "But I think we can prevent it. They cannot burn anything with a fort full of soldiers laying there sick in their beds. They cannot blow it up with people inside. If they try to

160

bring the guns and powder outside and bury it, we will kill them. If they bury it inside, we will dig it up."

"True."

"The soldiers will not stay in a fort with a lit fuse and tons of gunpowder. If we time our attack correctly, we can seize everything in there. We can run in and extinguish the fuses."

"Perhaps. But who wants to run toward the lit fuse?" asked Osceola.

"I will," said John. "I have been inside that fort many times. I know where the armaments and powder are stored."

"I will go with you," said Yancy. "You find 'em and I'll follow behind you and snuff 'em."

"You?" laughed Osceola. "Yellow Beard, you're the slowest runner in all Florida."

"True enough," said Yancy. "But a slow waddle with the right amount of wisdom is sufficient in almost all arenas of life. You will appreciate that one day. Those fuses can get tricky once you're right up on them."

"I hope your waddle doesn't overtake your wisdom," Osceola said.

"Eagerness is grand, lad. But let experience handle this one. It will be fine, I promise you. I am vastly experienced handling gun powder and fuses. If you need a fuse snuffed, you better make sure it's done proper and with finality."

"Yes, that is true," nodded Osceola. "But do you plan to simply run past the guards?"

"That will be your role," said John. "You attack any guards at the fort. Kill them once they are gone, but you must chase them away immediately, before the fuses can burn down. The soldiers will not want to linger with tons of lit gunpowder close by. I would think it would not take much to get them to bolt. Once the last guards are gone we can run inside."

"That is not much time," said Osceola.

"I have blown forts before. Whatever fuses they leave will be long and slow, to give the sick wagons time to get down the road," said Yancy. "Get those guards out of the way fast and we'll have time."

"You're sure of this?"

"Sure enough to risk my life," Yancy said. "Just make sure none of them return while we're inside that giant bomb."

"They will not," said Osceola. "I will attack the sentries at the gate and chase them away. I will attack the wagons, but only from behind to also chase them away. I have no interest in killing a wagon train of sick men. But we will make sure they run far away and do not return. I will block the road with all my warriors."

"Excellent," said John.

"It will be a joy in my heart to watch that plantation burn," said Osceola. "We will leave nothing but a pile of ash."

"Yes, but we do not need to burn it right now," said John. "There are many valuable things on that plantation beside the rifles and powder. The food from the fort does not need to be carried away. There is comfortable shelter there for hundreds of people. We would be as safe there as anywhere in Florida. We would be dry. The soldiers will not return for months, not until after the seasons change."

"I will not live in any of the white man's buildings," said Osceola. "There is evilness inside them."

"Nobody is asking you to," said John. "Just that there is much we can use. We do not need to waste time or energy moving it."

"Very well. It is agreed," Osceola said. "But the sugar mill must be burned until the flames are visible for a hundred miles. Let our allies watch in awe, and every soldier and slave owner tremble and quake with fear. Let them all see that Florida is ours! Let our people know we have the power now."

"Yes. A flame like that will signal our great victory. However, there is also no need to waste all that rum," said John with a grin. "There are enough barrels of rum in the warehouse to burn the place fifty times. Saving some to have a little sip from time to time would not be so bad. We will burn the house and shacks before the army returns."

"There will be no drunkenness, nor pointless mayhem and destruction," said Osceola. "We must be firm on that point."

"Are you saying you won't drink the white man's rum?"

"No. I never said that. I just will not sleep in his house or slave shacks. Those must burn, too."

"Of course, after we're done using them for the people that need them. Let those houses be homes for once, not prisons."

***

A dozen mounted dragoons waited fifty yards from the fort gates as the twenty-two wagons full of sick men rolled out in the morning. Once the last of the wagons was a half-mile down the road, three more soldiers, the ones who'd struck the fuses, rode out of the fort. All the riders moved a little further down the road.

"Yiii-eeeeee," Osceola howled, and our sharpshooters fired. Two of the dragoons were shot from their saddles and the others slapped spurs to their horses and tore off after the wagons. Our warriors poured out of trees screeching and howling.

The wagon drivers yelped and cursed and lashed their long blacksnake whips. The harness mules lurched into a gallop and the bedridden soldiers clung desperately to the side rails as the wagons bounced and jolted down the road. Two hundred of Osceola's warriors swept in behind and blocked the road as John and Yancy sprinted through the gate.

Long minutes had passed. The wagon train was long gone, and wisps of black smoke curled over the palisaded walls of the fort.

"What you reckon, Pete?" asked Virgil.

"I don't know," I said. "Those soldiers could have rigged it up, expecting this. Set a trap to blow us all up."

"Yancy seems mighty smart in these matters. I reckon he could recognize a trap if there was one there," said Virgil.

"We'll know soon enough," I said. "And then there won't be any doubt to it."

"No doubt to it for miles around, maybe," Virgil said. "Reckon we should be picking out trees to land in?"

A single gunshot came from inside the fort. The rest of us rushed inside at the signal and extinguished the small fires the soldiers had set. Little damage had been caused, and all of central Florida was now under Seminole control.

***

Men with picks, timber axes and sledgehammers swarmed the sugar mill. Most were men who'd once labored in it, or the nearby fields, and had escaped its horrors when the war started. Others had just run off that morning. They clanged and banged and chopped with fury.

A crowd gathered on the manicured lawn and the colonnaded porches of the mansion to watch the demolition. Barrels of rum and kegs of beer were tapped. Fiddlers whipped their bows and tub thumpers pounded out a happy, foot-stomping beat. Dancers kicked and clapped and spun each other with joy. Beef from the Army's herd turned on spits above glowing coals. Our families joined us. More people emerged from the surrounding swamps and forests.

The dismantling continued throughout the day. Spectators cheered as pipes and pistons and gears collapsed. They hallelujahed and praised the lord when the stone walls and heavy lumber frames collapsed and the five-hundred-gallon boiler vats dropped.

Toward dusk, gunpowder and rum were packed into the wreckage of the sugar mill and the celebrating crowd was ushered into the safety of the trees. The fuses were lit, and everyone cheered as the flames and sparks raced up the cord.

The explosion knocked half of us over and blew through the trees like a hurricane. Blue, white and yellow flame shot far into the sky. Bits and pieces of metal and wood showered down as the people ran out of the trees in a delirious celebration.

"Our flame of liberty burns bright, brother," shouted John as black flakes wafted through the air around us.

"Glorious," said Virgil. "That there is the sweetest sugar I've ever seen on any plantation."

***

After two days of feasting and a day of rest, the task began of turning the plantation into a livable village for five hundred hungry people, with more streaming in every day. Many people wanted to loot the mansion immediately, and Osceola wanted to burn it. The Women's Council forbade it. He was a war chief, they said, and this was a peace camp. He had no authority here. He huffed around for a while but never protested further.

The Council, which included my mother, declared the house off limits until everything could be sorted out and put to its best use. Guards were posted at the doors. The Council assigned duties to everyone. Slave shacks, barracks, overseer houses and any other livable shelters were cleaned out and reoccupied. Chickees went up in the lawn. The brick kitchen house bustled with activity, and food was abundant. Two huge copper sugar cauldrons had turned into stew pots hanging over never-ending fires. The storerooms had been left well-supplied with beans, yams, rice, and potatoes. Cellars were packed tight with jars of preserves and jellies, pickles and relishes, canned fruits and vegetables. There were beef cattle and dairy cattle. The smokehouses were still full of hams, bacon and pork shoulders. There was even a large cache of precious coffee and salt.

**

"Your wife sent this to you," I said, handing Jovis a pitcher of sweet tea and a ham sandwich wrapped in paraffin paper.

He was a small man of sixty or so years, the color of wheat with hazel eyes and neatly trimmed gray hair. Until a few days ago, every breath Jovis had taken had been as a slave to the Clinch family. For the past twenty years Jovis had served as General Clinch's personal man-servant. Jovis and his wife, Esther, had been responsible for keeping the rest of the mansion staff on their duties.

On his first day of freedom Jovis had knocked out the front wall of his two-room cabin and called it his veranda. That's where he sat now, smoking his pipe on a massive maroon and gold overstuffed chair. The wood was heavy cherry, with a thick-maned lion engraved above the head rest.

"Well, bless her heart, and yours too for fetching it to me. Just set it there on the table. I don't want to eat and stain this fine chair," Jovis said. "Please, have a seat. I can't let a guest stop by without offering a seat on my new sofa."

"It is a fine chair," I said, setting the food and drink down. "I've never seen a finer chair. A fine sofa, too. Right up there with the chair. Appears to match it."

"Special delivered," he said.

"I helped deliver it," I said.

"I always did fancy this chair," Jovis said. "It was Massa Clinch's reading chair."

"That's what I heard."

"For twenty years I watched Old Massa sitting in this chair with his feet up, sipping his bourbon. Most nights I'd be wondering if that would be the night I snapped and did him in. But then I'd think to myself, I'll just keep on persevering and one day I'll have me a chair like that one. One the white folks tossed out probably, but still a fine chair," he said. "I never really expected it to be true. It was just something I told myself to keep going."

"And now here you are."

"Yes, sir, now here I am. And not just in a chair like his but the exact same chair. And he just got it re-stuffed in the past year or so."

"Ain't that something?" I said. His eyes were on the kitchen house. "You just sitting here watching those women work?"

"Sort of. It's a rare thing for a black woman to have the chance to cook, simply for the pleasure. Most of them women, they been cooking for the Clinches, or them like 'em, all their lives. For once, they get the same fine cuts that the master's family got. No mistress of the house watching over, no fear of threats or screams of displeasure. Those women have children. For the first time ever in their life, they can give them what they have cooked for the Massa's children all these years. I expect that's mighty satisfying. A completely new pleasure," he said. "I enjoy watching folks enjoy themselves."

"Feeding this many people is a pleasure?"

"You best believe it is," he said. "Just look at them faces."

"What's really going on up in the big house?" I asked.

"I wouldn't know. Why do you ask?"

"Your wife and my mother and those other women ran me out of there, and they run off nearly all the men. They pulled all the drapes and won't let anyone inside. Nobody will say, but I see them all chatty and giggling. They are planning something, I can tell. I expect you know what's going on up there," I said. "What's the big secret?"

"You will find out soon enough. Them houses have secrets you'd never want to know."

"I have my suspicions. I heard piano music and violins and a horn of some kind. They were playing music like I have heard in St. Augustine."

"The ladies have a little celebration planned, a little music show of some sort. It was your mother's idea. She says she wants to give people something they've never had. Something they will always remember. But I was sworn to secrecy, so that is all you will get out of me. Ain't no use of you pestering me about it further," said Jovis. "If you let on I told you that much, we'll fall out."

"I won't say a word. You can tell me."

"I am not speaking on it further, young Pete. In great part, I owe my long and fairly easy life to keeping the secrets of the big house. I don't see no reason to stop now," Jovis winked. "I've never worked a day in those fields out there. But if I told what those ladies are fixing up, and ruined their surprise, I reckon I'd be chopping from daylight to dusk and sleeping with the hogs."

"I won't let on," I said.

"You won't, 'cause you won't know," he said and took a long drink of tea.

***

Promptly at seven, Jovis met us at the servant's entrance. His demeanor was courtly. He was dressed in an immaculate black suit with a long-tailed jacket and plum colored waistcoat. He wore a white ruffled shirt and white knotted cravat and white gloves. Yancy was beside him, looking just as regal, though much more uncomfortable. His burgundy jacket strained at the shoulders and the shirt collar points dug into his newly trimmed beard. The green vest that girdled his belly seemed to hinder his breathing.

"What do you make of this, Pete?" asked Virgil.

"It's hard to figure," I said.

They led us down a hallway and up the sweeping stairway, past more of our men with quizzical looks on their faces as they were being directed into other rooms by old men dressed like Jovis, men who had worked in this house for a long time. The women were unseen, but I heard their excited laughter and chatter from down the long hallways. Someone played a piano.

***

"Your changing room, gentlemen," said Jovis.

We entered a bedroom that was bigger than most houses. Arranged on chairs and mirrored dressers were neat stacks of brightly colored European style formal clothes: Shirts, waistcoats and cravats as green as limes, yellow as lemons, red as cherries and purple as plums. Along with them were more sedate long-tailed jackets and trousers. I saw the closet full of colorful swallow-tailed frock coats.

"The ladies have already picked out your ensembles, based on your size. If the drawers is a little too loose, I can pin them up," said Jovis.

"If they's too tight, well, best not get too exuberant in your Grand Jetes."

"Our what?"

"You will find out soon enough. Just get in these fancy ball room clothes and make haste about it."

"For what purpose?" I said.

"For a ball, of course. For what other reason would you need ball-room clothes?"

"Well, I guess we don't need to speculate further on the reason for all that scrubbing and bathing we was ordered to do," grumped Virgil.

"That would be correct," said Jovis.

"I never seen such fine clothes," said Virgil. "Where'd you get all these fancy suits?"

"General Clinch has twelve children, most of whom are grown," said Jovis. "They all flit between here and their city houses, living here more than not. There are twenty bedrooms in this house, and they were about always occupied, and packed full for holidays. Uncles and cousins pour in during the season. Other dignitaries visited often. Generals came and brought their staffs with them. Mistress Clinch, she loved to entertain. She always had the latest fashions brought in from Charleston and Jacksonville for her daughters and sisters and made sure the gentlemen were also suitably attired."

"I never seen so many clothes in one place," said Virgil.

"Everybody was here for the Christmas holidays, when news came of the attack on Fort King," said Jovis. "A packed house that left out of here in a ferocious hurry."

"Looks like they run out of here nekkid," said Virgil.

"Not quite, but not more than the clothes on their backs," said Jovis. "When word first reached here about the attack on Fort King, everybody started packing up, getting their carriages ready. Then word came of the Dade massacre, and it became a panic. When news arrived of Call's defeat, they just about lost their minds getting out of here. Clothes was the last thing on their minds. They were fighting each other over seats in the carriages, real hair-pulling and eye-gouging by the ladies. I never seen the like. There was brawling by the gentlemen, which left me less impressed. Some between the ladies and the gentlemen. All us slaves run off and watched from the trees. Buggies was colliding and horses was running off before they could get hitched up, dragging people by the harness. There simply weren't enough carriages, and some folks run off and left their kin. Those pretty ladies in their fine dresses looked mighty glum riding out of here in the manure wagons. They sho' wasn't worried about their closets."

"Ain't that something," said Virgil.

"Now, let's get you dressed and go meet your ladies," said Jovis.

"I don't think I care for this," said John with a stone face.

"Oh, swallow your spleen, lad," said Yancy. "Your wondrous mother said just once in her life she wanted to see her boys all primped and preened in finery, so seeing her boys all primped and preened in finery is what she will get."

We stripped down. Every man in the room bore the scars of a lifetime of hardship and battle. The runaways had vivid whip scars across their backs, rough-edged ridges running from shoulder to waist.

"I don't see how men can wear these constricting clothes," said John once we had most of them on.

"You'll adjust," said Yancy. "I've seen souls entering Newgate with more enthusiasm than you're showing. The ladies have planned a fine event for you, so I'd expect a bit more of a show of gratitude on your parts. If you're smart, you'll just play along."

"Why didn't you tell us beforehand?" I asked Jovis.

"Because I expect the majority of you would have high-tailed to the swamps before coming to a ball in the Massa's house."

"No, I wouldn't have," I said, knowing very well I would have considered it strongly.

"Sure," said Yancy. "It ain't all about you anyway."

I stared at my reflection in the floor length mirror. I had on a blue silk tailcoat, waistcoat the color of a roseate spoonbill, white ruffled silk shirt and tan buckskin trousers. They chafed instantly but Jovis said they fit perfectly.

"How am I supposed to put this on?" I said, fingering the cravat.

"I'll give you a hand, laddy," said Yancy.

Yancy folded, unfolded, and refolded the cravat at my throat. He crisscrossed, uncrossed, knotted, un-knotted, re-knotted and fluffed until I was left with a large billowing knot kept in place by a ruby brooch that stabbed me.

Next Yancy fixed Virgil's cravat, who was resplendent in a burgundy velvet tailcoat, lemon yellow waistcoat and crisp cream-colored trousers. He would have looked like royalty if the trousers had reached below mid-calf and his shoes weren't battered brogans.

"Bloody marvelous. Ain't you all just the image of dusky, dashing Beau Brummels," beamed Yancy. "My swamp tromping hellcats turned into regular high society exquisites. The Pinkest of the Pinks."

***

The oval ballroom was like being inside a cloud. Every inch, from floor to the pinnacle of the arched ceiling, was flawless alabaster. Hundreds of candles glowed from crystal chandeliers as big as carriage wheels and candelabras the size of big buck antlers. Mirrors with heavy gold frames lined the walls and reflected the light like suns. The floor had been chalked in a design that looked like a large coach with a dozen spoked wheels. Wavy flourishes connecting the wheels. A round plat-form was in the center of the dance floor. On the stage, my mother sat at a white pianoforte, wearing a gown that glistened like pearls. Jovis and three men dressed just like him stood on the stage, tooting horns and tapping bowstrings.

"Gentlemen, your attention please," announced Jovis in a loud voice. "Please prepare yourself to accept the ladies."

Yancy and the Clinch men arranged us in a line curving away from the grand archway. They told us to stand right there and be quiet. Jovis stood at the archway and extended his arm, holding his hand like he was accepting some delicate, precious item.

"What's this here?" muttered Virgil under his breath.

"Probably the reason they didn't tell us beforehand," I said. "I'm feeling pretty rabbity."

"Miss Ophelia Duncan," announced Jovis in a loud, formal voice. His voice cracked at the end.

Jovis's seventeen-year-old daughter Ophelia stepped through the door wearing a gown the color of the sky above the Gulf. She was ra-diant, smiling broadly but looking like she might cry, too. She placed her white-gloved hand over her father's forearm. With a face full of pride, Jovis escorted Ophelia to Tim, the first man in line. Tim had once been a Clinch horse groomer and I knew he and Ophelia had planned to jump the broom. Ophelia looked Tim in the eye with tenderness, bowed her head and performed a perfect curtsy, holding the edge of her skirt out daintily. Tim placed his left arm across the small of his back, palm out, and bowed like he was meeting a queen.

"Shall I have the pleasure of dancing with you?" Tim said, stutter-ing out the first word. Ophelia whispered yes and they promenaded hand in hand down the line to some cushioned benches beside a long table holding platters of nuts and cheeses and pickles.

Jovis returned to the doorway and called the next lady. One at a time they came out, wearing striking gowns of every color of the rainbow, flower and bird. Their shimmering hair was arranged in towering coiffures, coiled, woven or in long braids down their backs. As Jovis escorted them past me I caught whiffs of orange peel and lavender, cloves, violets and bee balm. Seven more down and Virgil was the end man on the line.

"Gentlemen, I present Naomi Hampton," Jovis said.

Naomi stepped out in a peach-colored gown. Her skin shined and her eyes were bright. She smiled like the happiest woman in the world. The wide gilt mirrors that lined the walls reflected her a hundred times and she walked toward Virgil, her fingers curled over Jovis's arm.

"Oh, my lawd, ain't that something?" Virgil gasped.

Two small grinning faces peaked around the partition. With nervous smiles but in perfect step they went to their mother. They wore little gowns identical to hers and tiny white gloves.

"Mr. Virgil Hampton, I present Primrose and Posie Hampton for their debutante ball," announced Jovis.

Virgil stopped breathing when his wife and daughters stood before him.

Holding hands, they swept a foot back, dipped and curtsied.

Virgil placed his big, calloused hand behind his back, palm out, the other across his belly. He bent solemnly at the waist, then rose and looked into the eyes of Naomi, and then his girls.

"Shall I have the pleasure of dancing with you?" he said.

"It would be my heart's desire," Naomi said.

***

174

Willet came around the curtain in a shimmering lavender ball gown. She smelled like honeysuckle. There was no more buckskin hunting shirt. Willet's gown was cut low, and her shoulders were bare. The tight bodice pushed her breasts up. Long sparkling earrings dangled and swayed. Her hair was in shining braids coiled on top of her head. Though I'd never said the word, even in my head, I knew Willet had become a beautiful woman by the standard of any tribe, village or even nation. Now this.

"Will you do me the honor to dance with me?" I finally stammered out after I had answered her perfect curtsy with an awkward bow where I got light-headed and thought I might fall on my face.

"My fondest wish," she said.

"Do I look ridiculous?" she whispered as we walked to the end of the line. "You stared at me like I had three eyes."

I was still stammering my thoughts around in my head. None were ready to be uttered.

"It's so silly you are speechless?" she said, a slight cross look on her face.

"No. The furthest thing from it. You are…beautiful," I finally said. "Dazzling is the word that comes to mind. The right words do not come to mind."

"I feel awkward enough without your teasing," she said.

"But I am not joking. Not even a little bit," I said, squeezing her hand. I held her eyes with mine. Now I felt awkward and light-headed again. "Not at all. You are beautiful, Willet. I've known it for some time."

"Thank you," she said a little bashfully. "You're a handsome man yourself when someone else dresses you."

"I had no idea you were interested in such things," I said.

"I'm not. Not really. Such a thing never crossed my mind before, really. I thought it was silly when your mother first proposed it, but it's all rather nice. The dances at the trading posts always looked enjoyable. I have seen glimpses of formal ones like these a few times in the city, when I was living with the missionaries," she said.

"That's the first time I've heard the Presbyterians were proponent of waltzes," I said.

"No, that's not really the missionaries' position," she said. "But I saw the forbidden bacchanals. And heard them condemned enough times to make them sound appealing. Everything is much more fun when it is supposed to be sinful, don't you think?"

"I hadn't really considered it," I said.

"Well, I suppose I can't explain my irrational enjoyment otherwise."

"I don't suppose your pants are as tight as mine," I said. "That may be why you're enjoying it more."

"I wouldn't think so," she said. "But I think this will be great fun. A masquerade ball like the European aristocrats might be enjoyable someday, but I could never imagine making a habit of it."

"When did this idea come about?"

"Well, once your mother saw the piano, and we found these beautiful garments, what reason would there be not to put them to use?"

"Of course," I said.

***

Jovis and Esther stood hand-in-hand in the center of the room as the orchestra played a melody I remembered from years before in St. Augustine. The elderly couple bowed and curtsied to each other as the spectators gathered around. They stepped away and began their dance, gracefully swirling around the room with their chins high and faces serene. Dipping under elegantly arced arms and floating toward each other on tiptoes with fluttering fingertips, their dance looked like the courtship of waterbirds.

"You expect me to do all that?" I whispered to Willet.

"Of course not. That is just the minuet, the dance to open the ball. They will be the only couple doing that. Jovis and his wife have probably served at a thousand such affairs. If anyone knows the steps, they would."

"They seem to," I said.

"Look at their eyes, when they meet," said Willet as Jovis and Esther fluttered around each other.

"What?"

"Nothing."

***

The dance master called lively steps. Couples wheeled and pinwheeled, passing under arm bridges and promenading hand in hand down the rows. The couples on the dance floor were mostly older people who had served this house or another all their lives. Now they laughed and smiled as they skimmed along the chalked loops and curls.

"Just watch for a little while," Willet said, as the dancers whirled about the ballroom. "Yancy is a fine dancer."

"He is nimble for a fat guy," I said, watching Yancy skip around, swinging his arms and prancing like a colt.

"How is Virgil doing so well?"

"I suspect he was tutored by Yancy. They have dancing instructors in London. Caper merchants, Yancy calls them. Some in the British military sought them out. Yancy and your mother showed me."

"I'm relieved. That would explain why I saw them dancing together out in the woods the other day. I was more than a little concerned by that," I said.

"Come on, just follow me," said Willet, pulling me onto a chalked wheel. "Your mother and Yancy showed me the steps. Listen to the dance master and follow the chalk lines on the floor."

"If you insist, and promise not to complain of broken toes afterward," I said.

"I promise I won't complain to you directly," she said. "My understanding of affairs such as these, though, the women must gossip about such things afterward."

"Is that so?"

"It is, to my limited knowledge."

"And what do the men do?"

"Oh, that's quite secretive, I think," she said. "Mostly lie about stolen kisses, conquests and such. Men are the same everywhere, whether it is the Massa's ballroom or the Dance of the Green Corn."

"You seem to know much about it."

"You seem to worry too much."

***

"Miss Willet, don't you look spectacular this evening," said Yancy with a deep bow. He took her hand with a grand gesture and kissed it.

"Oh, stop," she said.

"Well, it is true."

"Well, get a good look then. I do not expect we'll get invited to many more plantation balls," she said. "Especially since we came to this one quite spectacularly un-invited."

"That's a point to be considered," he said. "How about you, lad? The suit a good fit on you?"

"I have no idea how it's supposed to fit, but I, for one, am relieved not to worry about any upcoming soirées."

"Care for a toddy? Maybe that'll brighten you up a bit."

"Why not?" I said. "It is a soirée, after all."

There were rows of liquor bottles of all different shapes and colors. Outside were barrels of beer and apple cider. Some stern, older women had volunteered to guard the liquor. They used long silver dippers to fill the delicate cups from crystal punch bowls full of bright, frothy red or green liquid.

"Are you sho' you's old enough to be drinking likker?" demanded the large woman staring at me in disapproval. Her crossed forearms were big as hams.

"A couple snorts of the good stuff, Nelly Fae. I'll keep an eye on him," said Yancy, putting his arm around me and giving me squeeze. "No more than two though. These sweet little drinks will sneak up on a lad."

"He won't sneak one past me," said Nelly Fae, with ominous lidded eyeballs that would have punched me in the head if they could.

"That's good," winked Yancy, grinning ear to ear. "Three drinks and these two get horny as goats."

"Yancy!" Willet yelled and punched him in the shoulder.

"Lawd Jesus," said the woman, eyeballs now wanting to slap Yancy around. "You won't be getting no punch from me with talk like that."

"Now, now, Nelly Fae," said Yancy. "No need to be so dour. It ain't been all that long ago you was known to take a stroll in the orange orchard."

"Yancy Yarbury, you keep talking and you'll be wearing this punch," she said, filling three cups for us. Yancy grabbed a bottle of clear liquid and tossed a big splash into our drinks. Nelly Fae squint-eyed him, but he didn't care.

"Come along, kiddos," said Yancy.

"Why did you say that to that woman?" said Willet.

"Oh, that's Nelly Fae. She loves me," said Yancy. "I knew her at the Negro Fort, before she promoted herself admiral of the ardent spirits. She was a runaway from Georgia and stayed at the fort for a good long while. A real looker back in the day. Until we got here, I hadn't seen her since that day. Didn't even suspect she'd survived."

"And you met again here?" said Willet. "Twenty years later?"

"Aye, and don't let that serious demeanor fool you. She was known to kick up her heels and enjoy her frolics with those lusty young men manning the fort," said Yancy. "Somewhere along the line I guess she got the holy spirit and a fondness for taters and syrup."

"Sounds like you knew her well," said Willet.

"Now, I never dallied with her, mind you," said Yancy. "But lord she was fine."

***

"That concludes the more formal part of our evening. Open them windows up and tell those people outside to come in here and bring their cups. There's a toast to be made," Jovis announced after perhaps ninety minutes of dancing. He put down the fiddle and raised his glass. The men on stage did the same. Curious people crowded in, chattering with excitement, quickly filling the dance floor.

"This toast is to General Massa Duncan Lamont Clinch, without whose generosity these festivities would not be happening," shouted Jovis. "I've been waiting my entire life and never expected such a moment would come. Now, let's kill that yaller cat!"

Jovis and the musicians whooped. The room burst alive with euphoric people hooting and howling as Jovis and the banjo pickers and the tub drummer and the tambourine player whipped into action, high stepping and stomping as they played and bellowed out the song.

"Juba dis and Juba dat,

and Juba killed da yellow cat,

You sift the meal and ya gimme the husk,

you bake the bread and ya gimme the crust"

***

As the evening wore on the partiers wandered through the house, admiring the luxuries their labors had produced. Down every hallway and in every parlor hung oil paintings in thick gilt-edged frames. Most depicted valiant steel-eyed champions leading men into action against daunting enemies or crashing waves. Some of the visitors were quite impressed, some not as much. Some had never been in a building before that wasn't a shack or a slave pen.

"Like that one?" asked Yancy.

"Very much," I said, gazing at a glorious battle. "They are rousing."

"I'm stirred by such works myself. I used to visit the museums in London when I was a lad. Paintings are very popular with the exquisite set," said Yancy. "On a busy day, a good finger-smith could slip out of there with the fat wallets of many a preening art lover."

"Is that the only reason you went?"

"Not at all," said Yancy. "That gold frame, there? It cost as much as a good field hand. The painting by itself cost a field hand and his entire family. Me and my lads never could have pulled off a heist like that, though, nor know of a way to get rid of the pictures if we did. We

181

cased it out though, several times. We had high aspirations, me and my lads did. If only the magistrates at Old Bailey hadn't got involved."

"I think they're exciting," I said.

"You're young yet. There will come a time soon when you won't. I've seen a hundred battles. That don't represent none of them, and they sure smelled worse," said Yancy.

"Is that supposed to be Clinch?" I asked, looking at the next one, a painting of a blue-caped officer astride a rearing horse. With pointed sword, the officer led a charge against some red-coated soldiers and a cannon on a hillside.

"Looks like him. But I suppose big hams and paunch could be a family trait," Yancy said.

"If that's him, he looked a little different at the Withlacoochee, didn't he?" I said.

"Now that you speak on it, he was going the other way, wasn't he?" said Virgil. "The rear-side of that man on the horse does have a familiarity to it. That's really all I seen of him."

"He was courageous when we had Gaines trapped at the river," I said.

"He blundered into that one backside-first too," said Yancy. "Ironic. And I suppose one could say there's a good bit of irony there."

"What's irony?" asked Virgil.

"Us standing looking at his picture while he ain't," Yancy said.

"This here ain't but one lesson after another," said Virgil.

***

Back in the ballroom, Jovis and the musicians cackled and howled as they called out the songs.

"Hambone Hambone pat him on the shoulder.

If you get a pretty girl, I'll show you how to hold her.
Hambone, Hambone, where have you been?
All 'round the world and back again."

The singers and dancers hopped and stomped, bobbing their heads on stiff necks, shaking one leg and then another, and flapping their arms like bird wings. Wild abandon swept through the room. The dancers shook, bobbed and flapped and swung each other and flung their limbs around with a freeness I had never witnessed before. Gray-headed people bent from a life of hard labor kicked up their heels. Little children skipped and darted between the dancers. Young and old high-stepped and hopped until the whole house shook.

Willet and I were caught up in the excitement. Shiny with sweat and laughing with joy we twirled and swung, strutted and peacocked and slapped out the hambone beats. Our men cut dashing figures, but none came close to Wild Cat. As the son of King Philip, Wild Cat had attended many balls of St. Augustine privileged classes. He came in wearing a blue velvet jacket and lemon-yellow waistcoat that looked tailored for him. A cravat the size of two was pinned up under his chin. A tower of Egret plumes waved above his silk turban. Big silver hoop earrings bounced as he capered about like a show horse.

"The women seem to love Wild Cat," I said when we took a short rest.

"He is easy to be enamored with," she said. "He has a strong spirit."

"Many came hoping to meet with Osceola," I said.

"Osceola will not attend," Willet said. "He considers it frivolous. Osceola also says there are bad spirits here. He says there is too much soul sickness to come inside."

"He's probably right."

***

"What are you smiling about?" I asked Willet. I was warm and happy, more than a little intoxicated.

"What Yancy said," she said. "Perhaps we should have that third glass of punch. And then do a little more dancing."

"You think so?"

"I don't suppose I'll wear a dress like this again anytime soon," said Willet after we sat down with fresh glasses of brandy.

"I probably won't either," I said.

"But you might like these lacy under-drawers I found in the lady of the house's chiffonier. Should I decide to invite you into my boudoir?"

"You have a boudoir and lacy drawers?"

"All fancy ladies have boudoirs," she said. "The frisky ones have lacy drawers. Camisoles and pantaloons and such."

"You're a fancy lady now?"

"Fancy enough. And frisky, too. Have you had enough of the dance?" she asked. "Have you finished your drink?"

"I believe so," I said. "Did you have something else in mind? Regarding these pantaloons?"

"I do. I was planning to drop them," she said. "Come with me."

We left the ballroom and walked down the hallway, past the watchful eye of the ancestors of Gen. Clinch and Nelly Fae. Willet went into the bedroom first, lighting the wall lamp which she turned down to dim.

She walked behind a satin screen in the corner and told me to wait on the large, canopied bed. I heard clothes rustling. Willet came around the corner in a white corset, stockings to mid-thigh held up by be-ribboned garters, bright white. Nothing else. She walked toward me.

"What do you think?" she said.

"I don't see any pantaloons," I said.

"You're quick," she said. "Want to wrestle?"

***

During our stay at the Clinch plantation our days were filled with care-free leisure. The weather was mild and food plentiful. People sat on whitewashed patio furniture in flower covered gazebos and pushed each other in swings under the sprawling oak shade trees. People wandered over the fifteen acres of landscaped lawn and garden terraces. The old men fished in the creek or played checkers or whittled dolls and toys while they smoked corncob pipes. Women sat in circles and shelled beans or sewed clothes. Rowdy young men ran races, had wrestling matches and played day-long, collision-filled stick-ball games in the horse pasture. Blossoming girls strolled across the vast lawn, wearing bonnets and holding pink umbrellas. Children played as children should. Young people courted and the old people smiled, remembered, and wished.

Virgil and I were sitting in the grass, watching.

"Boy, ain't this living?" said Virgil as I slathered a biscuit with jam. "We is in the land of milk and honey."

"I sure can't argue that," I said.

"Too many of those and you won't be nobody's fastest runner much longer," Virgil said.

"I am like the bear. I store the sweet energy for when I need to fight," I said. I'd already eaten three biscuits and was looking for a shade tree. "I just hope nobody feels like fighting for another hour or two."

"I never would have imagined this in a million years. Sprawled out on the Massa's well-kept yard, struttin' around the big house like we owned it. Cutting de pigeon wing an' frolicking all night in his London fashions. It sure is a step up from what I was doing this time two years ago," said Virgil.

"Sure. Unless you get yourself killed," Yancy said.

"Kilt or not, it's a step up," said Virgil. "That General Clinch, he sho' know how to throw a party."

"You think we should send him a thank you note?"

"We probably should," said Virgil. "I suppose you would have to do that, seeing as how I can't write. Thank him for that, too."

"I'll do that," I said.

"Let him know I said he has fine liquor and prime beef. That the more I learn about him, I wisht I would have killed him at the river," said Virgil. "I reckon that's it."

"It makes your point, I think," I said.

***

In October word came that Call was finally on the march from Talla-hassee. He had recruited a thousand mounted volunteers, mostly from Tennessee. Laughing Boy had recruited a thousand Creek from Alabama. The column was coming to teach us a lesson.

We packed all the buildings on the plantation with gun powder and rum. Then we waited for the column to get close enough to hear the blast and see the flames. When it was, we lit the fuses and ran for the swamps.

The plantation was flat by the time Call arrived. Nothing stood higher than the weeds in the cane field. Every building was reduced to rubble. Charred circles covered the once gorgeous estate. Thick smoke hung over the ground. Ash and black dust covered hundreds of acres.

Call stormed around the lawn in a rage until his voice left him and he sagged into the arms of his aides. There was little he could do to punish us. His army had galloped too far, too fast, trying to reach the flames of the burning plantation. His horses would be too spent to travel for days, as we'd expected they would be. At night, we came to the edge of the trees and taunted them with song and the calls of swamp haints.

When Call started again, we waited for him in a swamp south of the plantation. We were badly outnumbered and expecting the worst, but our ally nature saved us again. The black skies ripped open with roaring wind, sideways rain, thunderclaps and lightning strikes. The storm landed like a hammer on Call's volunteers as they crossed a saw grass prairie less than a mile away. The blinding rains blew for hours and then the eye wall of the hurricane struck with fury. Frothing brown waves and roaring winds carried away wagons, mules and men. The following morning Call's army was scattered for miles. Their supplies were gone, and half their horses drowned. Call took the remnants of his army home.

Chapter Eight

JESUP ARRIVES
DECEMBER 1836

We had enjoyed peace since the hurricane had defeated Call. The storm had not harmed us. As we always did at such times, we just dug our defensive holes a little deeper in the mud and tied everything down. Our families were twenty miles away from the fiercest of the wind.

We made the most of the time, harvesting our hidden gardens, smoking meat, repairing what was needed and preparing for whatever would come next. We were anxious about the uncertain future but remained hopeful. At times we traveled to the larger villages for festivals and reunions, but mostly we waited. When word came that a new general was coming to Florida, we knew the hard times had returned.

"Who is this new general? Do you know him also?" John asked Yancy.

"I know of him. Gen. Thomas J. Jesup. He concerns me a great deal. He is an exceptionally brave man, no doubt about it. He has won medals for valor and had two horses shot from underneath him at Scott's great victory at the Battle of the Chippewa."

"That is of no consequence. We have fought brave men before and sent them running," said John.

"Yes, exactly. We have defeated them, which is why they send Jesup. He is different. He'll be slow, methodical, and thorough. He's been the Quartermaster for the entire American Army for years. He is a bean counter, not a glory seeker. He is the man who watches the bean counters. I expect his strategies will be markedly different."

"How so?'

"Everything in his past says he's a studious planner. Good quarter-masters are like that. He came to do a job, not throw a parade. Men like him don't just rush off on a whim. Those others charged in here without having studied properly on it," said Yancy. "Jesup won't leave his men to wander aimlessly through the swamps. He will not march without enough supplies."

"I see," John said. "He might even want details on where to cross the rivers. And when they are flooded."

"Yes, exactly. That's what bean counters do. He's a bean counter, and we are the beans."

***

Jesup's armies plodded. His engineers and axmen constructed perma-nent roads and bridges, strong enough to support heavy supply wagons and cannons. His engineers built blockhouses and supply depots every second day. In each new fortification, Jesup left a company of men and stockpiles of powder and bullets, bacon, and corn. Patrols prowled the swamps. The rivers were no longer our moats. Instead, steam powered boats chugged down them loaded with fresh supplies.

Within days of leaving Fort Drane, Osceola had become gravely ill. Now he could barely lift his head. His body burned with fever and shook with chills. He was wracked with a cough that left him in painful spasms. The sickness that ravaged the soldiers, but rarely touched us, had stricken him. He was sleeping a few yards away, quieted by lauda-num and a strong broth Susan had prepared.

"We must restore Osceola to health," whispered John. "There is much yet to be done. Our fight has barely started."

"I wouldn't count on it. That's a churchyard cough if I ever heard one," said Yancy.

"Don't speak of such things," said John. "No. None of us can put fire in the heart and iron in the spine like Osceola. He is the fire that holds us all together. The people know Micanopy and Abraham and many others would betray them for a life of ease in the West. The other chiefs do not have the confidence of the people."

"Those things need to be spoke on," said Yancy. "You can't find yourself in the middle of a war with no general. There are others that can lead. Wild Cat. Alligator. Sam Jones. Yourself."

"Alligator is wise, but he has none of the fury that pulls others behind him. Wild Cat is fiery, but rash. He lives and fights for today and doesn't consider the future. He needs someone beside him to cool his head. Sam is almost seventy years old. They are all good men, and would attract a following, but not a unified following. I fear we will splinter, and all will be lost," said John.

"You're leaving out someone. You," said Yancy.

"The Estelusti might follow me. I doubt the Seminole would be so eager."

***

Two months had passed since Jesup had invaded Florida with ten thousand soldiers. Patrols were relentless. The MacCuaigs attacked with savagery. The soldiers found our buried caches of food and destroyed them. Our cattle herds were captured.

The worst of the barbarities occurred at the end of January. Wizened old Chief Osuchee had made a camp beside the Hatchee-Lustee Creek, thought to be far away from prowling slavers. A few wounded warriors were recuperating in the camp, but most villagers were old people and mothers with small children.

The camp had been discovered and massacred by the MacCuaigs and a band of vigilantes. From infants to old grandmothers the bodies had been mutilated and molested. Noses and ears and hands and feet and private parts had been cut off.

Chief Osuchee had been scalped and decapitated. His head, with spectacles over eyeless sockets, had been placed on a Philadelphia newspaper. The front-page editorial decried the Army's practice of paying the Creek bounties for capturing slaves. A smile had been drawn in blood.

***

"I will speak to them," said John. An army patrol with a white flag had been at the edge of the cove for several days.

"It could be a trick," I said.

"I think not," John said. "We have watched them for two days and gone completely around them and found no one following. We should find out what message they bring."

"I will go beside you then," I said.

"What is it you wish?" said John to the tall, thick bearded captain.

"I wish to speak to John Horse."

"I am John Horse."

"Outstanding. I am Captain Mallory. General Jesup wants a parley with all the important players in this drama. Osceola, Micanopy, King Philip, Abraham," said Mallory. "He wants you, specifically. He wants to talk peace."

"Peace under what terms?"

"I could not answer that. Hence, the parley. The message I was sent to deliver is this: We don't need to kill any more of your people.

However, we are prepared to kill everyone until there is no one left to kill. General Jesup does not wish this to happen. He wishes peace."

"How magnanimous of him. You want to talk peace after the way the MacCuaigs slaughtered those at Hatchee-Lustee Creek?"

"These are my orders," said the officer. "I was to relay that the destruction at the Hatchee-Lustee was only a small demonstration of the fury and power that you can expect for this point forward. Or we can have peace and we will demonstrate the benevolence and mercy of the Great White Father."

"A demonstration of ruthlessness. Of a father's barbarity," John said.

"Use whatever nomenclature you wish. I did not come to argue semantics. The time for that is long past."

"Murdering women and children is not power. It is cowardly," said John.

"Those women and children fought fiercely beside their men. Of that you should take pride," said Mallory. "They were combatants."

"I will pass the message to the chiefs," said John.

"Do not tarry. General Jesup is under great pressure to be more aggressive. We are extending an offer of a truce until a council can be held. We will chain the MacCuaigs. They will halt their raiding until you come in for a parley, as long as that parley is held promptly. But I cannot stress this enough: If there are any attacks against our people during this time of peace, the General will come blazing with every gun he's got. And he's got ten thousand of them. Do you understand?"

"Completely," said John. "He wants peace."

***

The officers and chiefs sat facing each other under an arbor of canvas and palm leaf. It was a warm day for this time of the season. Some of our men were bare chested, showing their tattoos and battle scars. Most wore hunting shirts and a little bit of finery. Every man in the circle was a veteran of hard fighting in Florida. Distrust and bitterness were on every face, whether it was red, black or white. Every Indian in the circle had lost friends or family, some at the Hatchee-Lustee. None of the MacCuaigs were in the council circle, though some loitered nearby, sneering at us. I didn't see Laughing Boy. Osceola was too sick to attend. We told Jesup that he refused.

John smoked a pipe and cooled himself with a big turkey wing fan. He would be the interpreter for King Philip, who had been chosen to speak for the Seminole. I sat behind John where I could hear every word and see every face clearly.

All around the field clusters of soldiers and Indians sat watching, brewing coffee or broiling meat over small fires. Everyone cleaned knives and guns. The grizzled Florida frontiersmen glared at us and spat tobacco juice in their fires. The faces of the soldiers were tired, like they just wanted to go home.

General Jesup sat cross-legged on the ground, ten feet across from John and the Seminole chiefs. He was thick-necked, and stern faced, a callous-handed man. He wore a uniform without the frills of the previous commanders.

"Gentlemen, this war has gone on long enough. It must end," said Jesup.

"You made the quarrel. You invaded our land," said King Philip. "Tell us what you came to tell us."

"I have ten thousand soldiers in Florida. How many of your fighters remain capable? I know it is less than five hundred. I know they are tired and hungry. We could wipe you out tomorrow," said Jesup. "I did not bring this huge army down here just to build forts. However, I restrain my forces. I do not attack. This is because I wish for peace."

"Peace to you means allowing your planters to take our lands and make us vassals of the Creek. To make slaves of our Black brothers. To put them under the whip of the Creek," said King Philip. "Peace to you means sending us halfway across a strange continent, to lands hostile to us, to a fate unknown. That is not peace for us. That is defeat and humiliation. You do not want us peaceful. You want us beaten. Powerless. Impotent."

"No, it is peace," said Jesup.

"Peaceful, perhaps, but not peace," said King Philip. "The people of the Hatchee-Lustee are peaceful now. That is the peace you wish for us."

"I'll certainly give you that option should you persist," Jesup said.

"Telling a man that you will not murder everyone if he grovels is not peace," said King Philip. "It is submission. It is castration. It is surrender. It is the end of a people. But it is not peace."

"I'm extending the offer," said Jesup tiredly. "I am not the one dictating the terms. Or choosing the vocabulary."

"It is not right what you do."

"I have no time for lofty ideas like right and wrong. I am not a missionary. I am a soldier. It's an unpleasant job, so I'll make it as horrible as I can to bring about the fastest resolution," said Jesup. "I'll destroy you. I will use any means necessary."

"That is already clear."

"However, you'll need for nothing if you comply," said Jesup.

"Hogs awaiting slaughter need for nothing. They are happy. We are a humble people. We need for nothing now, except to be left alone. Why do you persecute us so? We do not want these annuities," said King Philip. "That is how you would control my people without using guns. Giving it to us will only make our people soft and fat and lazy. We will be dependent on them, and you."

"That is not the intent of this order," said Jesup.

"That you fight so hard to impose this joy and a better life upon us makes me suspicious," said King Philip. "Whatever you give, you can take away. You try to beguile us with false words and free trinkets and gifts that would then imprison us. You want us to be like the Creeks. To grow fat and lazy and enslave our Black friends to work fields larger than any man needs. That is not how the Seminole want to live."

"Why does your government think it can tell us to obey their decrees? What gives them such arrogance?" snapped Wild Cat.

"Good grief. At this point, because we have more guns. Because we can," said Jesup. "I didn't invent the concept. When diplomacy fails, bring in the armies. It has been that way throughout time. On all continents. By all people."

"And what of the Estelusti?" said John. "The Black Seminole? What of us?"

"Those that are the bona fide property of a Seminole, that have lived all their lives and their parents lives amongst the tribe, will stay with the Seminole," said Jesup. "Those that cannot be proved to be Seminole property will be returned to their lawful owner."

"Unlike you, we do not keep on a tally sheet which humans we own," said King Philip.

"You should probably start," said Jesup.

"And our other Black brothers that fled the plantations to join our fight? What of them?" said Alligator. "Those that fought beside us? We would be betraying them, abandoning them. Condemning them to slavery, or worse. Execution, for many."

"That is going to be a very difficult issue," said Jesup. "If they cannot speak the language of the Seminole, they will not be considered bona fide property. Slaves that pick up guns in revolt face execution. That is law. Not a military matter. We have no power to emancipate anyone."

"Only to kill them by the hundreds, women and babies," said Wild Cat.

"I'll not coat it with sugar," said Jesup. "Those slaves will never be emancipated. Many will be executed, as you say. To send a message to any that might consider revolt in the future. That is a separate issue over which I have no say. It has no bearing on this situation."

"Then we also send a message," said Wild Cat. "It has every bearing on this situation. Those people risked their lives fighting with us. They would face certain death or extreme suffering if we abandon them. We will never agree to return them. If you come to the land of the Seminole you will die. We will fight and spill blood until we are left alone or dead. That is our message."

"Dead it will be then," said Jesup. "I will leave you with this stern admonition. I am prepared to continue this war for as long as it takes. I don't wish it to happen. However, if you continue to resist I will unleash Laughing Boy MacCuaig and his Hell hounds with no restraint until you are dead. Everyone."

"We need to discuss this ourselves," said Abraham.

"As you certainly should. Also, I hope to meet with each of you individually," said Jesup. "I would like to hear what you have to say, in private, and without fear of ending up like Charley Emathla."

"Charley Emathla was a traitor to our people," said Alligator.

"I leave you to consider it, and the ramifications if you don't comply. We will meet again in two weeks. A truce will be in place until our discussions are over."

***

Jesup welcomed us to walk through his camp. He had invited newspaper and missionaries so we would feel safe. He told the chiefs to feed their people from heavy iron kettles full of boiling sausages and crabs and potatoes and corn. Steers were roasted. Bread and pies baked in ovens assembled on the spot. There were contests, races and wrestling. Jesup had a band, but it was a couple of old bearded fiddlers and a blind man with a Jew's harp.

The soldiers never harassed us. The cooks and men at the barbecue pits were cordial. Their overwhelming might was obvious. Jesup showed off his three new cannons, blowing up piles of wood three hundred yards away.

John, Yancy and I stopped to watch a chess tournament. Soldiers, civilians and a couple old Seminole army translators sat studiously at a dozen boards set up on stumps and blocks of wood.

"Do you play?" asked General Jesup, walking up beside John.

"I do," said John. "Just because we are untamed does not mean we are unlearned."

"Outstanding. So do I," said Jesup. "Excellent stimulation, and a fine way to learn your opponent."

"It is," said John.

"Could I interest you in a game?"

"You interest me in many ways, General," said John. "A match would please me."

"Outstanding," said Jesup. "Who is the young man?"

"My brother Pete."

"I see. Well, it is wise to learn the ways of diplomacy while young," said Jesup.

"Is that what this is? Diplomacy? More of your diplomacy before you bring on the cannons and hanging ropes?" asked John.

"Most diplomacy ultimately comes at the point of the gun. Polite and sterile as the envoys make the discussions out to be, that's simply a fact," said Jesup.

"Perhaps," said John.

"Still, it can all be achieved as gentlemen," said Jesup. "Let's discuss it soon. I will supply the brandy, cigars, and chess board."

"I look forward to it," said John.

"You're Yancy Yarbury aren't you?" Jesup said, eyeing Yancy as he stood over John's shoulder. "Quite audacious and bold of you to stroll through an American army fortification."

"I am indeed Yancy Yarbury, your humble servant," said Yancy. "No boldness involved. I knew you were a man of honor, and no harm would come to any in our party. A gentleman and all that."

"Yancy is my interpreter," said John.

"You speak English better than most of my men," said Jesup. "You spoke it will enough at the Council. You're speaking it now."

"Am I? Your language seems to have so many double meanings when it comes to the Indian. I want to ensure I don't make a mistake in interpretation," said John, smiling.

"I see. I suppose you have a point. Still, I think I'd prefer to hang you, Yarbury," said Jesup. "It's a shame you weren't blown to bits with the rest of that insurrectionist rabble at the Negro Fort."

"I'm flattered to have achieved such eminence in your thoughts," said Yancy. "And now here we are. I shall keep my opinions of you private. For the greater good and all that."

"Such nobility coming from one who waged war as a pirate against the United States," said Jesup.

"You know I did no such thing. You are just repeating the fantastical fabrications of your political liars and agitators in Washington," said Yancy. "I fought against you as a soldier of the Crown. I was a peaceful civilian minding my own business when you attacked the Negro Fort."

"Bah."

"Bah it out your ass. You were not there," said Yancy. "You want to try to solve this problem your government created, or obsess over my past of more than two decades ago?"

"Oh, I suppose I'll let bygones be bygones. For now. For the greater good," said Jesup with a cold smile.

***

The following afternoon, Jesup welcomed us inside his tent. We sat in camp chairs around a table with a chessboard in the center. A bottle of brandy, open box of cigars and clean ashtray were on a wicker stand. Jesup poured rum into three tin cups and a cup of cider for me. He gave John and Yancy each a fat cigar and passed a candle in a brass holder around to light them. I was thankful the tent flap was up for ventilation.

"Nice cigar," said Yancy, refilling his rum cup.

"Cubans," said Jesup. "By the way, you'll no doubt be pleased to know General Scott, with whom I rarely agree, mentioned you. He said I should hang you if I had the opportunity. Something about a wineglass and hat."

"Is that so?" laughed Yancy. "How is your fat friend? He wasn't here long, was he?"

"I'm sure he's comfortable wherever he is," said Jesup. "I trust you enjoyed your stay at the Drane plantation."

"It was grand. The amenities could not have been more pleasant, or generous. I put on a few pounds," said Yancy. "It is a shame we didn't leave it in better condition for Governor Call. Pass on our apologies, will you?"

"Enjoy your mirth," said Jesup. "It may not last much longer."

"But our memories shall last a lifetime," said Yancy.

"Let's discuss it as we play, shall we?" said Jesup, turning to John. "Black or white?"

"You open," said John.

"I understand Abraham still has much sway with Micanopy, but I'm told his influence wanes among the Estelusti," said Jesup, advancing his king's bishop pawn two squares. "Am I told the truth?"

"You are," said John, answering with his pawn.

"Am I told the truth by those who say you now lead the Estelusti?" asked Jesup, pretending to study the board and then moving his bishop out.

"You would have to ask the Estelusti," said John.

"I have, and that is what I'm told. That you speak for them."

"I will speak for them only after I have given them a chance to speak for themselves," said John.

"Fair enough," said Jesup. "But I am also told you are a worldly man. A well-read man. That you might have a better understanding of how things work than most Negroes. Have I been informed correctly?"

"As long as I have my interpreters with me," said John, puffing out a large cloud. "Micanopy has his sense-makers. I have mine."

"I'm told that you are more wily even than old Abraham," said Jesup.

"Did you bring me here to insult me?" said John as he captured a pawn. "The mules that pull your big slow wagons are wiser than Abraham."

"You've had a falling out?" Jesup said caustically.

"Abraham has many faces. One for you. One for Micanopy. One for the Estelusti. Others at his convenience. Not wily, but a schemer nonetheless," said John. "Micanopy is old and lazy. He has let Abraham guide him too much on too many matters. Now Abraham thinks the war is lost so he uses his wiles toward retaining his status and comfort. Not the best interests of the Estelusti, no matter what he might say in council."

"Yes, and he thinks highly of you too," snorted Jesup. "I'm glad you see things exactly as I do."

"Probably not exactly," said John, moving a pawn. "Tell me what it is you want to tell me."

"I understand what my predecessors in this war did not," said Jesup. "Those in Washington and the newspapers can call this the Seminole War all they want, but it's a Negro war. Micanopy and the Seminole chiefs do not understand they really do the bidding of the Estelusti when they fight us. I understand it is no longer Abraham, but you, that puts iron into the spines of chiefs that otherwise might have little. I know that if I remove the Estelusti from the equation, the Seminole chiefs, most of them anyway, would accept the terms of the treaty."

"I know Abraham tells Micanopy to seek his best deal, to negotiate," said John. "He denies it, but I know better."

"The way of life for the Seminole would be relatively unchanged if they moved west. As long as they still had the Estelusti to perform most of their work for them," said Jesup. "But I've had other discussions with Micanopy. About the permanent manumission of the Estelusti and their heirs. He demands payment for you, a huge amount of money."

"This does not surprise me. How much?"

"The going rate for skilled tradesmen, and he claims every single one of you is a skilled tradesman. You are walking gold. With all the money he would get for selling his Estelusti he could buy more slaves. Plantation slaves that would be forever grateful for the ease of life of a Seminole slave. He could buy some docile ones that would behave as proper slaves, to be worked hard in the fields and build wealth for the chiefs. They would not be such a pain in the ass."

"I see."

"Another consideration is simply confiscating every Estelusti we capture and awarding them to the Creeks as the spoils of war," said Jesup. "Manumission or confiscation of the Estelusti would leave Micanopy and the Seminole in a bad situation. No more free labor. No allies. A disastrous financial loss. Micanopy didn't like that idea. Not at all."

"Either he sells us to you, or you just take us, is that it?"

"It's a cutthroat world," said Jesup. "Everything is on the table right now. He says you are betraying him by trying to get a separate freedom, to no longer be his serfs."

"I see. And you put that idea in his head? He is too simple to think of that on his own."

"Of course, I did. And I could see he was pondering the merits. He realizes he is in a dire situation. He will lose his wealth if the Creeks claim you, if we confiscate you, or if you are manumitted. And, of course, if you simply run off, or get killed fighting," said Jesup. "It is the Negro who could well end up in a bit of a pickle if they lose the security of a purported Seminole owner."

"What is your point?" asked John.

"That it is time for you also to take your best deal. It is time for the Estelusti to lay down your arms and convince the Seminole to surrender. Seminoles that surrender can take their Negroes west. I will be generous on the awarding of legal title. Your life can return to the way it was. For your personal help in this, there will be substantial financial considerations."

"You seem to think everybody is swayed by money," said John.

"Yes, I do. I've yet to see evidence to the contrary," said Jesup. "And I'd much rather bribe someone than shoot him."

"And you also pay Seminole who betray Estelusti," said John.

"Those who help pacify the Estelusti, yes, I do," said Jesup. "Handsomely."

"This is how you divide us," said John. "Gold for them to betray us. It is also an abomination that you hire the MacCuaigs to hunt us."

"You and I are at war. The Creek are our allies. That is how it works. You don't like it, save your people and move west. Is it better to live, or die? I tell the Creeks not to shoot, but to capture these valuable blacks that are worth gold. The Creeks would happily murder your people by dozens, hundreds, if that bounty wasn't keeping them alive."

"How noble," snorted John.

"Those in Washington are desperate to end this expensive war. I know several that are cordial to the idea of a path toward manumission for the Estelusti, or at least establishing your own land, separate from the Seminole. Land of your own. Self-governance. I will do my best and try to convince Washington that this is the best course. Of course, most resist that idea, but not all. There are some important people, powerful people, in Washington that ask for your good faith effort in convincing the Seminole to put down their guns. It would greatly help your chances to be manumitted."

"I don't believe you can ensure that."

"No, not yet I can't. But there have been preliminary discussions."

"What of the runaways that risked their lives for us?" asked John.

"My personal opinion is that slavery is the greatest abomination on earth," said Jesup. "But freeing slaves is also not my problem, not unless I'm ordered to do so. As for the runaways, that's a civilian legal matter. A slave revolt is a very serious matter. Those runaways have killed people. Those that are unable to speak the Seminole language will be returned to bondage. I have no say in it. Nor have I had any desire for a say in it. That could change, possibly, with some compromise from you."

"This is not a slave revolt. This is war, as you yourself have said many times," said John. "I am a free man, fighting to keep that freedom. We are a free people, and you need to recognize that. You are fighting men, not menials. That is my word to you. Those men are soldiers of a sovereign nation, the Seminole nation. They must be considered prisoners of war and not enslaved."

"There is no sovereign Estelusti nation. Those are not free men. They are revolutionaries and mercenaries," said Jesup.

"We just declared it so. As your countrymen did, so do we," said John. "No difference. We declare ourselves a free nation and a free people."

"You'll have a hard time convincing their masters of that," said Jesup.

"You have a hard time convincing me that men have masters," said John.

"The prisoner of war idea for the slaves will never be accepted," said Jesup. "But this is a chance for you to save your people. Surrender yourselves peacefully and go west, with a possibility of real freedom. If you don't, it will mean annihilation for your people. Do you want to end up like Nat Turner and his group? A hundred dead Negroes with their severed heads stuck on fence posts until they rotted off. Nat Turner is burned in people's minds."

"In yours, General Jesup?" said John. "Are you worried about more slave rebellions in other states?"

"I'm a Virginian," said Jesup. "How could it not be?"

"And that's why you make war on us?"

"That's why I offer you life and a chance at freedom," said Jesup. "Would you need to go on a murderous rampage if you had freedom?"

"No, we would not. But what is our guarantee? What of the Creek?"

"I'll make the MacCuaigs go away if you'll stop fighting."

"You seem to have great magic when it suits you," said John. "I don't think you can pull off that trick."

"I can keep them away from you while you are in Florida. I give you my word I will do my best to make sure the terms of the treaty are honored and that you are treated fairly. You do have some allies in Washington. It would take some time. Your people would live on the Seminole reservation, at least for now. But your people would no longer be the slave of the Seminole, nor would they be Creek property," said Jesup. "We will have strict rules in place forbidding this, should they try. It's your only hope for your people to survive."

"Is it?" John said as he took Jesup's rook with a knight, a move Jesup had not seen coming. Jesup stared hard at the board, both fists buried in his cheeks. He was down two pawns and a piece and didn't seem to have an answer. He moved a knight's pawn one square.

***

The conversation slowed as John asserted control of the board. His bishops lurked behind a full wall of pawns.

"I capitulate," said Jesup, laying his king down. "That is what a wise man does when the cause is lost. Faces the facts and moves on."

"On a sterile board with no bloodstains, perhaps," said John. "Where the games is over, but none of the pieces are enslaved."

"Agreed, but still it's a lost cause. You know that," said Jesup, pouring brandy for everyone. "Why not save everybody a bunch more pain and hardship? Why continue a hopeless fight?"

"Because it is a righteous fight. Defeat nor death alter that," said John. "Do you have children, General?"

"I do."

"Are they well? Do armed child stealers prowl near your home, waiting to snatch them and sell them into slavery? Does an army chase them through swamps, not even allowing them to rest or eat?"

"No, of course not."

"Would you submit your children and grandchildren for some safety of your own? To be ruled over by someone like Laughing Boy MacCuaig. Would you really do that?"

"No, John, I don't see how I would," said Jesup. "But you need to be reasonable."

"Reasonable? What is reasonable? Were the men that established the freedom for your country being reasonable? Why should we not desire the same? Those who would give up essential liberty to purchase a little temporary safety deserve neither liberty nor safety. Benjamin Franklin said that," said John. "My children will not grow up as the chattel of the Creek. Give me liberty or give me death! That is the American founder Patrick Henry."

"I'm aware of who said that," snapped Jesup. "You think mighty damned highly of yourself, don't you?"

"No higher than any of the men that signed your own Declaration of Independence. No higher than the men who said all men are created equal. I am a man. I am an Estelusti, a warrior and leader of my people, not a fool. Freedoms you permit me are not freedoms. Those are simply the times you let me off the leash," John said. "I am as good as an American, or Frenchman, and I am as good as you. Only that and no more. As good as your damn Texians who fight for their freedom now. With rights the same as any. Go free them and leave us alone."

"If only I'd been given that option," said Jesup.

"Now you see how it is with me and my people. Same as any man. We do not fight for gold. We do not fight for land or trees or these waters full of fish. We do not fight for a way of life. We fight for our very lives. We fight against the enslavement of our families," said John. "What kind of man would surrender his children to that fate?"

"A poor one, I suppose, but it doesn't have to be that way," said Jesup.

"And what about Wild Cat? What does he say to you on the matter?" said John.

"The words between Wild Cat and myself will remain that way, although I'm sure he'll tell you," Jesup said. "But someone is getting betrayed, and it is not the United States Army. It does not matter a whit to me who does it first, or a hoot what their reasons are. Nor will I lose any sleep over the consequence to those who do not. I have a job to do."

"Just a job to do, right?"

"Exactly. And I'll tell you something else," Jesup said from deep in his chest. "I'm enjoying the weather here in Florida this winter. I have been in Florida in the summer previously. It is hot and miserable. I hated it. Don't drag this out until the summer when I'm hot and miserable. You really won't like it. Just put down your guns and let's start working on the things I've proposed."

"I think not. Do you know who else put down their weapons and came along peacefully?" said John. "The ancestors of these slaves with us. My ancestors. The ones sent across the ocean in the diseased belly of a ship. And now look. No, I think I'm not interested."

***

That night we gathered around the sofkee pot.

"He lies. He lies to all of us," said Wild Cat. "He tells each of us what he thinks we want to hear. He intends to separate us using lies and deceits. As long as we hold together, he cannot defeat us. Not without great cost to his army."

"You tell the truth, brother," said John. "Sadly, Jesup tells the truth also. It is as he says. Now we fight two different wars. Jesup is clever. We are pitted against each other even as we fight against the Americans. The Estelusti want to leave the Seminole, and Jesup hints he can do that. But Micanopy and the Miccos want money for us. The Seminole now fight to keep us, as we have great value. We are no longer allies, but property. It can never return to what it was."

"That is not so," pleaded Wild Cat.

"It is," said John. "Perhaps not to you, but to many of the other miccos, especially the most senior, the most affluent. Those with the most Estelusti and easiest lives. Micanopy and the other wealthy chiefs now see us as a bargaining chip. They will fight only until their life of ease in the west can be guaranteed."

"That's just about always how wars end," said Yancy. "The rich still end up with all the chips, just slightly shuffled."

"What will you do, papa?" John asked Yancy. "Perhaps it is time to take my mother to safety somewhere. Germaine could take you to the Bahamas, or even to one of the free American states."

"I will stay beside your mother," said Yancy. "If we can find peace here in Florida, I will happily stay. If removal to the west in inevitable, I will go and try to find peace. If it is a fight, so be it."

"There ain't no choice for some of us," said Virgil. "Some of us are facing execution and our families put in chains. Don't see no way around it unless I can get out of Florida."

"Germaine could also take you to the Bahamas," said John. "I would hate for you to go, but you must do what is best for your family."

"I reckon I already am doing what's best," said Virgil. "I am standing up. I am a free man fighting them that would throw chains on my children. Find me something better than that."

"There ain't nothing better," said Yancy. "But no one would fault you if you took your woman and babies to safety."

"No, sir. I ain't running away. I did not get my freedom just to spend it running from them that aim to harm me. That ain't no better life than what I had," said Virgil. "I got me a little something now. Ain't no MacCuaig putting me off it."

"Hooah," said John.

"The soldiers came and destroyed the fields of my village. They stole my cattle. We face great hunger. People have reached their limits. They are frightened," said Coa Hadjo, micco of some St. John's Seminole. "My people suffer too much."

"You knew suffering would be a part of it," said Osceola. "Did you think the others sacrificed their freedom so you could continue to enjoy yours in comfort? That is foolish. And selfish."

"We should make our best bargain."

"Why?" asked John. "Because Jesup has promised you a hefty reward if you can persuade us to surrender? He offered me the same bargain, to abandon my friends. To betray my brothers. Is that not true?"

"Yes, he made that offer. But I am not thinking only of myself. We have had many men killed. We live in hiding and fear. This is no way to live," said Coa Hadjo. "Jesup offered another way. We would be left alone if we return all our runaway Blacks. I propose we do so. They are a burden. They cannot live in the wild like us."

"The Blacks are our allies. We are not in the slave returning business," said Osceola. "You confuse us for Creek dogs."

"But Jesup says he will convince Washington to leave us alone if we return the fugitives. He says all his officers and many more in the army feel that way," said Coa Hadjo. "Many of the runaways wish to return anyway. They suffer severely in the swamps."

"We all suffer," said John. "They have the right to suffer right beside us, if that is what they desire."

"They desire to be back with their old owners where the sweet yams can be counted on. Their children cry," said Coa Hadjo. "They were not meant for this life. They are farmers, that is the life they know. Jesup is too relentless for them to grow crops. What little we Seminole can hunt and find in the forest is meant for us, not to be shared. It is not our role to ensure the safety of runaway Negroes. They eat our food and contribute nothing if they cannot farm. Our obligation is to our own people, not to them. We must think of ourselves."

"In that case, we Estelusti must also look for ourselves. Many of the enslaved are our family members. They have fought beside us from the beginning. They fight beside us now," said John. "Jesup also told me my people would be freed if we abandoned you. So, you see, he says one thing to you, another to us."

"John Horse, we will fight beside you to the end," said Wild Cat. "It does not matter what comes out of their lying mouths. The Army will not stop until all Black men are in chains and all Seminole are dead. We both fight for our very lives."

"There is much to consider," said Coa Hadjo.

"There is much to consider only if you are a coward and want to go be the white man's boy but want to do it gracefully," coughed Osceola. "That is the only consideration."

"How many times must we force our children into the swamp? To abandon our belongings and live on roots and palm cabbage? That is a heavy cost on the mind, hearing hungry children. They will leave us alone if we return all the remaining runaway blacks," said Coa Hadjo.

"Speak the truth! That you have already taken two hundred Blacks to General Jesup's fort!" thundered John. "You have surrendered others so you can live in comfort. I was waiting for you to admit it."

"Is this true?" demanded Osceola. "Did you collect a bounty on them too?"

"There were few fighters among them. It was women and children and old people. They were tired of the hardships. My payment was very small," said Coa Hadjo. "Many of our Chiefs are now willing to do this. Negro freedom is not our war. We owe them nothing. Let them fight their own war. The sooner we all surrender the blacks, the sooner we can go about our lives, even if it means in the western lands."

"Coa Hadjo, you did not capture me!" shouted Virgil. "I am not yours to return. If you try to turn my wife in, I'll cut you open and feed you to the alligators."

"You can't speak to me that way," said Coa Hadjo.

"I'll speak any way I wish," said Virgil. "I'm a man with natural rights to be free same as you claim to, or anyone else. Same as the white folks. Same as anybody. You ain't my chief nor my master!"

"That is our gratitude for their fighting beside you?" said John to Coa Hadjo.

"You fight for yourself," said Coa Hadjo. "Don't pretend otherwise."

"I will not allow a single black to be sent in chains to the plantations, not while I can still breathe or fire my rifle," Osceola promised. "If I hear of anything further from you, Coa Hadjo, I will kill you. No council will stop me."

Chapter Nine

FORT DADE CAPITULATION
MARCH 1837

Twenty days later, the Seminole chiefs signed the "Fort Dade Capitulation of the Seminole Nation of Indians and their Allies." The surrender ceremony was held at Fort Dade, which had been built on the site of the battle. An abandoned plantation east of Fort Brooke was turned into a refugee camp. Jesup promised any person claiming to be Estelusti would remain safe from capture until the courts could determine their status. He forbade slave trackers from coming within a mile of the camp. Soon, eight hundred Seminole and Estelusti were living there in a field of tents and old shacks. Flour and corn and potatoes were distributed. A herd of cattle was provided. Steamboats waited in Tampa Bay to take them across the Gulf of Mexico. John, Osceola, King Philip, Wild Cat, and Sam Jones refused to sign. Instead, we spent the days spying on the encampment.

"Isn't that your friend?" I asked Virgil, pointing to a man in a miserable procession of gaunt, barefoot, and ragged people trudging down the road to surrender themselves.

"You are surrendering?" Virgil said, walking up to the men. He saw Fredrick, a man who'd toiled beside him on the Gentry Plantation and fought beside us in every battle. Fredrick's wife led a bony horse with two dirty, hungry-looking children and a baby on its back.

"Our little ones cry. They can't rest, they are hungry," said Fredrick. "The mother of my baby gives poor milk because she has so little to eat. We simply cannot continue. We just can't."

"They will cry more if they grow up under the lash of an overseer," said John.

"Being a slave is bad. Watching your family starve is worse," said Fredrick. "I do not want our children to grow up slaves. I also don't want them to starve or be shot down like varmints in the swamp. And ain't nothing going to change. It's what's going to happen anyway, and there's no point in this suffering."

"If your children get sold away from you it's going to be mighty hard living too. It is hard living, but we ain't got no overseer," said Virgil.

"You think I ain't thought all that through!?" Fredrick shouted, anger and pain rushing out. "Of course, that would be mighty hard. I suspect having them die in my arms from hunger would be mighty unsettling, too."

"I'm sorry. I didn't mean that in no disrespectful way. I'm facing a hangman's rope," said Virgil. "Hopefully you ain't."

"No, I don't figure I am facing a rope. But I imagine I'll get whipped something fierce," said Fredrick. "It don't matter. We can't go on."

"When you surrender, tell them we stole you," I said.

"Don't expect that will spare me any lashes. They's whipping away on folks for allowing theyselfs to get took," said Fredrick. "For not fighting harder against having freedom imposed upon them. I just got to accept it, I reckon. I'll just take my lashes. Take 'em, and with every stroke pray that my children will be spared. That I don't get sold off away from them before they's growed."

The friends tearfully embraced a few times and then Fredrick continued on down the road with his family. Virgil never looked back at him.

***

"How are you today?" I asked Jovis, reposing on a hammock of heavy fish net strung between two trees. I had just plopped down in the one beside it.

"Missing my chair, but this will do fine for now," he said. "I think a man could get accustomed to this life if he could be left alone."

He was drinking rum with sugar and fruit juice. He and Esther had come with us after we left Fort Drane, as had several more who had been enslaved there. They'd adapted to life in the wild much better than anyone expected, smiling through the hardships and sleeping on the hard ground and eating from communal sofkee pots.

"You think that will ever happen, that they'll leave us alone?"

"From what I know of the men who visited that house to converse with Massa Clinch, no, I don't expect that will ever happen."

"Why are they like that? You probably know them better than anyone, even Yancy," I said.

"I don't reckon I do. Only the devil knows men that visit the St. Augustine Cathedral and the St. Augustine slave market on the same Sunday," he said.

"I've seen those markets," I said. "I don't want to end up in one."

"Nor I," he said. "But I don't reckon I'll be asked back to serve in the big house."

"Well, not that one, anyway," I said. "Not even a chimney was standing when we left."

We were quiet for a few minutes, watching some hawks in a whirling, diving courtship dance in the sky above us.

"I ain't been whipped in forty years," he said.

"What's that?"

"It's been forty years since a man laid a lash on me," he said.

"That's a long time," I said. "That's good, I guess, is what you're saying."

"I don't know what I'm saying, except maybe, if someone was to ask me how my life had been, I'd say good, I ain't been whipped in forty years. I got me a good woman, Esther. I have three children I haven't seen for almost as long as I ain't been whipped. Not a thing to my name, and never took a free breath until a few months ago," he said. "Don't ever get yourself like this."

"I don't expect to," I said. "I expect to fight it to the death."

"You do that," he said. "That is about all I have to say on that. I sure wish I had that chair back."

***

A messenger reached us with grave word from the camp. President Van Buren had rejected Jesup's proposal after attorneys for the plantation owners sued the United States government. The planters demanded immediate payment of hundreds of thousands of dollars for the illegal confiscation of their property. To the planters and Van Buren, the right to claim ownership extended beyond the runaways. Children, and even grandchildren, of long-ago runaways could be taken.

"I didn't expect we could count on Jesup talking Van Buren into manumission for the Estelusti," said Yancy.

"I thought Van Buren was a northerner opposed to slavery."

"Not exactly. He's one of the many that claimed to be morally opposed to it but lacks the courage to act. It wouldn't be politically expedient for him."

"What does that mean?"

"Van Buren has made statements to the effect that slavery is a moral evil, yet he has slaves scrubbing the floors and cleaning the thunder pots in the White House. As a child, his family was wealthy and owned slaves before it was outlawed in New York. He was Jackson's vice-president. Jackson could never have been president had it not been for Van Buren's back room deals between his powerful New York donors and the planters. Cheap cotton and sugar come at a price for some," said Yancy. "So, I'm dubious about the whole 'morally' opposed, but there you have it."

"I had hoped for better," said John.

"It is better, but only a small increment. Van Buren is some different from Jackson. If the freedom of the Estelusti was to benefit him in some way, he wouldn't oppose it. Whereas Jackson would fight it with a frothing mouth regardless. Van Buren's an overly ambitious political animal. And by political animal, I mean a man who will make abnormous promises to everybody, with the intention of keeping only the beneficial."

"So couldn't his promise not to interfere with southern slave ownership also be a promise he plans to break?" said John.

"Unlikely. That's rarely how these things work. Any others, yes. But not that one," said Yancy. "He's wanted to sit in that White House for a long time. He won't fritter it away over a bunch of Negroes. Not that man."

***

Within days the people in the camp were begging for help. Although Jesup had issued orders banning the MacCuaigs, they raided in the night and stole our people anyway. Any Seminole that acted to prevent it was savagely beaten. The food stores issued to the prisoners were stolen by the MacCuaigs.

"What can we do?"

"If the MacCuaigs can steal the people out of the camp, so can we," said Osceola.

"The camp is well guarded."

"The guards no longer care. They will not try to stop us. I have spoken to many of them," said Wild Cat.

"Why is that?" asked Virgil.

"They were told they could keep their land if they joined to fight against us. Now they are finding out they were lied to and swindled like the others. Their land in Alabama is being taken anyway and their families also forced on the trail west. Many plan to leave soon and find their families. Some may even join us."

"Ha! And he wanted us to lay down our guns and trust him? Now look at the fools that did," said Osceola.

"Yes. Jesup cannot be trusted," said Wild Cat.

"Jesup could not prevent it. The blame is on the white father in the White House," said John.

"That is not important," said Osceola. "If we do this, we must force every person to leave whether they want to or not. We cannot allow them to be used as hostages again. Or leave them so they can run and alert Jesup."

"We should leave Micanopy to explain to Jesup why the people are gone," said Wild Cat. "Let him face Jesup's wrath."

"No. Bring Micanopy and the other chiefs out, so they can face our people's wrath. So he can be held accountable for his betrayal," said Osceola. "Let the people decide what to do with them. All those who took the Judas silver from the Americans should explain why they allowed our friends and families to be stolen and enslaved. Explain why they brought the people to a camp to be mistreated and abused."

"It will be harder for Micanopy to convince Jesup he played no part in the planning if he is gone in the morning, too," said John. "An Indian tribe kidnapped their own chief?"

"Yes, that is good thinking," said Wild Cat. "I would like to see that fat cow explain to Jesup how we kidnapped the chief of the nation."

***

Two hundred Seminole and Estelusti warriors crept through the forests to the mile-wide encampment. Quiet as ghosts we went tent to tent and shelter to shelter. The people had been prepared and hurried away, barely making a sound as they followed their guides toward the swamps and freedom. Once the camp was cleared, we gathered outside the tent of Micanopy.

We silently slipped into the wall tent of the snoring chief. Two of Micanopy's youngest wives were inside. They were awake, their eyes wide-open in fear. But they had not alerted Micanopy.

"Wake up Micanopy, it's time to go," said Wild Cat, poking him under the chin with the point of a buck knife.

Micanopy jerked awake with a snort and startled gasp. He wore a look of complete shock as he looked at the men surrounding his bed, his jaw and tongue working furiously but futilely to form words.

"There is no reason for me to go. I have made my agreement. I will honor it," whimpered Micanopy.

"You come or you die," said Wild Cat. "You betrayed our people. Brought them here like lambs to slaughter. You will not lie here in sloth while the others suffer greatly."

"You will kill me if you get me out of here," said Micanopy.

"That is not mine to say," said Wild Cat. "But I promise you I will kill you if you don't."

John appeared with the sputtering Abraham, pushing him by the neck of his nightshirt.

"I hope now you two will be happy with the choices you made," said John. "And that your bribe money has been sufficient."

"I don't wish to go back out on the trail," said Abraham. "The war is lost."

"Good. Because you stay," said John. "Only you, by yourself. With no one you can manipulate. No one to do your bidding. Just you, to explain to Jesup why this plan you agreed to has fallen apart."

"You are breaking the agreement and will cause more war," said Abraham.

"No. Jesup broke the capitulation when he allowed the Negroes to be taken," said John. "You should have spoken up then, to Jesup. But you remained silent for your own comfort and safety. You no longer speak for any Estelusti. Your chief is going to answer to his people, without you there to put sugar in his words."

***

Although Jesup stormed and swore vengeance, there was little he could do immediately. It was the end of summer season, the time of storms, constant rains and sickness among the Americans. He had too few healthy soldiers and the floods prevented supplies from traveling. We returned to our hammock deep in the belly of the Withlacoochee Cove and the soldiers stayed at their coastal forts. The MacCuaigs still prowled around the edge of the Cove but never ventured too deep into our watery wilderness.

I was naked beside Willet on a bed of green moss. The sun was drying us after we had spent the morning swimming in the spring nearby.

"It saddens me to think about life if we are forced west, even if we are left alone out there. I think our hunting days will soon be over, whether we remain in Florida or not. The big plantations run the animals away. The land they want to send us to is not hunting land. It is farming land. I do not want to be a farmer. I would rather be a fine lady in a soft bed with a virile young lover in it."

"Is that so?"

"It is. I have become accustomed to it, and I find it to my pleasure."

"And I'm a virile young lover?"

"Well, I really have nothing to compare it to, but from what I've heard, yes," she said.

"That is a good thing to know," I said.

"I will miss the hunt. I prefer the hunt to the cooking and women things," she said. "Well, except the one."

"It's a very important one," I said and kissed her.

The hard months of fighting had changed us all. We had all suffered. Some had broken, and some had toughened up. Some had become aged by worry and a few had grown despondent. Willet had transformed into a beautiful woman. She could fight or run all day and was even more tireless and spirited when making love. I knew I loved her, and I could not live without her. I worried about her every second, wished this war to be over, and wondered what our life would be like once it was.

"What do you think we should do?" I said.

"Continue the fight."

"Yes, but for how long? I do not want to spend my life fighting for this land."

"We're fighting for our freedom," she said.

"I can fight for my freedom anywhere," I said.

"What do you mean?"

"That perhaps I wouldn't mind going west. Beyond the Oklahoma territory, though," I said. "Even further west, where skin color does not matter. We are not bound here. Micanopy cannot hold us."

"We don't have the freedom papers the whites demand," she said. "Those Certificates of Freedom."

"That's why I said further west, where it don't matter," I said. "There are free lands out there."

"Where?"

"Out there in the Indian lands. California. Mexico. There is not slavery there."

"We can't leave the fight."

"No, not now. When all this is settled. I wish to be an adventurer," I said.

"Being in the middle of a war isn't enough adventure for you?" she said.

"It's not the adventure I chose for myself," I said. "I want to choose one. A big grand one."

"This is more than grand enough for me," she said.

"You know what I mean. We can fight for our freedom anywhere."

"You would likely have to," she said.

"Will we ever have a choice in that?"

"Who can say?"

***

A circle of men sat around the council house when we returned to our island. Wild Cat and several men from his village were there. Osceola was sitting up, propped against a rolled-up pallet in the center of the circle. The sickness was killing him. The continual fleeing through the swamps, hiding from the probing MacCuaigs hastened it. He was too weak to fight, or even walk much of the time. His big strong body was bones and sagging, discolored skin. He came to live with us, as our remote island home was just about the safest place for him. Visitors came and went every day to council with John and Osceola. Wild Cat came by often.

Mother hurried to meet us, worry and sadness on her face. It was a look I had seen often recently, even though she tried to hide it. This looked worse than before.

"What's happened?" I asked her.

"Gen. Hernandez has captured King Philip. He promises to hang him in a fortnight if Osceola does not agree to come in for a parley," said Mother as we walked toward the debating circle.

"King Philip has always stood beside us. I cannot let him hang," croaked Osceola weakly. "I must save my brother."

"We must do what we can for King Philip, but getting captured is not the answer. They will arrest you and any that come with you," said Alligator.

"We don't know that for certain," said Wild Cat, no longer his cocky, jaunty self.

"Jesup isn't allowed to keep his promises of fair treatment, even if he wanted to," said John.

"Which he sure don't right now," said Yancy. "He was publicly humiliated by our escape. He wants revenge. He wants blood."

"Yes. I fear King Philip will be hung regardless," said John. "I don't mean to speak coldly of your father, Wild Cat, only of Jesup and the past deceits of the Americans."

"I fear you are right, brother," said Wild Cat. "But I plead with you to prevent it, if at all possible. He has always been a great warrior and leader for you. A hangman's rope is no way for such a man to die."

"Return to Jesup and tell him I will come for a parley," Osceola said.

"So Jesup can hang you too?" said John. "There will be treachery."

"I know this," gasped Osceola, weakly dropping back down. "I have but little life left in this body anyway. I do not believe we can fight much longer. Our Chiefs are worn down. The fire of battle is out of their souls. Many have lost sons. Their families grow hungry. Villages and fields have been burned. Too many cattle seized. They will starve us if they cannot defeat us in battle. Perhaps Jesup will be satisfied taking me, declaring victory, and then leaving the rest of you in peace."

"I will go with you," said John. "I think we cannot trust them. My heart is very heavy but I also know that we cannot fight any longer. I want to hear for myself what the soldiers have to say."

"It is settled," said Osceola.

"Hooah!" shouted Wild Cat, embracing his friends.

That night they shared some whiskey. It was just Osceola, Wild Cat and John. Old friends and rivals and bold, fearless spirits. They talked and laughed and drank well into the night. I could tell there were some tears, too.

***

"Brother, if you go, then I also must go," I said to John in the morning.

"I cannot stop you," he finally sighed after staring hard at me for several seconds. "I would forbid you if I could, but I cannot. You are grown. However, today, as your chief, not your brother, I command you to stay hidden and watch. This is not for your safety. This is because there must be a witness. Someone needs to speak the truth about what happens at that council. It would be good if it was you."

"What do you mean?" I said. "Do you expect treachery that extreme?"

"I do not know what to expect," said John. "Treachery, that much is certain. How much treachery? How extreme? Only that is uncertain."

"Then you should stay and be the witness," I said. "You are the leader of our people."

"But I may speak louder for my people as a martyr, if it comes to that. That is a possibility," said John. "A strong one."

"Then allow Osceola to be that man," I said. "He is dying anyway."

"No, I cannot," said John. "He is my friend. My ally. He needs me there. And he is not Estelusti."

***

The location for the parley was a grassy meadow a short distance from Fort Peyton. Jesup had promised provisions for all who came. The sun was shining bright, but the wind was cool.

Osceola was very sick, but he put on his best bright blue calico shirt, red leggings, and a new turban with fresh egret plumes. He wore a necklace of silver crescents and silver hoop earrings. He walked with a whalebone cane. John would serve as interpreter. Wild Cat was there.

Two hundred people followed them. They were our weakest and our sickest. They suffered so badly they didn't mind being taken prisoner, not if it meant food and shelter. Willet and I watched from the trees at the edge of the meadow, close enough to hear John and the others. They sat facing a pole with a white flag fluttering in the breeze.

At noon, General Hernandez and a column of three hundred mounted Dragoons trotted down the road. Hernandez dismounted and faced Osceola. Some of the dragoons formed a line behind Hernandez.

The others continued slowly walking their horses in two lines snaking around our people.

"Why have all the blacks not been returned as promised by Coa Hadjo?" demanded Hernandez.

"Coa Hadjo speaks for no one. He is a weakling. Take him. He is a burden anyway," said Osceola. His voice was strong but his hand on his walking stick trembled.

"The Blacks must be returned," said Hernandez.

"They are not ours to return. They are free people, to our God, to your God, to nature, to man," said Osceola. "To everyone but your laws."

"That was a very nice speech," Hernandez said and tipped his hat. At that signal, the dragoons stepped forward with their bayonets leveled, forming a tight circle around our people.

"You are our prisoners," said Hernandez. "Comply and no harm will come to you."

"We have a flag of truce!" Osceola tried to shout, but the words came out in a raspy whisper.

"I noticed it on my way in," said Hernandez. "I will not honor it, as you did not honor the agreement of your people to remain at Fort Brooke."

"This is unspeakable treachery," said John.

"This is no more treachery than your escape from our camp after accepting terms of surrender," said Hernandez. "Where are all your warriors?"

"They all got the measles and could not come," said Osceola.

"Is that so? I wish them well, and that you recover soon from your own illness. But we have been deceived too often. Now this is the way it is. It is necessary for you to come with me," said Hernandez.

"If so, it is the way of cowards and deceivers," said Osceola. "A path with no honor."

"You have fought well, Osceola. Your valiant fight does you and your people the greatest credit. However, it is time to bring this to a close. You are sick. Your people are tired and hungry. You will all see the good treatment that you will experience. You will be glad that you fell into my hands."

"Perhaps," Osceola said, weakly. "Perhaps you are right."

"I am pleased you are a man of reason," said Hernandez.

"Where will you take us?" Osceola asked.

"From where you will not escape this time. Fort Marion at St. Augustine."

Chapter Ten

FORT MARION
NOVEMBER 1837

"I know someone inside," said Jovis. "His name's Leander. He is the prison cook, owned by Gen. Hernandez. He is a good man that has been running the prison kitchen for a couple decades. He's been there so long he can go about any place he wants to, into town and out to some of the farms to buy supplies."

"Myself, I don't believe there's any way to break someone out of that prison," said Yancy. "The walls are solid stone, strong enough to withstand naval bombardments, and the only way out is through a guardhouse and bridge over a moat."

"Nothing is impossible," I said. "Our people are ready to give up. We need John and Wild Cat. We must at least look and see."

"If anyone would know a way out it would be Leander," said Jovis. "But I've been inside there. I agree with Yancy. About the only way out of there is gluing you some bird feathers together and flying out."

"Perhaps there are underground tunnels or something," I said.

"Why hasn't your friend flown the coop?" Yancy asked Jovis.

"He is an old man, even older than me. Where would he go?" said Jovis.

"Would he help us?" I asked.

"Possibly. To a certain extent anyway. He has a comfortable life now, so I don't expect he'll want to take any huge risks. But he can be trusted. He will know where our men are, and where the guards are. If there's a crack anywhere, Leander would know."

"You have been in there?" I asked Jovis.

"I have, on many occasions with General Clinch," he said.

"Are the guards the same soldiers that were at the forts?" I asked. "The soldiers that fought in the field, or have been to our villages?"

"No," said Jovis. "Most were soldiers once, but long ago. Now they'd too old or crippled up to go out on campaigns. The officers have grown lazy with the easy, boring duty of the fort. The entire place is poorly run."

**

"I weep every night for John," Mother said. "I miss him terribly and worry of his fate. But I do not want to lose two sons. You could be easily recognized."

"There's little worry of that if we play our roles well. I have been going into American forts since I was a young child," I said. "No one expects danger from a simple-minded Negro."

"That was a different time," she said. "Now there is a price on your head."

"They will not be expecting anyone to break into the fort, only out," I said. "As long as I play my role well, I will be fine."

We sat at a fold-up table inside a tent glowing with the light of candles and lamps. Mother held a long red candle, dripping wax to seal the letter I was taking to the fort. For days she had practiced the ornate signatures of the provost marshal and Reynaud Garza, a local farmer. Garza owned about fifty slaves and supplied the city and fort with a good share of the farm products they consumed.

Garza was not a cruel master like the MacCuaigs. The slaves on his place were not whipped. Families were not separated and sold away. None had run away or joined the rebellion when it started. Still, they often helped us. The wagon drivers had come by with their travel passes for Mother to copy. They had brought pen, ink, wax seal, the special paper and wax candles for the seal.

"The plan is risky. Extremely dangerous," said Mother.

"Life is full of risks, Mother. It must be done," I said.

"It both fills my heart with pride and fear when you sound and behave so much like your father and brother," she said. "But right now all Negroes are looked at with suspicion. The MacCuaigs travel those roads, looking for runaways, paying rewards to those who reveal fugitives."

"Yes, but it is quiet around St. Augustine. There has been no trouble there. The Mayor and Provost Marshal have banned the MacCuaigs. Patrols of soldiers keep them off the nearby roads."

"Banned them? How so? Why?"

"The MacCuaigs kidnapped two local farm slaves as they drove a wagon to market in the city and sold them as their own property. Now the soldiers patrol the roads to protect the wagons."

"When such evil and deceit is in your nature, no one is safe," said Mother. "But don't trust the soldiers to protect you."

***

Our war had not come to St. Augustine. Other than the first fiery days of the slave revolts in Mosquito County, all the fighting had been on the other side of Florida. In the city of St. Augustine, black people still walked freely. They were too important to the city's commerce to lock away. They were craftsmen, housekeepers, laborers, wood cutters and buggy drivers. Slaves unloaded the cargo from the merchant ships in the port. They mingled with the soldiers, merchants, shoppers and sailors that congested around the carts and open shops. No one paid us any mind as we drove the battered farm wagon toward the fort.

Up close, the massive stone Fort Marion was even more imposing. Tall watchtowers and fortified guard posts projected off each corner. Uniformed men peered over the high walls at us as we rolled up to the guardhouse at the bridge. Two blue coated soldiers stepped out.

"Whoa up," I pulled back on the reins. Willet sat beside me wearing a washed-out dress she'd pinned up to distract the soldiers from anything we might be doing. We had a wagon bed full of pumpkins. Three thirty-pound gopher turtles lay on their backs in the straw.

"Have your pass?" said the soldier looking at us closely. "Don't think I seen you before."

"Yas suh, I finally gots me promoted to wagon driver, yas suh. Taking in a load to the kitchen nigga," I said, handing him the pass and grinning. "Massa say he ain't got enough hands for all this work 'dis fort giving him."

"And a pretty little gal helper, ain't that nice," he leered. "Pretty little punkin' picking pickaninnie. How 'bout that, boys?"

The other guards laughed. About four or five of them gathered around, hoping for a peek up or down the dress Willet was swishing around, showing her legs. One of the guards, the one skinny one, hopped up in the bed of the wagon and started moving the pumpkins around, peering underneath. Cursing at the ugly turtles overturned in the straw.

"More turtles? I ain't eating no more turtles," the guard said. "Damned old mud meat."

The man in the back hopped down and the other waved us across the bridge.

***

We entered the courtyard. Soldiers and civilians loitered about at tables and benches, playing cards and socializing. Most soldiers were older men that did not look fit enough for long marches or enduring much hardship. A work gang of black men and women toiled around the fort, wearing gray uniforms with bright orange stripes sewn on the sleeves.

The kitchen building was at the far corner of the courtyard, fifty yards away. No one paid us any mind as our old mules pulled the wagon up to the door. A burly, thick-necked man stepped out. Silver grizzle covered his head and cheeks, and his skin was black as coal. He wore all white, with the apron smeared with fresh food stains. He eyed us suspiciously as I got down off the wagon.

"Who are you?" he asked.

"We're from Garza's. Punkins and fresh turtle meat," I said, picking up one of the turtles by the tail. In the turtle's panic, his short scaly legs clawed the air with the speed of molasses.

"I never sent nobody after any turtles," he said. "I get more turtles than the men will eat."

"Perhaps this note from Senor Garza will explain it," I said. I handed him the sealed page and he opened it. Leander stared at the note with intense concentration. I knew the letter itself only quoted the prices that Garza expected to ask for next year's steers. Below the signature were some minuscule symbols that didn't make any sense to me. Jovis said they would mean something to Leander, whose brow furrowed. He turned silently and motioned for us to follow him inside.

"Get us some cool tea, Billy," Leander said to a hulking boy standing in the kitchen. We sat down at a table as the boy lumbered off.

"Don't worry none about speaking in front of Billy," Leander said as the boy walked away. "He's a mute with the mind of a child. How is Jovis?"

"He is well. He and Esther are adapting to the easy life of the Estelusti. They have built a cabin on our island, which so far has been distant from all the fighting," I said.

"I was worried about him and Esther after I heard of the attack on the Clinch plantation. I'm happy they are doing well, that they have found some peace and freedom for however long it lasts," said Leander. "Ol' Jovie used to be a hellion back in the day. Don't let them big house manners fool you."

"He told me a couple stories of his youth," I said. "We met many of the Clinch plantation people."

"Ever come across a gal named Nellie Fae?"

"Sure. We met her."

"How's she doing?"

"Just fine, I guess. Found Jesus."

"Is that right? I never expected to hear that."

"Thickened up some, according to a friend of ours."

"Is that right? I reckon me and her might have us a baby somewhere. About thirty years old now. No idea where he might be now," said Leander wistfully. "Anyway, I reckon Jovis told you me and him was tight as peas growing up. He grew up being groomed to be a manservant to the massa and my mammy ran the kitchen."

Billy sat a pitcher of tea on the table and returned to his chores.

"Lord, Jovis chafed at working in that house," laughed Leander. "Us that worked in the fields hated the highs that served in the house, all their airs and pretensions. But Jovis was different. He rankled and resisted working in that house, but if he acted up to get sent himself to the fields, his mammy and them would suffer for it."

"He got to see the house burn."

"That had to be satisfying."

"It seemed to be."

232

"This stone fort ain't likely to burn."

"It's not difficult having a mute and an imbecile for a helper?" Willet asked, watching Billy peel potatoes.

"No, I wouldn't have it any other way. He is the perfect companion. Don't speak a lick, hence, can't bitch and complain. Strong as an ox but meek as a lamb," said Leander. "You should be happy, too. There is plenty of snitches around this fort, trying to improve their situation in life. Some that would tell on a soul for a bigger hunk of bacon. Billy ain't smart enough to think like that and couldn't make himself clear even if he did."

"I hadn't considered it like that," she said.

"I have growed mighty fond of that boy," said Leander. "I have others that work for me, in the kitchen and repairs and such around the fort. That is a duty that has just been entrusted to me over the years, mostly due to the habitual drunkenness of the prison superintendent. Most of the time, I keep the others out of here. They come in, stir some pots, peel some taters, serve the meal lines, and then I run them out. I don't need 'em around much, and idle hands ain't nothing but trouble and bickering. His quietus is a blessing."

"I expect so," I said. "About the note. Jovis said you might help us."

"Yes," said Leander with gravity. "Those scribbles on the page is our code from years ago. We would carve them in a tree or fence post to send a message. I never expected to see that again. What is it you need?"

"We plan to break the Seminole prisoners out. One is my brother."

"To bust them men out? That's impossible. Have you all lost your senses?"

"Perhaps, but we must try regardless."

"And how exactly do you plan to do that?" he said.

233

"We have no idea. Jovis thought you might have some ideas."

"Lord A'mighty," sighed Leander. "The trials and tribulations I suffer."

"Are there no cracks in the wall, a tunnel we could escape through?"

"No. Where do you get such ideas?"

"Just something I read," I said. "I see that our people are allowed out of their cell in the daylight. They are standing right over there. Is there no way to overpower the guards and run them out?"

"No. Impossible," said Leander, sadly. "The fact is, I've studied those walls myself, many a time, for many a year. That was before I earned the privilege of going into town. I've studied the roads on those times I've ventured out of the city. I have studied the tides. Hell, I've looked at the clouds and birds and wondered if I could make me a set of wings and fly away... That seems as likely as you getting your people out."

"Can't you consider it some more?"

"I will, son, I will. I will put my heart and soul and prayers into it, but I just don't see how."

"You have a lot of big knives in here," Willet said. "Can we smuggle some into the prisoners and they could use them to escape?"

"Another story book tale, I take it?" smiled Leander. "No, the soldiers come in several times a day and count the blades, down to the dullest butter knife. A missing blade would get me lashed and sent to the cruelest sugar field. Or shot. I will not risk that, and such a foolish attempt would be suicide anyway. The jailers and soldiers here may be of poor quality, but there's still a couple hundred of them with enough guns to blow you all to pieces."

***

Over the next few days, we frequently came and went from the fort. We brought in several loads of stolen farm vegetables or fruit stacked on a thick bed of straw. The food should have gone to feed our hungry people, but we needed to keep the deception going. Each day we brought in another pistol safely buried under the straw until we had six hidden away in Leander's crawl spaces.

We worked chores alongside the slaves of the fort, pulling weeds, painting walls and cleaning stalls. We toted and pulled and fetched. Always we watched the routines of the men atop the walls and in the guard posts, looking for weak spots.

We hadn't brought Virgil at first, worried he might be identified, or that his size might be intimidating and raise suspicions. Leander said people here had heard of Virgil, but no one was looking for him. On the farms around the St. Augustine, several men close to Virgil's size toiled in the fields. More worked on the docks. We saw no wanted posters nor heard any loose talk of reward seekers. Virgil insisted on coming. Satisfied he wouldn't stand out, we took him on the next trip.

"Who is this?" the guard at the bridge demanded the first time we brought Virgil with us.

"This here Bubba. He don't speak much. Don't understand much neither," said Willet.

"Why'd Garza send a big dummy?" the guard asked.

"Don't nobody consult me on such matters. The old fool cook has a fondness for 'em, I guess. Maybe they can't complain about his cookin'," Willet said. "I expect there's some heavy totin' to be done. That's what he's mostly good for. Totin' or digging. Some pulling. He's almighty stout. Ain't no one better at totin' than Bubba here. Dumb as a rock, but, boy, he can tote a whale."

"I ain't seen no whales in the fort since I been here," said the guard. "You ain't got a pass for him?"

"I 'spect it's in this here," Willet said, leaning over and letting her loose shirt fall open as she handed him our passes. The guard looked down her shirt longer than he looked at the papers.

"Well, it ain't," the guard finally said. "It don't say nothing about no third person, no big idjit."

"I only brung the pass massa gave me," I said. "You knows I can't read what's inside them words."

"Hey, you dummy, you got your papers?" demanded the guard, slapping the side of the wagon.

"Yas sah, this right here," Virgil said, and handed the man some folded paper.

"This ain't a pass," the man scoffed. "It's a letter from your master asking the major out to supper."

"He said I was to give it to you," said Virgil.

"I ain't the major," the soldier snapped. "But you got to have a pass to enter the fort."

"That must be the other one then," Virgil said, and handed the guard a forgery. He waved us through.

***

Billy was wolfing down a big platter of eggs and grits when we walked into Leander's kitchen. Leander filled coffee cups and sat them on the table.

"I have pondered out an idea on what might just work for you," said Leander. "It's audacious and will likely get you killed, so it's probably the sort of hopeless adventure that would appeal to a pair of swashbucklers such as yourselves."

"More appealing than digging a tunnel into the ocean, hopefully," I said. "That's the best I've come up with so far."

"Here's my idea. From time to time, the commander gets a generous spirit. He has kegs of beer brought in from the city and treats the guards," said Leander. "He'll have me send the boy around with buckets of beer to all the guard posts."

"You want to get them drunk?"

"As a start, but I was thinking a step further. They might not notice a few nice slugs of laudanum. Not until they woke up and found the prison cell empty."

"We would wait while they drank the beer?"

"An especially rare treat includes a bottle of rum, if all the reports have been good," said Leander. "I guarantee the laudanum in a slug of rum would go unnoticed."

"That is wonderful!" squealed Willet. "But how do we get over the wall or out the gate?"

"At the end of that corridor is a stairway that goes up to the sentry box on the northwest corner of the fort. That is the only point of the wall you could go over undetected," he said. "I know the guards that work that post at night. You will have to approach them a little different, but it could be accomplished."

"Why only there?" I asked, looking out his window at the walls and guards in towers. "Those walls are very long. Isn't there another place we would not be seen?"

"Trust me on this one. I've looked it over plenty, especially when I was first here and thinking heavy on escape," Leander said. "That side of the watchtower is in complete darkness once the moon passes over. Anywhere else, you'll be in the sightline of at least three other posts and have to avoid a foot patrol on your way out."

"What if we brought a boat into the lagoon?"

"I'd strongly advise against it. This fort was built to sink warships so I just about figure it could blow the hell out of a little fishing boat.

And these cannons are a whole lot better than those built three hundred years ago."

"Only if we were seen."

"You would be seen. The lagoon has two patrol boats in it at all times, with a warship anchored offshore. Men on foot walk the beach and edge of the lagoon," said Leander. "Your only chance is to sneak back down the peninsula and through town."

"Where will you get the laudanum?"

"Ah, the hospital storerooms have plenty. It has come in with the regular deliveries for years, and we've yet to have a battle that required it," he said. "The surgeon uses a lot of it for the dysentery and various complaints of the soldiers."

"And they would just go to sleep?"

"I'll stake my life on it," he said. "They will gulp that beer down like they was in a desert and be out fast."

"That much might kill them."

"It might," he said. "I won't lose sleep over it. But if you don't make it over that wall, they'll hang you, regardless."

"How many guards will we have to deal with?"

"If you're lucky?"

"We can start there."

"You'll need to take care of the two stationed at main corridor inside the prison part of the castle. Your boys are behind a door down one of them dark, dungeon hallways," said Leander. "After that, two on the bastion. That's if you're very lucky."

"Which door is it?" I asked.

"I've never been down there for years, personally, nor do I have any desire to go," said Leander. "They still got the bones of dead Englishmen down there."

"Doesn't your boy know which door?"

"Of course he knows, but he can't tell you how many doors, or which door," Leander said. "He can't count that high. And if he attempted it, I wouldn't trust his figuring. He is mighty slow between the ears."

"Well, that's a problem," I said.

"I figured you came in expecting to encounter one or two," Leander said.

"The only way to know for sure is to go down there. I reckon you should start taking their meals down regular, so no one suspects you later," said Leander.

"Will they suspect us now?"

"I doubt it. From time to time, I have others deliver supper to the guards and inmates down there. I don't mean nothing that would bring no shame on you, Miss Willet, but I suspect you can most easily disarm them with your charms."

"My charms?"

"The men stationed here see few women. I know most of the guards. They are an uncouth, vulgar lot who are not welcomed by neither the society ladies nor upper-class whores of town," he said. "Instead they frequent cribs on the waterfront. Most of the cribs belongs to the MacCuaigs. I figger you have heard of them?"

"The whores are slaves?"

"Yes, and the men that have been here a long time have developed a fondness for pretty young Negro girls. Except they don't leave them pretty for long. Some get their enjoyments being dreadful rough on those little girls working the shacks. You'll need to be mighty careful about it, but you might have to give them some ideas, you know what I mean? I don't mean to shame you, but that may be the only way they'll let their guard down," said Leander. "The two in the bastion you must cross are two of the worst when it comes to getting drunk and beating on little colored babies."

"Then will we find another way," I said.

"I will not wilt from this challenge," said Willet. "Please continue, Leander."

He looked at me and I looked away.

"Most of these broke-down loafers ain't smart enough to question a gift like we're about to give them. Thing is, the two posted up there in the southwest bastion are foul cretins. They are hateful and suspicious of everything and everybody. Both of them fought in the first Seminole war and took some bad wounds at the hands of some runaways who'd joined the British. They ain't forgot. In fact, they fester their hate, and have a particular dislike of me," Leander said. "They are always accusing me of giving extra food to the slaves assigned to the fort, or allowing stealing, things like that. They complain I send them up food that ain't cook done. They don't like any nigras in no positions of importance like I got is the thing. They don't like me one bit, but maybe we could use that, too. They might even suspect I was trying to poison them."

"Then why would they drink the liquor?" I snapped. "This is a bad plan. It is much too dangerous."

"No, I understand," said Willet. "I will pretend to drink some, then they will not believe it is poison. They will not believe I am poison either."

"Yes, I think so," said Leander. "I sure don't mean to shame you none."

"It's no shame," Willet said. "I will use the weapons I was both blessed and cursed with. No man will shame me, and I have something for any that might try."

***

"What are you two doing down here?" challenged the guard standing at the thick door to the prison corridor. It was our first time delivering the supper buckets.

"Leander the cook sent us down here," Willet said, kinda wiggling a little. "That boy got himself in some trouble or sumpin'. He is slow in the head."

"We've noticed," said the soldier leering at her. He leered for a good while, and she encouraged it by wiggling a little more.

"He's 'specting us back shortly," Willet finally cooed.

"Come on then," grumbled the guard and we followed him down the dark hallway barely lit by flickering torches along the wall.

"Take them buckets in and be quick about it," said the guard opening the heavy door. "Watch yourself, though, them injuns ain't to be trusted."

Holding a candle in one hand, I carried the buckets to the shelf as the jailer ordered, picking my way through the men seated cross-legged on the straw covered floor. Their eyes registered surprise but no one uttered a sound.

"Dey sho' is scarity booga-man men," Willet said loudly as I shuffled past John and whispered to him. I could see her in the light of the doorway. She was batting her eyes at the guard, keeping his attention on her body. "They is sho' nuff savages. And ugly. Mighty ugly. And smelly. Dey smell dis bad when dey was brung in?"

"They sure did," said the man. "Godless heathens."

We wheeled the heavy supper cart up the ramp to the guard post on the southwest bastion, to the two men with a grudge toward Leander. They were both big, thick men. Emil and Hector were their names.

"Leander said that shif'less boy has ternt lazy," she said.

"Sure nice not to have to look at that slobbering dummy right when I'm setting to eat," said Emil. "Don't help my appetite any."

"He can't hep hisself," cooed Willet.

"I reckon not, but it is a heap more appetizing when a delicious little thing like you brings a man his supper," he said. "Look, I'm took to drooling myself."

"I don't mind taking some men their supper," she smiled shyly. "Not always. Just depends."

"Depends on what?" he said.

"Different things," she said. "Whatever on a girl's mind sometimes I reckon. Sometimes it's a shiny coin or something pretty."

"Is that right?" he chuckled.

"I want to buy my freedoms one day. That takes lots 'dem coins."

"I reckon it do," said Emil.

***

Every night for a week we carried supper buckets to the prisoners and guards on the wall. Willet kept her blouse low and open and her skirts high and loose. She always smiled like a coquettish simp at any soldier she caught looking.

"I'd like to cut that one's liver out, the way he paws at my legs," Willet said as we approached the drawbridge.

"You show him plenty of them," I said.

"I have to keep their attention," she said. "You jealous?"

"Probably something along those lines, and a little more. I would like to cut his liver out, too, when he paws you. But no liver cutting," I said. "Not until we free John. Then you should do it with a dull, rusty blade."

"Hey little gal, why don't you come down here and pass the day while them dummies with you deliver their goods?" hooted the one they called Hubbard from the guardhouse. The gang loitering nearby joined in the catcalling.

"Now, you know Massa Garza don't 'low his gals to dally with no soldier mens," Willet teased. She stood in the wagon bed and leaned into the straw, giving them a good look down her shirt as she scooped up two cantaloupes. She stayed bent over as she held the fruit toward the soldiers. "But he did send these juicy melons. Don't they look tasty?"

"Oh, my, yes indeed they do. I'd sure like me a taste of them melons while they's still ripe on the vine there," said Hub, guffawing and rubbing his grimy hand up the inside of her thigh. "Don't they look sweet, boys?"

The others joined in the laughter. Willet grinned and swayed back and forth, spreading her feet so she could get low and show them about everything.

"Maybe you soldier mens should talk to Massa about me visiting you out here some time, if you got a little coin or something purty for me, in case you want to squeeze my melons."

"Peel 'em and lick 'em more like," laughed a guard.

"That might be two dem coins," said Willet as I snapped the reins, and we rumbled through the gate.

***

"Sho' wish I could come with you," said Leander. "There's folks I would sure like to see one more time, but I reckon I don't know many folks out there anymore. Few on the plantations live to be my age."

"There are still a few, maybe more than you would expect. Nelly Fae."

"Maybe so."

"The offer is open to come," I said.

"If I was about 20 years younger, I'd be right with you," said Leander, rubbing his chin and grinning. "There was a time, when I was a young buck in Georgia, I led the patty rollers on some merry chases. I had gals on half a dozen different plantations. I was scairt half to death when those hounds was baying, but boy I felt alive, and on the way back home, just smiling and humming and skipping along. Free for a little bit. My own damn man."

"You must have liked those girls a lot, to risk getting caught," Willet said.

"I sure did. Every single one of them. There were times I took a licking, but it barely slowed me. Every second of it was worth it," he said. "They whupped me, but never lamed me. Nor kilt me obviously. They always knew I was sparking, not running away, since I got caught skipping along, grinning like a fool and not paying attention. Hardly running away type behavior. Still, I paid the price. These days I don't think I could handle the running, nor tolerate well getting shot at. Sure could do with a randy sparking though."

"They do make it hard on us," I said. "I suspect it's about to get a lot worse, when Jesup finds his prize prisoners gone."

"Tromping through them gator filled bogs ain't for me," said Leander. "Ain't no way the boy could survive out there, and I could never leave him. They would likely just shoot him like a crippled horse. Nobody but me can make ourselves understood to him."

"Sadly, I'm sure you are right on both counts," said Willet.

"You all getting out of here alive will be good enough for me," said Leander. "Now, I've collected everything we'll need, and plotted this all out."

***

"Raise a good knot on the boy's head, but don't crack him until he's snoring good from the laudanum," said Leander, with some sadness in his voice. "And I reckon I best have a fat one, too."

"I do not like doing it," I said. "I feel heartless watching that simpleminded boy grin at me, and knowing I'll have to club him. And you."

"I reckon we're just doing our part. I know enough about ol' gentle Billy there to know he wouldn't mind a knot and a headache if he thought he was helping someone else escape misery," said Leander. "Don't feel bad about it, son. We must make it believable. For me and the boy's sake, more than anybody. No one will believe we was overpowered unless there's signs of a scuffle. I'll put enough in his tea that he'll be asleep for hours. Another good thing about Billy, if he wakes up, he can't yell for help."

"I hope no harm comes to you because of this."

"Well, it's my own plan that I thought up. If harm comes, I have no one to blame but myself. I been in tight fixes before over the years and I know how to play to the buckras if I need to. I have me a story already cooked up," he said. "This might be my last chance to be a big aggravation in their side. That always pleasures me. It will to my grave."

"I expect they'll be aggravated alright," said Willet.

"I'll deal with it. Let's get back to the plan," I said. "I'll put on the feedbag extra-big for the boy."

***

Billy smacked his lips in bliss as he chewed the fat off the pork bone. He'd gone through a stack of fried pork chops, three big buttery yams, and a gallon of greens and rice. As he was mopping his plate, Leander gave him a mug of tea, heavily sugared to cover the laudanum.

"Poor fellow only has eating as his one pleasure in life, and he's enthusiastic about it," said Leander, smiling sadly at Billy. "I'll pack my pockets with biscuits for him, too. It might be a bit before they discover us tied up in here if they're all out chasing their prize prisoners."

Billy grinned and waved at all us watching him eat, and then his head hit the table. He was snoring like a boar hog as Virgil lugged him to the heavy iron stove.

"Thump away," said Leander, chugging a slug of laudanum and putting his arm around Billy's shoulders. "Make sure my gag is good and tight. It falls off, I won't have no choice but to start yelling for help."

After they were both snoring, Virgil cracked them both on the back of the head hard enough to raise a nice lump. Then we tied them tight to the cast iron stove.

***

I pushed the cart of supper slop buckets now carrying a bottle of laudanum-laced rum and Virgil carried two buckets of beer. Willet carried a basket filled with long loaves of bread.

"What's all this here?" Burris the guard asked. He was old, paunchy and slow moving.

"I dasn't rightly know," said Willet batting her eyes. She used pins to tighten the waist and shorten the hem of her dress and had fixed her shirt so it was low and open. "We's the bringers not the senders. We just heard one of them general mens's telling the cook ever'body was getting extra rations of beer and a bottle of rum. They told the cook to tell you men it was for all the hard work you been doing, especially seeing as keeping them nasty injuns and such is so perilous. That's what I heard."

"About time someone appreciated us down here," said the guard named Reyes.

"Yas suh, sho'nuff sounds like them that sent us knows yo' efforts," said Willet.

"I ain't ungrateful, but this is peculiar," said Burris.

"Well, I know I ain't supposed to spill this, but I heard something else," she said, flirty as can be. "I heard them say they ain't telling nobody yet, though. Says a big surprise announcement is coming someway. Only them tippy toppest ones knows. Something about most of you soldiers is going to march out of here tomorrow to put down them Seminoles raiding south down the coast. Said it would keep you warm tonight 'cause you might not be back for a good long spell."

"Us? March out of here? Most of us ain't marched no further than the courtyard for ten years!" gasped Burris, staggered.

"They was talking urgent-like," she said. "So I reckon it might be emnint."

"Lord A'mighty," the man shook his head in disbelief.

"I reckon dummy here will drink the liquor if you don't want it," she said. "But we got to get them Indians fed and move on to them other tasks laid upon us."

"Yassuh, I'll set myself down and drink ever' drop if you'd allow me," grinned Virgil. "It'd be mighty precious to me and not a drop would be spilt."

"That ain't likely, dummy," said Burris.

"Yas sah," said Virgil, dropping his head. "Sorry, sah."

"When are we supposed to pull out?" said Reyes.

"Well, now, I don't know. They don't tell me everything."

"Come on, damnit, let's get to drinking," said Burris. "This shocking news calls for a bender."

The first guard took a long slug of rum. He handed the bottle to the second and then unlocked the door.

"It is good to see you, brother," I whispered to John as I set a supper bucket down. "The guards will be asleep soon. We will come for you then."

As we left the cell, the guards were passing the rum bottle and slurping the beer. We took the empty cart down the hall and waited around the corner. Within a minute, the guards were slurring. Their heads drooped and bodies sagged but the bottle continued to pass until Burris fell off his chair and cracked his head.

"Whaffa thit Burf?" Reyes garbled, reaching toward the fallen man. He tried to stand but instead toppled onto his partner and did not move.

Virgil took the five-pound pistol and gave Reyes a tremendous whack that echoed down the stone hallways. Then he did the same to Burris.

"They were already out," I said.

"Don't you think it would look mighty suspicious if Leander and the boy has knots on their heads, and these here guards don't?" said Virgil. "They might be unjustly accused of aiding in our escape. As one somewhat knowledgeable about escapes, maybe I should give them each a clout. Just to be safe."

"You're right. We can't leave anything to chance. It would not be proper if they were unjustly blamed."

"Hooah," said John when I opened the door. "Have your friends had too much to drink?"

"Yes, in celebration of your freedom," I said as Virgil dragged the snoring guards into an empty cell across the hall. Willet quickly tied and gagged them.

"What comes next?"

"We must go down this hallway and up the stairs to the sentry box. That is where we go over the wall."

"To the sentry box? Where are the sentries?"

"In the sentry box, waiting their supper. We have the same gift for them these men received," I said. "Laudanum in the rum."

"What if they don't want the rum?"

"Then we'll kill them," I said and handed him a pistol from the breadbasket.

"You will be punished if you stay," John said to Osceola.

Our dying war chief was too weak to escape. King Philip would stay behind too. The sickness was not killing him, but old age and the wet, dark dungeon were.

"That is of little concern to me," Osceola said. "They bring nothing I fear. I could well be dead before your escape is discovered. I am too weak. I cannot even walk down the hallway. If they execute me, perhaps I could have a warrior's death after all. Hooah."

Five more of the twenty people in the room were too frail to attempt an escape. We all embraced tightly and said our final goodbyes.

*   *   *

"Hallo up dere, supper coming," Willet sang out before she showed herself in the archway that led from the stairs onto the wide, walled bastion. Virgil and I followed a few steps behind, carrying beer buckets and supper pots.

"There ain't but two of us here," chuckled Emil as he looked at all the food and drink.

"Something extra for the bestest mens I reckon," she said coquettishly.

"Ain't likely," he snorted.

"Them was my precise orders. I heard the general with my own ears order that lazy cook to do it up right. He was a hollerin' something fierce," Willet said. "He says it a 'pology for all that cold food the other dummy brought."

"The general? I ain't seen him," said the soldier.

"He come in bright this morning, but I never seen that myself. But when I was emptying the mornin' slop jars, I heard him say it through the door. I don't reckon no other man be cussing like that lessin' he was the general."

"Did he now? And he come all this way just to send us some beer and rum?"

"How's I to know his reasons for coming himself?" Willet said with exasperation. "But I heard him say double rations and spirits, and we been toting all night. I reckon he come all this way to personally deliver the marchin' orders to you all, not the food orders, though, if I was to figure on it."

"Marching out? To where? Who all?" he demanded angrily.

"Lordy, I don't know. I reckoned you knew. To fight injuns somewheres," said Willet, acting shaken. "I'm just doing as I was told, trying my bestest not to get my ass whipped by that bastard old cook down there."

"Leander? He mistreats you?" said the guard, his voice loud with excitement from all these recent revelations.

"He's whupped me ever' day since they brung me here," she said sadly. "I'd ruther be back on the farm hoeing and scraping. Least I didn't get whupped out there."

"I'll have a word with Leander," he boasted. "That flouty nigra needs to be set back in his place."

"He's a mean ol' task masker. I been running ragged all over this place since we come here to work. He don't never let me stop. I am sorely tired. Reckon I could just rest a bit?" said Willet, almost in a swoon.

"Sure, little girl, you can rest here a little bit, but them two dummies have gotta wait down below."

Virgil and I walked back down a few steps and sat in the shadows. I could still see Willet as she squeezed past the men and sat down facing us. She laid out the meat and bread and rum on a checked cloth. The guards sat cross-legged facing her.

"I seen you batting them big eyes of yours at me when you was down there unloading that wagon yesterday," Emil said. "Like maybe you had a little itch."

"You reckon I think you're special or something? I ain't got time for them thoughts, even if I was allowed to have them."

"I seen your titties yesterday, too, when you was down below there. I seen 'em when you came through the gate."

"Oh, no you never did no such thing," she said, but she'd flashed the men on the wall plenty.

"Did too, didn't we Hector?"

"Like some jiggly chocolate pudding with a black cherry on top," said Hector.

"Now, you boys is ornery. But maybe you be right accurate with them colorful descriptions. I expect you might want to see them again to be sure. You can tell me more of them adoring words if you's a mind too," she whispered. "I kinda like it."

"I suppose we got a few seconds we could spare," said Emil. "I reckon we're entitled to a few feels for us being kind enough to let you join us, and since I'm about to set that old Leander straight for you. He won't bother you no more."

"You can do all that?"

"Course I can. Now, forget about him. This won't take much time at all, what I got in mind. Just open your shirt a little more and lean over this way."

"Might be nicer if I could have me a little sip of that rum."

"Sure, honey, that would be just fine," chuckled Emil, handing Willet the bottle which she pretended to gulp.

"Hooey, dat hot, but sho' is good," she gasped.

"Good, honey, that's dandy," Emil said, taking three big gulps. "Now pull that dress down off you."

She did as they said.

"Ain't that nice, Hector," said Emil.

Willet moaned and leaned back. Emil and Hector passed the bottle and fondled her. They never heard Virgil as he stepped forward and swung his three-pound, stone-headed club with the strength of Sampson. The force lifted Hector about three feet in the air and he farted like a whale as his head caved in.

Emil whipped around and my club caught him square in the mouth. Blood and bits of white flew out as his head jerked back, but he was strong as a bull. The blow seemed to barely faze him. He lunged for my feet but Willet jumped on his back and slit his throat.

We were quickly away, creeping through the narrow alleys and backstreets of St. Augustine. Without waking anyone but some boney-ribbed curs we were out of the city and to our dugouts hidden on the banks of the San Sebastian River. Traveling by night we moved south, toward the Kissimmee River and our new camp, below Lake Okeechobee.

Chapter Eleven

LOXAHATCHEE
DECEMBER 1837

As expected, Jesup was in a fury. He declared us a people without honor. He said he now had no choice but to exterminate us like vermin. Five thousand soldiers were immediately on the march, coming at us from four directions. All field commanders had orders to kill or capture any Seminole or Estelusti on sight.

One column moved down the east coast. A second column moved south along the St. Johns River. Another came at us in boats from the south, up the Caloosahatchee River. The fourth column, a thousand men led by Colonel Zachary Taylor, marched down the Kissimmee River.

Patrols of MacCuaigs and Creek mercenaries ranged far ahead, never allowing us to rest. Every day there was another running battle. We could only flee further south, living in temporary camps filled with the smell of medicine pots, melting lead and strong, greasy alligator broth to heal the sick and wounded.

***

Taylor bulled his way down the Kissimmee and at last our chiefs decided to turn and fight. Taylor chose the battle, but our leaders chose the battlefield. Now we waited in the swampy thickets on the northern tip of Lake Okeechobee with our backs to the water. We were surrounded on three sides by miles and miles of open marshes and saw grass prairies. The closest land was the tip of a large pine forest two miles away. The army would come from there.

Four hundred warriors would face the enemy, and another hundred elders and wives had stayed to reload our rifles and tend the wounded. The rest of our people had crossed the forty-mile-wide lake to safety, into the Big Grassy Water that the Europeans called the Everglades. No army could ever penetrate the Big Grassy. The soggy, dreary, reptile-ruled place would not sustain us for long either, but the army would never reach us. What happened next, no one knew, but here we made our fight.

We had left a trail of cold campfires and abandoned huts for the soldiers to follow. And at each campsite a few of our people stayed behind. They were too sick and frail to continue, but would act as our tricksters, sending the soldiers into our carefully laid trap. The captives told Taylor less than a hundred of us were still willing to fight, and that our spirit was broken. They told Taylor we were lying helpless in the bushes like a wounded rabbit. After dickering for a warm fire and a bowl of stew, the prisoners pointed the army right toward us.

***

I had spent the last days perched in a tall pine with my spyglass, search-ing the far trees for a glimpse of the oncoming army. This morning they had arrived, coming out of the trees as expected.Colonel Taylor and his staff stood between the forest and the saw grass prairie, staring our way with field glasses. Tents and tables were set up. Couriers scurried around. In the dark pine forest behind them I could see glimpses of many more soldiers.

Several times during their march we had lured the soldiers into tromping across wide, wet prairies like this one, full of ponds, puddles, sinkholes and ankle-breaking underwater roots. The previous fields had been much smaller than this one, but still took hours to cross.

We had watched with amusement as they slogged through the mire, flailing at the savage grass that slashed their faces and tore their clothes. We laughed out loud as they exhausted themselves battling the hostile sludge all day, only to reach our defenses and find us gone. This time, however, we did not run away. We were few, but we were more than one hundred and we were more than willing to fight. Somewhere hidden in the clumps of thick, towering grass our bravest men lurked. They were down in the mire with all the slithering things, waiting to draw the soldiers further into our trap.

***

Bugles and drums sounded. Lines of soldiers came out of the trees. The first two hundred soldiers had hacked about a quarter of the way across when our first skirmishers popped up and fired point-blank into them. Before the soldiers could react, our men were already far away down the alligator trails.

The soldiers gave chase through the mud and weeds, but quickly fatigued. No sooner would the soldiers slow than another of our men would jump up and fire or take a soldier from behind with a knife to the throat. Soldiers responding to the victim's cry were leapt upon by more of our hidden men. For three hours the soldiers chopped and slogged their way toward our stronghold on the lake, dodging blades and bullets from our daredevils in the grass.

Finally, the first soldiers fought their way out of the tall grass and reached the edge of our moat, a hundred-foot-wide slough of thigh-deep floodwater. The murky water was strewn with weed-draped dead-wood. The soldiers were so relieved to be out of the saw they didn't notice the grass where they stood had been freshly scythed. It was so short it barely covered their shoes. The soldiers had nothing to hide behind, not even a twig. More soldiers congregated at the water's edge, staring at our hiding place but seeing nothing of concern. Finally, some officers had chopped their way across and into our gunsights.

"Fire!" Sam Jones shouted. Three hundred rifles blasted and the soldiers reeled in shock. We snatched up our second and third rifles and fired. Our bullets left many on the wet ground as the others stampeded back into the tall grass. We moved back a hundred yards and waited.

An hour passed before we heard orders being shouted and the sounds of many feet tromping through the mud. The soldiers massed just inside the grass and fired a volley that went over our heads. We returned fire and they retreated. Over the next hours we exchanged volleys half a dozen times, but the army never attempted to cross the slough. As dusk approached, our ammunition was nearly gone. Word came that a force of soldiers had finally turned our left flank.

"It is time," said John. "We have punished them severely and our people have had time to get away."

"They can have this little bit of mud," said Wild Cat. "They will need it to bury all their dead soldiers."

We slipped back through the brush to the dugouts lining the shore of Lake Okeechobee and paddled away quietly. By the time the army discovered we were gone we were a mile away.

***

We camped near the headwaters of the Loxahatchee River. A month had passed since we'd faced Taylor's army at Lake Okeechobee. It was a great victory for us, but only fueled Jesup's rage. He once again allied himself with the MacCuaigs and their Creek soldiers. Patrols of slave hunters swarmed through the swamps like a nest of angry snakes. Every day we heard of another barbarity against our people. More people were losing hope. Children suffered from hunger. Our food stores were depleted. We ate koonti bread and palm hearts. We net-fished enough to keep from starving completely.

I was sitting by the fire with Virgil and John when Tohechah, an old Seminole man, walked into camp. He had been with those who had been captured with Osceola.

"Fredrick is dead," said Tohechah, scooping out some thin sofkee.

"What happened?" asked Virgil.

"His wife and children was sold to a man in Georgia. Just the wife and children, not him. He charged Jesup with a hammer, and they shot him dead," said Bascom. "That is what the soldiers do now with the runaway families. They split them up and sell them outside of Florida. They separate any slaves that conspired together. That includes husband and wife. And children."

"Damn him," swore Virgil.

"Jesup said he will cease this practice when John Horse surrenders and brings the Estelusti in. He says now the responsibility for this suffering is on you, as you have shown no Black Seminole can be trusted."

"He puts the responsibility for this pain on me?" said John. "Yes, how dishonorable of me to escape a prison after being captured under a flag of truce."

"That's what he says."

"Now you deliver messages for Jesup?"

"I take no pleasure in it, nor any pay, if that is what you believe. He has made these announcements in the towns and the holding camps several times. He said if he catches Susan and your children or sisters before you surrender yourself, he'll sell them off and you'll never see them again."

***

"What are you thinking so hard on, Virgil?" I asked two days later. He had barely said a word since Tohechah had come to camp.

"About what Tohechah said. I do not want to be blamed for other families being split up. The images of them bawling babies being took away wears hard on my mind."

"That's what he's trying to do," I said. "Corrupt our minds like that. Nobody is responsible for those families being ripped apart but Jesup and Jackson. Certainly not you, just trying to keep your own family from a life of bondage. You cannot surrender. They will hang you."

"I know, just, sometimes it was a whole lot simpler being a slave. Never have to ponder such things. Never had to ponder many things, and the things I could ponder only saddened me. I know they intend to hang me. Maybe that makes my choice to continue fighting or taking my family back to slavery easier. But them others? Forcing a soul to make that choice for his children, slavery or death, is a torture created by Satan himself."

"And Andrew Jackson, I guess. And Jesup."

"The only worry I have is the fate of Naomi and the children."

"Have you heard your daughters speak the Muscogee language? They speak it very well, and better every day. Naomi, too. Your son speaks Muscogee as his first language," I said. "Mother and John are confident they will pass as Estelusti if she has a few more months to work with them."

"I sure hope you're right," said Virgil.

"If not, John says he will get them to the Bahamas once…"

"Once I'm dead? No reason to be shy or sad about it. It has already been decided. Now it's just got to play out," Virgil said. "In the meantime, I got all these memories to savor. I spun my woman around on the ball room floor, under crystal chandeliers and her in her silks and satins. We drank French brandy from dainty cups, and I loved my Naomi in the massa's chamber. I'll always have that."

"It was something, wasn't it?" I said.

"Yes. Not many can say they burned the house where evil abides," said Virgil. "That damned old sugar mill that broke so many of my folks. Burned that old bastard down, too. Yes, I did."

"In spectacular fashion," I said.

***

We waited for battle in the shadowy Loxahatchee swamp southeast of Lake Okeechobee. The soggy land on which we stood was underwater much of the year. It was a place fit only for the creatures that thrived by slithering, swimming or burrowing deep in the mud. Centuries of strong ocean winds had bent the trees in odd and eerie angles. The bare limbs curled like bony fingers beckoning one into the unknown, and the silver Spanish moss draped from them like cobwebs.

This battlefield had not been chosen as our others had. The fight had begun by accident two days before, when a few of our hunters surprised a small patrol which had come ashore from a convoy of army supply boats. More fighters from both sides rushed to join, and the little skirmish soon became a desperate running battle across miles of swamp. The surrounded soldiers finally reached their boats but left behind two of them full of desperately needed food and ammunition. Jesup responded quickly and large units of American reinforcements poured in from all directions.

***

Several hours after sundown we sat around the fire. We no longer had the natural allies that had carried us through so many battles. This time the army would have to cross another saw grass prairie, but this one was less than half the size of the Okeechobee.

"I believe this is my last battle," said John. He rolled his red war club in his hands. It was a gift from Mateo. "I can feel it. In my dreams the shadows come closer each night. It is time. We have no place left to go."

"You can't think that way," I said. "There will be no one to lead us if you are killed."

"Look where my leadership has gotten us so far. On the verge of extinction. If any of our people survive, then they can worry about who will lead."

"No one could have done better," I said. "We are but a few hundred. They are many thousands; with all the rifles and bullets they would ever need."

"Perhaps," said John. "But that does not change our predicament. And that is why I tell you this now. You are ready to lead. Listen to our mother. She is wise. She is excellent counsel. She knows much about the world. But our people will need a young man to lead them. One with fire in his belly. And steel in his spine to face our enemies. Mother is wise, but she cannot lead in battle."

"I don't have those things you said," I replied.

"But you do. Others see it even if you do not," he said. "You will find you have it when it's called for. Do not doubt yourself."

"I think you want to see more than is there," I said.

"Whether I say it or not, it is true. It will only reveal itself when your moment comes. You must always be ready for it," he said. "The freeing of Virgil's family was one such moment. Freeing us from the castle another. Those people's lives depended on you, and you performed magnificently."

"That was different," I said.

"I am not sure why you would think so. You have it in you."

"I do not want the burden," I said.

"Neither do I, never did I, but here we are."

"I don't wish to speak on your death," I said.

"Speaking or not speaking doesn't change it," said John. "I am merely saying I am prepared for it, as you should be. This is where we are. Perhaps war wasn't the way, but those cards have been dealt."

***

Mateo walked into the glow of our campfire. He was no longer Mateo the grandfather, the whittler and arrow maker. A bold stripe of green war paint covered his upper face, to aid his sight in the dark, smoky wilderness. His freshly shaved head, shoulders and chest were yellow, the color of the warrior who has lived his full life and will now fight to the death. He would give no quarter. He would accept none. He walked with vigor. His black eyes had fire in them. His shriveled body was strong and straight. His chin jutted out and his nostrils flared.

Willet followed slightly behind Mateo as he walked across the clearing and greeted me with stout slaps on the shoulders.

"He comes seeking redress for the battle of Horseshoe Bend," she said after Mateo walked on to John.

"He comes seeking a warrior's death," I said. A dagger and red club hung from his beaded belt. A bow and two quivers tightly packed with arrows hung over his shoulder.

"Hooah," she said.

"Hooah," I said.

"Hooah," Mateo said.

***

At sunup I climbed a tree. The soldiers stood in formation and the cannoneers were unlimbering their guns. However, this time, instead of elevating the barrels to bombard us, they kept them level, pointed straight into the tall saw grass that hid our skirmishers. The cannons roared and bucked and billowed smoke. The thick cloud lifted from the guns and our hidden skirmishers came sprinting back toward us, faces full of terror. The cannoneers reloaded and blasted a dozen more volleys of shrapnel, until a wide smoldering path had been cut through saw grass.

The cannons paused and elevated. They roared again. The first cannonballs soared harmlessly overhead but the gunners adjusted quickly. I scurried down my tree and got flat behind it as trees cracked and splintered and the soggy ground shook.

When the cannons went quiet. I went back up the trees. Lines of infantry marched toward us. Behind them, more soldiers dragged sleds through the soft mud. Each sled held a wooden frame containing numerous tubes not much wider than rifle barrels and about twice as long. The soldiers dragged the sleds until they were five hundred yards from us, still safely out of rifle range. Once they stopped, cannoneers loaded the tubes with long narrow rods that had metal canisters attached and heads that were shaped like arrowheads the size of gopher turtles.

"What are they doing?" asked Virgil.

"They're pulling up sleds filled with some kind of gun with a lot of long skinny barrels, with some kind of spears or harpoons or something in them," I shouted down.

"Congreves. The infernal screaming rockets, those bloody bastards," said Yancy. "They can't hit a target ten paces away, but they'll shoot clean through a bystander and leave a smoking hole where his entrails used to be. They'll make us deaf, and possibly set the brush afire if it ain't too wet."

"What are we supposed to do?"

"Dig some holes, for starters," Yancy yelled.

The rockets whistled and shrieked and soared high in the air before plummeting back to earth, jerking and twitching and spitting fire and sparks. The muzzle-loading many-barreled guns could be reloaded as fast as a rifle and the sky filled with long sparkling tails, some shooting up and some whistling and spasming back down at us. Cannons joined the flaming spears. The earth trembled and shook. Trees ripped apart and arm-length splinters hurled through the shadows. Blasts of fire and flash rocked the swamp. Shadows in the smoke, wounded men staggered through the burning bushes, their bodies pierced by wooden spikes.

Finally, the cannons and rockets stopped. Damp brush smoldered and dying fires crackled and sputtered. While we had been face down in the mud, deafened and blinded by the barrage, the soldiers had crossed the prairie. They stayed massed inside the tall grass, not exposing themselves as earlier soldiers had done.

***

The American bugle blew charge. Soldiers and Creeks charged into the slough until the frontline bogged down in the jumbled deadwood, submerged roots and sucking mud. The second and third lines blindly rushed in until they collided with the floundering first line.

Most carried more than one gun. We held our fire until the slough could hold no more enemy. Our bullets ripped through them and when the smoke cleared, bodies draped the gray logs and bobbed face down in the water. Instead of retreating, the men behind the carnage surged forward. Screaming Creeks and bearded men with long bayonets slogged through the mud in waves. Pushing dead and wounded out of the way, they charged up the bank and bulled their way deep into the thicket. Shotguns blasted away the brush and the Indians hacked their way toward us.

I retreated back into the brush and reloaded. A Creek war ax seemed to float above the palmetto bush in front of me. I aimed ten inches below the handle. There was a scream of pain, burst of red mist and the tomahawk spun through the air. I heard running footsteps and brush breaking. I fired again. A bare-chested, war-painted Creek collapsed forward, dead but still on his feet.

I crawled behind a tree and left him there, draped in hanging vines like a scarecrow. A bayonet probed through a hedge wall in front of me. I scurried backward through the thicket like a crab, listening to enemy shouts and footsteps. I heard grunts and curses, the heavy blows of stone war club heads and the shattering of bones. I heard the ting of clashing sword blades and bayonets and the boom of pistols. I caught glimpses of blue uniforms and white plumes. Thick smoke lingered. Ash had fallen from the fires. Everything was gray except the red blood that dripped and sprayed from every bush.

I fought when I had to and hid when I could. My face bled, my knuckles were broken, and my head throbbed. I'd been hit in it, first by a tree limb, then a club and fist and finally a gun butt. I had lost John and the others. I turned and ran.

***

I finally reached the Loxahatchee. The air coming off the river was clean, and I sucked it in. I was silent except for the sounds of pain. The birds had left us to our destruction. Their perches had been blasted apart by cannon balls and set on fire by rockets. Willet and John were there. Willet was bloody and weeping.

"Where are the others?" I asked.

"Virgil and Yancy have taken our powder and lead across the river. They are unhurt. Hooah," he said.

"Hooah," I said. "Where is Mateo?"

"He died a warrior's death. He fought bravely and killed an enemy in his last battle. It was as he wanted it."

"I'm sad for you," I said.

"He died standing up, as he wished," Willet said. "There is no need for sadness."

"Hooah," I said. "Then why do you weep?"

"We'll speak on it later," she said. "We must rest now and get ready for the soldiers again. Hooah."

In the morning we waited at the ford. This was our final moat. At midmorning, the first soldiers came out of the woods. Half a dozen soldiers were testing the water's depth when our first rifles fired. Two soldiers fell backward into the water and were carried away as the others scrambled back onto shore. We fired a few more shots and all the soldiers ran for the trees. For the next hour no one else approached the river.

***

"They are not retreating," I said after I came down from my pine-top perch. Darkness was almost complete. "There are many thousands camped in the trees."

"Now don't start singing your dismal ditty just yet," said Yancy, lighting a cigar. "They have the numbers, aye, but we have the lions."

"Our lions are pretty well shot up," John said. "And they have those rockets."

"Too wet to do any good here, even if they could drag them through the swamp to get close enough."

"What is that noise?" asked Virgil. A slight breeze carried the noise of the soldiers to us through the heavy river fog. It had been a hot day for the season, but it cooled quickly. River fog rolled in heavy.

"Bagpipes, those cruel, merciless fiends," said Yancy.

"It sounds like demons screeching bloody murder," said Virgil with a slight tremor in his voice. "I don't need to be hearing that all night."

"More like hogs squealing as they're butchered," said Yancy. "I underestimated the depravity of those foul heathens. One ain't supposed to be tortured until after the battle."

"It's some unsettling," said Virgil.

"Yes, that is why they do it. Or simply to be annoying as hell. But the pipes have been used to unnerve the enemy since ancient times, to announce the Barbarian hordes was coming through," said Yancy. "Though I had never given that idea credence, I'm reconsidering. Coming through the fog, it's down-right eerie."

"It will be rough to listen to all night," said Wild Cat.

"A wee bit of pirate juice might make the pipes less irritating," said Yancy, pulling out his beaten-up old canteen. He'd had it since his early days in the British Marines. He had freshened the paint of Calico Jack's smiling skull.

"I will," said John, sitting up.

"The fiercest bunch I've ever fought beside," bellowed Yancy. "Hooah!"

"Hooah," grunted John and Wild Cat, clicking their cups and drinking them down.

I took a big gulp knowing I'd hate the burn and the taste. Within seconds I felt the numbing warmth and held my cup out for more. The fear and shock seemed to drift off a little. I poured some more in my cup.

"Not too much, now," he said. "Ya don't want to be laying here drooling and all owl-eyed staring at a flock of moons if the damned slavers try to cross. That was the downfall of many a brave buccaneer, including Jack's lads, ultimately."

"That was almighty something," said Virgil.

"The space between life and death, that's where we are the most alive," said Yancy to Virgil, clicking his tin cup. "And now to savor the wonders of being alive."

"We lost many men. We lost Mateo," said Virgil.

"Aye, we did," said Yancy. "Ask the lass how she feels about it."

"I am sad for me. Not for him. He died with valor, as he wanted," said Willet. "Remember his last moments as heroic. Remember his life. Do not mourn his death."

"It still makes me sad," said Virgil.

"Few ever know this moment," said Yancy. "Are you more alive now, when you risk death, or when you was bent under a hot sun but got your slops at night?"

"After what we just went through, I reckon I'm a sight livelier than most. I feel like I been teetering between them two for way too long," said Virgil.

"That's a fact, lad. There is a certain fatigue that comes with it," said Yancy.

"I would prefer not to go just yet," said Virgil. "I am just learning what this world holds. And I sure would not want none of you killed. You are my family. My closest friends I ever had in my life."

"It is tragic that the closest friendships, the tightest bonds, are forged at times like these," said Yancy. "But they carry on past mortality, if that is cut short. Battle brings the most euphoric of feelings, creates the closest intimacies of humanity. 'Tis a genuine pity so much suffering is attached with it."

"Seems suffering is attached to everything," said Virgil.

"Fear not death for the hour of your doom is set and none may escape it," said Yancy, filling and raising his cup. "To Valhalla."

"What's Valhalla?" asked Virgil.

"The glorious place where valiant Vikings go when honorably killed in battle," said John.

"We ain't Vikings," said Virgil. "Is we?"

"Who says we ain't? If the Creeks can play bagpipes, we can be Vikings. I see no reason we can't. I reckon we all got a wee bit of Ragnar Lodbrok in us when we are pushed into a corner. Us that's here anyway," said Yancy, pinching a drop of rum from his beard, licking his fingers. "This time tomorrow, we'll be drinking from the skulls of our enemies."

"You all go on ahead," said Virgil. "This here little cup is fine with me."

"Suit yourself," said Yancy. "I might go snatch me one now. Do you suppose those fellows bobbing in the mud back there would mind us removing their beans and enjoying a toast?"

"You go ask them. I'll stay put. I don't reckon my Naomi would care too much for cleaning that type vessel anyway," said Virgil.

"Fair point," said Yancy. "Truth be told, I've been told the Vikings weren't known for their sanitation. But they did scare the bejesus out of their enemies."

"My father killed enemies and died standing in his last battle. He is in Valhalla now with this Ragnar person. He always believed he would go to such a place," said Willet.

"Did he now?"

"Yes, with my mother. And his earlier wives. And he hoped for a few young maidens," Willet said. "I think that's the only reason he wanted to kill some Creeks so bad. To get a crack at some young wives."

"That buzzard," laughed Yancy, coughing, spitting out his drink.

"See, his spirit already outlives him and brings joy to his people."

***

I awoke at dawn with Willet tightly in my arms. Throughout the night we dozed, ate what we had and said little, too exhausted and too stunned by what we'd seen and done. We were both filthy, caked with mud and blood and black powder. Blood soaked the front of her ripped shirt, but she was not badly wounded. We jerked upright when we heard the shouting. I crept closer to the river and peered through grass.

"Get your damned men across that water!" General Jesup bellowed. He and several horseback officers were at the water's edge.

"General, I will not. Not without artillery. It's suicide," the militia officer beside him loudly protested.

"I will have you court-martialed," thundered Jesup. His face was full of red rage, and he spun his horse in circles, yanking at the reins.

"Have right at it," yelled the other men. "I'm a volunteer. My men are volunteers. We didn't volunteer for gratuitous dying, caused by a general with his head corkscrewed up his bunghole."

Jesup spurred his horse a few lengths into the river. He pointed his sword at us, posed like one of General Clinch's paintings. He stayed that way until someone shot him in the face. The bullet grazed Jesup's cheek and sent his eyeglasses twirling through a sunbeam. The horse bolted and Jesup cartwheeled off, landing on his face in the muddy water.

We howled with laughter as he wallowed around, cursing and spitting, screaming for his glasses. The whole cadre of officers sprang off their horses and ran to save Jesup, but one, and then all, slipped and fell in the attempt. We were laughing too hard at the panicked men falling over each other to shoot them. Jesup cursed and shook his fist at us as they dragged him back up the bank. Then our men shot his horse and the ambitious officer still searching through the weeds for Jesup's glasses.

***

The fog would not leave. It hung inside the sharp turns of the twisting river, held in place by the thick tree canopy. Gunshots broke the silence, but they did not come from across the river.

"They are behind us," said John. We listened as the shots grew in number and frequency.

"What shall we do?" I asked. No sooner had I spoken than a Seminole warrior staggered out of the brush and crumpled to the ground at our feet. Blood came from a bullet wound in his side.

"Soldiers! Soldiers! Creeks!" he gasped, eyes rolling around in his head. More blood leaked from his ear.

"How many?" asked John.

"Hundreds. Too many. We are overrun," the man panted. "They crossed far down the river and came in behind us."

"We are flanked brothers," shouted John to the men who had quickly gathered. "Follow me to the fight."

We sprinted down the trail passing more wounded Seminole dragging themselves away from the fight. We ran on until we reached a shallow lake that was now just a sunken field of mud and weedy, little ponds. The dome of a hammock rose above the fog a short distance away.

"Make a line here," John shouted.

We spread out and waited. Bagpipes keened through the cold, gray gloom. Gun shots came closer. A few musket balls clipped tree branches far above us. The first shouts of Creeks on the hunt reached us.

Shadowy figures moved in the fog like ghosts. Then bits of fleeting color floated in the drifting mist. War paint of red and black and yellow. Patches of pale blue army coats and white cross belts. The twinkle of a dangling feather earring. A bobbing toorie. An egret plume floating.

Laughing Boy's face appeared a stone's throw away. Fierce stripes of black and red showcased his wolfish sneer. Soldiers, MacCuaigs and Creek militia waded through the pond behind him.

"The longer we wait, the odds get longer," said Virgil to John.

"Well said, my dear friend," said John. "Hooah!"

"Go home, Pete! Please!" Virgil whispered to me, then bellowed "Hoooooah!"

Before I realized what was happening Virgil and John had charged the MacCuaigs. I followed them into the fog. Side by side they charged across the shallow water, their churning legs kicking up a wave. They fired as they ran, and their roars and huffs and growls sounded like a hurricane. They launched off a black log and landed in the swarm of MacCauigs with a clash like thunder and lightning and rolled through the red-streaked muck like an unbolted waterwheel.

I looked for a shot, but they were all too entangled. John pulled away to parry a bayonet when Carson McGillivray cracked his skull from behind with a war club. John fell face first into the water.

"It's John Horse! I want him alive!" shouted Laughing Boy. Creeks grabbed him by his feet and pulled him through the muck toward Laughing Boy. I hit McGillivray with a load of buck and ball and nearly blew him in half. I emptied my second barrel into a another MacCuaig just as Virgil hurled himself into the men pulling John away.

The MacCuaigs dropped John and surrounded Virgil. He brandished an ax in his left hand and swung a war club with his right. The Creeks stayed back like hounds, darting in as he swung at another of their pack.

I lurched toward them, but a bald-headed MacCuaig shot up out of the mud and tackled me. Blood gushed from an empty eye socket as he sank his teeth into my leg. We wallowed in a foot of muddy water as I clubbed him with my pistol. His jaws were locked onto me like a fighting dog. I pounded him with my fist and tried to kick free, but his grip was unnaturally strong. His bite was vicious. His bleeding socket slopped all over me as I gouged at his other eye and ripped off his lip. I found a rock under the mud and smashed his skull with it. Finally, his bite relaxed. I pulled my legs free and rolled over.

Spitting out mud, I crawled toward Virgil.

A Creek dove at his legs but Virgil's long club connected with the side of the man's head. More attacks darted in. Virgil swung but he couldn't get them all. They piled on around his legs, slipping and sliding off, crawling over each other and up Virgil's back. He hammered at them with his red war club until it shattered. Injured MacCuaigs fell but more leapt until the whole tower of them collapsed, churning blood-streaked brown water into gruel.

Virgil rolled free and stood as Laughing Boy charged, swinging his ax. Virgil threw his left arm up and blocked Laughing Boy's ax stroke, then drove the splintered club shaft through Laughing Boy's left eye.

A Creek in the brush fired. Virgil slapped the wound in his side like a bee sting. Another musket ball hit him, and he staggered backward, jerking the splinter out of Laughing Boy's face with the eye still attached. More guns fired and Virgil fell backward, still waving Laughing Boy's eye on the spike.

Creek ran toward Virgil to finish him but guns from behind me knocked two down and sent the rest to join those taking Laughing Boy away. I looked around and saw that half a hundred of our warriors had arrived. Yancy and Willet dragged John out of the mud and pounded on his back until brown water gushed out his mouth and he was wracked by violent coughs.

I slid through the muck to Virgil. A dozen dead men were mired in the mud or bobbing in bloody water around him.

"Well, I guess this is it," said Virgil, rubbing his hands over the leaking holes in his chest.

"You sure took a bunch of them with you," I said.

"I reckon that golden chariot be here in a minute to set me free forever. Tell Naomi and them girls I'll be waiting for them up there, in the Promised Land. I won't take up with no Valkyries. I'll be looking for you too, brother."

"I got things to do first."

"Yep. Tend to my little ones," said Virgil. "Keep 'em safe. Promise me that."

"I promise you," I said.

"I had me a taste of freedom anyhow, and it sure was fine. That apple was sweet," said Virgil. "Some real high living. Stormed a castle and loved my wife in the massa's bed. Ain't that something?"

"I was happy to share it with you," I said. "You've been a good friend."

"It's just a new thing, is all. Goodbye, Pete."

Chapter Twelve

THE END
JANUARY 1838

When the sun went down, we gathered our wounded and limped toward the river. I saw my friends laid out awaiting burial. Some were boys I had grown up with. Others were the older men who had taught us how to hunt and fish and told us stories. Fathers and brothers and sons sat in sadness and shock. We piled our guns onto the small raft and floated them across the Loxahatchee.

We were in ruin. Our losses had been severe, far worse than any other battle. Nearly forty of our warriors had been killed, and more than three times that were now disabled by wounds. Our camp was filled with wounded men on pallets of deer skins and palm leaves. Day and night our widows wept and boiled medicine pots and strong alligator broth.

Children wandered around wide-eyed, unsure of what they were seeing. Many were now orphans. There were few games of tag and no laughter.

Our cattle herds were gone. Alligators were butchered, the bones thrown in the pots to make a strong, fortifying heavy broth. I walked on a crutch Yancy had made for me, with my knee wrapped tight in sapwood and rawhide. Mother and Susan sat with Naomi as she sobbed quietly. Willet had quickly gathered up the children and taken them into the woods at the news of Virgil's death.

"He's resting in a peaceful place that gets good sun," said John. "He is beyond the reach of prowling Creeks forever. He is away from any land that could someday be plowed up for cane field. Hidden away, as our island in the Cove is. Flowers will grow there in the spring."

"Good. That is good," said Naomi. "I'd like to go visit him when we can, but it sounds fine. As long as he ain't gonna be on plantation land. At least there's that. He's out there free. That's just how I'm going to look at it."

That may have been how she looked at it, but she wept for a week. More bad news came quickly. Osceola had died in prison. Even in our miserable state we were all saddened. The sadness did not come from his death, which was long expected, but that he, our greatest fighting spirit, had succumbed in a dirty prison cell and not gloriously in battle. Now there was no one that could unite all the Seminole and Estelusti. Not that it greatly mattered. There were few Estelusti and Seminole to unite.

"I am so tired, Peter. So very tired," said Mother. She had been neglecting herself to care for others. Her cheeks were drawn, and her eyes had pain in them. Her hair had lost its luster, it was nappy and sometimes had bits of leaves or a briar in it. A streak of gray was above her left temple. There was a barely noticeable tremor in her fingers and voice.

"It has been hard," I said.

"Yes, I can see it on you also. You are quieter. Tougher. Harder. Your eyes are different," she said.

"I have seen much I did not wish to see. Done much I never wished to do. I thought I did. I was mistaken."

"Yes. Exactly. The ugliness and suffering. You're a man now. It is a proud moment in a mother's life, but a worrisome one as well. There are so many ways to become a man other than through war," she said. "I wish you'd been given that choice."

"John says we are lucky. That few men get to test themselves as we have. That few men have the honor of fighting for such a cause as ours, to fight for our people."

"Perhaps he's right. Perhaps he's not," she said. "But sometimes I miss my gentle boy."

"Am I not gentle with my sisters and the little ones?"

"No, you are very gentle with the children, perhaps even more so than before. Though I can see it is different now. Before it was enjoyment. Now I see worry when you play with them. That you understand how precious they are, and how quickly they can be taken," she said. "You always have one eye looking for danger. That is what I see in your eyes. I just see that some of the joy in the small pleasures in life has left your eyes. I hope it will return one day. You no longer look at things for the wonder they bring," she said. "Now you look at things to see if they bring death. And it's clear you can bring death, too."

"That's what's required of me," I said. "I'm not a frivolous child."

"I know this," she said. "I also must ask, have you considered what might happen if Willet becomes with child?"

"You know Willet. The only thing growing in her belly is the fire to do battle against the MacCuaigs."

"Tell her she cannot fight her best if her belly is large with child, or nursing a young one," mother said.

"She knows."

"Remind her. This is no time to raise a child, you are barely much more than children yourself."

"When will it be a good time to raise a child?"

"I do not know."

***

A week later Germaine unexpectedly arrived with two dugouts loaded with sacks of potatoes and barrels of bacon, dried fish and cornmeal. He'd also brought a few kegs of beer and a sack of salt. There were stacks of thick blankets and newspapers.

"This is most gracious," said John as Germaine walked toward us. "You took a huge risk. You brought so much; we may not have enough gold on hand."

"There was no risk," said Germaine. "I want no gold. Jesup sent me. He wants a parley."

"You are Jesup's envoy now? You bring us food to fatten us so we will go to slaughter like meek lambs?" John snarled, fists balling up and chest heaving.

"You can fill those children's bellies whether you come talk or not," said Germaine calmly. "Do not swell up on me, John. I am not your enemy."

John deflated, looking down, embarrassed.

"He wants to send an officer to you. Hitchcock. He is at my camp and will come to you. I will bring him alone. He will be blindfolded, and he will allow himself to be blindfolded the entire time if you want."

"He will be blindfolded?"

"Yes. I will ensure the blindfold stays in place. He will not discover your location. Captain Hitchcock is a very brave man," said Germaine. "Perhaps you should hear what he has to say."

"I respect that. I will see him," said John.

***

The following day Germaine returned with Captain Ethan Alan Hitchcock.

"Have you come to surrender?" asked John.

"No. General Jesup wants a parley."

"I would never trust him."

"John, please listen to me. Your brother Pete knows me well. He knows I've always attempted to treat the Estelusti fairly," Hitchcock said. "I know you lost many fighters at the Loxahatchee and that your people are very hungry."

"They would not be if you didn't burn our crops and eat our cattle."

"That's war, and I'm here to tell you, face to face, man to man, that General Jesup intends to further unleash every means of war and cruelty against you. No warning. No quarter. Jesup considers himself a man of deep honor. He felt he did everything in his power to treat you fairly and in return you made him look foolish. Now you face a horrible retribution."

"Your generals have needed little help from me to look foolish," said John. "That he intends further barbarism is hardly a surprise. None of this gives me reason to trust him."

"He says if you go to the fort, he will send some of his officers to be held as hostages until the parley is over. As a guarantee against treachery."

"You, yourself, will be a hostage? I do not want cowards or incompetents he wouldn't mind losing."

"I'll come. I'll be damn proud to come if it will help end this," said Hitchcock. "You can choose the hostages, any other than Jesup himself I suppose."

"Is that so?"

"It is. From my heart, John, my officers and I would like nothing more than to end this fight. We would like to stop and just walk away. No soldiers want to be here," said Hitchcock. "Many more of us fall to your swamp diseases than to your bullets. The soldiers wonder what the point is, fighting for land that can't be lived on, against a foe that can't be seen. You're a formidable foe, likely unbeatable in this terrain."

"Perhaps the Great White Father will give me a medal. What about you, Captain? How can you get more medals on your chests if you walk away?"

"The medals will be damned few for conquering what Washington thinks is nothing but a handful of savages in a jungle. Scott and Gaines have seen to that. They have soured public opinion against us for being down here. The leaders in Washington have grown weary of fighting this war. This war is expensive," said Hitchcock.

"If it's so expensive, why doesn't the government simply stop?" said John. "Make up some stories, cover some generals in medals. Declare victory and walk away? Take those that want to go west and leave the others of us alone."

"You seem to know quite well how that works. Your friend Yancy, I assume?"

"Where else? He is the wisest sense maker among the Seminole and Estelusti, but some chiefs shun him because of his skin. I think he understands you."

"Probably. He's been a warrior for a long time, and our men respect him as much as they hate him," said Hitchcock. "Truth is, there's a lot of men in our army who'd like to pin a medal on him for shooting Scott's wine glass. I may or may not be one of them."

"He could have killed him."

"I'm glad he didn't. Mostly because of blazing vengeance that would have been taken upon you. Not an Indian would have been left alive."

"He knew that."

"Scott will have a long time living that down. The other way he would have died a hero."

"That's what Yancy said."

"Anyway, back to what we were talking about. The war has gotten too big to just walk away from. Any leniency now would make us look weak. It would be seen as a defeat. It would encourage other tribes and slaves all over the continent to rise up. All the money spent so far would be wasted."

"That would please me," said John.

"I'm sure it would," said Hitchcock.

"The Seminole are using you, just as you are using them. But neither of you can win, or even survive if you continue. We are too many, too powerful. The Seminole are no concern of yours. They were not Estelusti. Think of your own first," said Hitchcock. "I have applied to be your agent in Oklahoma, to see you are treated fairly, and to the terms of any agreement."

"Free people don't need agents."

"I'm well aware, and that's why I volunteered for the position. The process would be gradual, over time. That is the best I can do. But you could live and prepare your children."

"Tell me, Captain. What further groveling would you have me do to receive this freedom you would permit me?" asked John. "Gradual, over time, patient. That is not freedom. You must understand liberty is equally as precious to a black man as it is to a white one, and bondage as equally intolerable to the one as it is to the other," said John. "Do you know who said that?"

"Yes, I do," said Hitchcock. "Lemuel Haynes."

"Yes. A free black man who fought for the Americans against the British in your war for freedom, your Revolutionary War. This is our Revolutionary War," said John. "That is why."

"Quite noble. But impractical. You are quite few, and we have thousands."

"I believe the same was said of your war for freedom from the British," said John. "Give me liberty or give me death. Are you aware of who said that?"

"I'm aware," said Hitchcock.

"Very well then," said John. "There you have it. We are no different. We believe the same things. We want the same things. We are not different men."

"I agree with you, John," Hitchcock said. "It has won me few friends."

"I will come in," said John, after sitting quietly for a few seconds. "However, as you can see, my injuries will prevent any travel for a while. I will send word when I can get around. It will not be long."

"We will give you some time. Seven days."

"Seven days is enough."

***

Zachary Taylor and Jesup sat across the table from John. There was no chess board. Taylor, an unkempt little man, stared at John with a fury. The American newspapers had turned him into a hero. They declared Taylor had achieved a great victory at the Okeechobee, because we paddled away after we had run out of bullets from shooting so many of their soldiers. Everyone in that tent knew the truth.

"John, you have fought well. You have earned my respect. The respect of many," said Jesup. "Now let's stop the killing."

"Have I earned my freedom?" asked John.

"You've earned the right to live a peaceful life," said Jesup. "You have fought tenaciously and honorably, but your people have suffered and endured great hardship."

"As the man who inflicted those hardships, I guess you would know," said John.

"The Seminole are beaten. The vast majority are on their way west or are already there. Osceola died in a white man's prison. Micanopy, King Philip, Coa Hadjo, Jumper have all been captured or surrendered. Most of the remaining Seminole chiefs want peace. What is the point?"

"The same point it was two years ago."

"You are the last Estelusti chief in the field. Do you want to be the last chief of your people? Do you want to see your people annihilated? Because that's where this is headed. You are on the brink."

"Tell me what you offer, and we will ponder it," said John. "We will think."

"The time for thinking has also passed. There is nothing more to think about. This army will pursue you until every Indian, every Estelusti, every maroon and escaped slave is either dead or in Indian Territory. That means all Negroes will be dead or enslaved," said Jesup. "It is time to move on and be done with it."

"So, what exactly are your terms? What riches do you offer me?"

"Listen to me, John. I don't have to accept any terms of surrender from slaves in revolt, or provide them aid and assistance. Do you understand what I'm saying? I could march ten thousand men in here under a black flag, and never have to answer a question about it."

"Conversations with men who say, 'I could kill you but won't' are always so pleasant," said John.

"I'm trying to save your life. You are a proud people. John, you are a proud man. I understand that, but your women and children are hungry. It is best this way. The Black Seminole will be under the protection of the United States Army."

"We no longer wish to be under anyone's protection," said John. "We wish to be free."

"I understand that also, John. You have been quite clear on that point. But the best I can do is offer you protection for the Black Seminole. You won't answer to the Seminole, nor directly to the Creek. Creek law will still apply, but I will order my men to enforce protection for your people. There will be an agent appointed to you."

"Just so easy like that suddenly?"

"Not easily and not suddenly," said Jesup. "Practicality and heated debate. It's tenuous. Your exact legal status is yet to be determined permanently, but this is great progress. There are many factors involved, what with all the planters making legal claims of ownership, demanding so many court hearings. We've had to bring in special judges. There are compensations to be determined. However, the number of people sympathetic to your plight is growing. You have advocates working fiercely on your behalf in Washington. It just takes time. Powerful people are reluctant, worried that they might get hurt politically."

"And we can choose our land, away from the Creek and their predations?"

"No, not presently. You will live on the land already designated, at least for the time being, while other arrangements are worked out. I cannot create land for you from the air," said Jesup. "However, no Estelusti will be anyone's property or bondsman."

"Certainly," said John. "This could be worked out while you sit in comfort of your estate, while we pick the cotton on Creek plantations in Oklahoma. The Creek do not honor white man's law. They honor only their tribal law, which claims dominion over the Seminole. We don't have the same risk in this game, you and me. They do not prey on your children."

"No, we don't bear the same risks, John. All I can give you is my word. I've learned a great deal from you and the Estelusti. You have earned my best efforts on your behalf. I mean that sincerely."

"And if we sign your paper, you will go from fighting with the Creeks against us, to protecting us from them?"

"Yes."

"Because the Great White Father loves his black Indian children so much? And now would take us as an ally? To feed and protect? Why would you do that? The same men who come to make war on us?"

"To bring peace."

"There was peace before you came," said John. "Why can't the new Great White Father declare the Estelusti a sovereign nation? Leave us to be free to forge our own way, whatever and wherever that may be."

"Even if that should ever come to pass, you could never be strong enough alone to defend yourselves. You would always need our protection, from Creek, or some of the wild tribes in the West. We can provide substantial financial incentives. Very generous annuities until you get your own land. I can see to it that yours is especially generous, given the influence you have. At this point, I'd just like to save your life."

***

"Hooah," John shouted when Wild Cat appeared in camp. As they slapped each other's backs there was happiness in their voices but tiredness in their bodies. Even Wild Cat was worn down and gaunt. He still had his fire, but some of the arrogance and swagger had been taken out of him. He hobbled as we walked to the sofkee pot. It was watery and there was little meat in it.

"I have news," Wild Cat said. "Jesup told the chiefs that they might be allowed to stay in Florida if they promise to stay in the swamps below Lake Okeechobee. However, first they all must gather at his new camp to be registered with the Government, where they will be fed and sheltered until all are accounted for. They must relinquish all the Negroes in Florida, free and slave.

"All Negroes?"

"Yes. The Seminole miccos would be paid generously for the Estelusti they claim title to, but from this day forward, any Negro, or Seminole found harboring one, will be executed on the spot. No appeals," said Wild Cat. "Verified Estelusti can remain with their Seminole owners, but must surrender immediately. Jesup has sent his proposal to Washington. His officers are also in support of his proposal."

"Is that so? He has a very different proposal ready on behalf of the Estelusti," said John. "And what do the Seminole chiefs say?"

"Most are already at the camp. That they are tired of fighting. They are now willing to accept just about any peace. Hundreds of Seminoles have already moved to a camp near the fort while they all await word. They have lost too much, there are too many hardships. They told him they would emigrate if they had to, but they begged to be allowed to remain," said Wild Cat. "His offer of peace and food was good for anyone that comes to the camp in the next ten days. The people are hungry. The food at the fort is plentiful and good."

"And the Chiefs agree, knowing Jesup's record of deceit and treachery?" asked John.

"At this point, I do not think they care. It wouldn't change anything," said Wild Cat.

"No, probably not," said John.

"And what do you do?" asked John.

"Hooah," grinned Wild Cat. "I live a warrior's life and I will die a warrior's death. And you, brother?"

"I do not know," said John. "For me, I would fight and die. For these children, scared and hungry, I cannot say."

"I'm sure he would welcome you at the camp," said Wild Cat. "But take a good look around before you go. It will be the last time you see your Florida homeland."

***

Jesup built a fort alongside the Loxahatchee River he named Fort Jupiter. Soon more than five hundred Seminole and Estelusti camped outside it. From treetops across the river, we watched. The days passed without incident. Indians and soldiers relaxed and settled into a casual and friendly routine. Shelters and chickees went up. The Seminole women sewed bright shirts and dresses from new reams of cloth. Cattle herds were tended. Cook fires burned and the pots were full and simmering. Children played games. Crowds of spectators watched rowdy stick ball matches between soldiers and Seminoles. Ceremonial councils, dances and mingles were held. Seminole men and their wives showed up in their newly stitched clothing, displaying the new baubles gifted from Jesup. Army bands played at the soirées and steers and hogs basted over barbecue pits. Handsome young soldiers in dress uniforms and curious young Indian maidens tossed come hither looks back and forth.

"What do you think?" I asked Yancy.

"I think I see a pig being fattened for slaughter," said Yancy. "They're sure free with the whiskey."

***

"Abraham comes," said a messenger. Weeks had passed with no word from Washington. The inmates at Fort Jupiter did not seem to mind. They ate well and slept in dry beds.

"What does that old turncoat want?"

"To talk to you. He says he has an urgent message but must tell you personally."

"I will go to him. He will not enter any camp I am in."

"Hello friend," said Abraham when we met him on the path a mile or so from camp.

"You are not my friend," said John. "You betrayed us."

"I made the best deal for myself, and my people," said Abraham. "So should you. You cannot win. You will likely die, taking our people with you. It is time. That is all there is to it."

"Is that the news you bring?" said John. "That's hardly news."

"No, I come to tell you all the people at the camp are now prisoners. Washington President Van Buren sided with the planters," said Abraham. "Jesup threw a big party. Barrels and barrels of whiskey. Our men drank until they were stuporous. Four hundred soldiers charged into the camp at dawn and overpowered us without a struggle. Many of the people were on ships going across the bay before they'd sobered up. The plantation Negroes amongst them are in chains. Six hundred people were captured."

"I'm sure no struggle came from you," said John. "You should have died fighting before bringing us word of such treachery."

"You cannot even feed your children. The children in the camp grow fat and healthy. Tell me again who is without honor."

John gasped at the deep cut of those words but didn't deny them.

"He wants you to come to a parley," Abraham said. "You and Alligator. Hitchcock and some officers stand ready to come here as hostages."

John spat at Abraham's feet.

"Then he says to tell you this. He broke no promises. He did his best to convince Washington to find other land for the Estelusti, and to allow the Seminole to remain in Florida. Washington refused."

"Bah. I do not want to listen to you. He got those people drunk and captured them. No doubt you played a part."

"The general says whatever your thoughts, he does not regret his decision. He said he wants you to understand that if he had given the people in the camp the opportunity, many would have fled to the swamps. Fighting would have started again. More people would have died. There is no need for that when the end is inevitable."

***

"I have broken my vow to live with honor. I have broken myself," sobbed John that night. "All our blood was wasted, only to bring our people to this humiliation, to being vanquished from our land and enslaved. It would be better if I had died."

"Nonsense," said Mother.

"Abraham was right. I cannot protect my family. The weight I carry is too much."

"Then it would be too much for any man," she said. "You are the best man among us. A better man than any that faced us. You have not failed. No one could succeed against those odds."

"I should have died as Mateo," John cried. "As Virgil did. With honor, on the battlefield."

"Put that behind you," said Mother. "I only want to keep my family alive and together. Do you believe your death would make things better? Look at the sadness on the faces of Virgil's daughters. Is that what you wish for your children?"

"I don't wish my children to ever look at my face in shame."

"Why should they? This is not dishonor. It is the cause, and the fight for the cause, that makes it worthwhile, right and just. Not winning or losing."

"Thank you, Mother. You lie so beautifully. But those words taste different on the tongue when it is my own battle," said John. "Very bitter."

"Do not use my father's death either, in your self-pity," said Willet. "He lived a long, full life. He gave me all he had to give. He gave his people all he had to give. You have much life left to live. Deeds you are yet called to do. Obligations you have made. You have much left to give your children. Our people need your strength now more than ever, not this."

John jerked at that.

"We need to see to the future of our people, not our gravestone," said Willet. "Do not be the chief of defeat. Be the chief that leads us in a new land, the wise man who rebuilds our people ever stronger. Would not that be better than martyrdom in a lost cause? You have done your job, my brother."

"Virgil was fighting for freedom. He did not die so we would meekly offer ourselves up," said John.

"My proud, noble son," Mother said. "Virgil fought for his children, not an ideal. That is the great reality when it gets down to it. All the other sounds wonderful, but at what price? People suffer worse because of this fight. As situations change, the objectives must change, John. Every commander knows that. When all the choices are poor, you are not standing up for what is right or an ideal any longer. You are simply picking one poor choice over another. It is not fair. But it is reality."

"But why do you say this to me now? You have always told me slavery is worse than death. If survival means enslavement, I will not choose it," said John. "We cannot shy from sacrifice."

"I know you want to save our people, but you are only a man, not a savior. Do not mistake the two. No man is a savior. You cannot do the impossible," said Mother. "Beware it is not your pride guiding you."

"It is not my pride, but I cannot meekly submit to enslavement. Inevitable defeat does not alter that," snapped John, sadness replaced by irritation in his voice. "It angers me to hear you say those words."

"I expected it might. Yet, the words are spoken. I cannot take them back. Nor do I want to. Given your reaction, it seems wise that I spoke them. I do not want it to be my regret that I raised such a fierce and resolute son, but obstinacy becomes a detriment. There are many lives at stake here. I ask you to really think about why you are doing what you do. Your own family. Your tribe. Battle Jesup to keep his word to us with every breath you take. Don't take the last breath here."

"What say you, papa?" John said to Yancy after a long, simmering silence.

"As a hot-blooded warrior in the field I've never bent a knee to any man, nor would I ever. As the fatherly figure in your life, though admittedly lacking the wisdom I wish, I'd like you to stop. Martyrs make wondrous stories, but those stories rarely delve into the tragic thereafters of the people left behind. This battle can no longer be won with rifles, but perhaps in the courts," said Yancy. "Consider it changing battlefields. Adjusting our strategies."

"Speaking to my fatherly figure, it sounds like you and my motherly figure have connived on concocting the most soothing of lies," said John. "What is your advice as a military man?"

"I take orders. I have loyalty. You are the commander. You are the leader of the Estelusti. I'm fighting if there's a fight to be had."

"No one chose me."

"Not to be overly dramatic, but the moment chose you. The people believe in you, as I do. By vote or de facto, you are the leader," said Yancy. "You can't shy away from it now, not when your people need you most. Getting yourself killed could be seen as shying from it. There is no shame to be seen anywhere in it. Mighty armies have surrendered under far less desperate odds. Those damned Americans have defeated the Brits twice, who up until fifty short years ago had the mightiest military on Earth. That is when they were just bratty colonies. Now America is a powerful, rich nation. They will keep sending soldiers."

"Naomi, what do you think?" asked John.

"I don't have a say."

"Yes, you do. You are part of this family now," said John. "It was to your husband I swore my vow. "Surrendering wasn't part of my promise to Virgil."

"No, it sure wasn't," said Naomi. "Your promise was to keep me and my babies free. You can't do that dead. I reckon it is risky to trust the word of that General Jesup, but me and my babies can pass for Estelusti better than many Estelusti. Only one man can protect us. You. I don't like putting that responsibility on you, but that's the truth. Anything other now is about you, not about what's best for a lot of people. You asked me, so I'm telling you. I think it's just best to move on out and start over. One new start is more than many get."

"What does Susan say?" asked Mother.

"She is tired. Our children are hungry," John said. "That is what she says. That this is no life. It's nothing but mourning and worrying and fretting, being hungry and scared, pouring it out to people that don't want to listen because they're already mourned out. That is what she says."

"Listen to her."

"Perhaps it is time I stepped aside," said John. "I feel you all are against me. You no longer have faith in me to lead. What say you Little Brother? You have been silent on the matter."

"We have faith in you to lead, otherwise we would encourage your pursuit of a glorious death," I said. "Soon the Americans will chase us into the ocean and shoot us down from boats as we swim for the Bahamas. If we do not like it on the new land, we will leave. We may need to cross mountains or deserts, but the West is a huge open place. We can go where Americans cannot. Mexico is much larger than America and has no slaves. I say we thank General Jesup for the boat ride that will take us to the border."

"Ha!" laughed John. "My brother, always the smart one. I will not tell him. He will make us swim across the Gulf."

"You see, my son?" said Mother. "We are here for you. I think you know what must be done but fear the condemnation of our people."

"I do not want to make Wild Cat my enemy," John said.

"Why should he be?"

"If he believes I abandon him," said John.

"Would he be your enemy, if the roles were reversed?" said mother.

"I cannot say. Three months ago, yes," said John. "Now I do not know. I will go see him."

"What will you say to him?"

"I do not know. I will think on it."

***

Jesup and John faced each other over the desk. John's face was drawn, his eyes bloodshot. His shoulders slumped. There was no friendly banter.

"If I agree to this, you must free Virgil's family also," said John. "Unequivocally."

"I told you before. I cannot protect runaways. I don't have the authority to free a slave's family," said Jesup. "Like it or not, that's a legal personal property issue. That's been made abundantly clear to me. Not a soldiering issue."

"The man died saving my life. And he was a man. Not a slave. Not a fugitive. Not someone's property. A man. A man who died saving my life," said John. "I will die saving his family's life if that is what you choose."

"Impossible."

"You must do it, or there will never be a deal. Never. Not with me," said John. "I gave him my word. I will never stop fighting unless they are freed."

"I simply can't do it. She doesn't belong to me. Only her owners can do that."

"The MacCuaigs will certainly never free her, not with what Virgil did to them. How is it you can decree that hundreds are thrown into chains, or sold, yet you cannot free one woman and her small children?"

"I cannot, but I can plead her case. I can tell Washington this is an imperative. But the fact is, it will come down to whether her owner wants to sell or emancipate her. Not even the President of the United States can force him to if he doesn't want to. Probably only the Supreme Court of The United States, if then."

"As I expected. Well, it is fortunate we have found a better way. Naomi and her children speak our language well and can pass as Estelusti. They will hide among us on the ship. The MacCuaigs are not on your army ships. Few know what she looks like anyway. Only you would know."

"You're asking me to lie. As a commanding general of the United States Army," thundered Jesup.

"To bring peace, you ask me to bow to an unjust authority. All I ask of you is to avert your eyes," said John. "Is that worse than following orders you believe personally to be immoral, killing and enslaving black people?"

Jesup's head looked like it was ready to explode.

"There is nothing you would have to do, really. Naomi and the children speak our language. If she's discovered, you just order the Mac-Cuaigs to pretend like she's Wild Cat's property," said John. "And sign this document."

"What's this?"

"Her mortgage, and that of her children, purchased by Wild Cat from a planter from South Carolina," John said. "You witness it, here and here."

"That's an outright forgery," shouted Jesup.

"No, it's an outstanding forgery, not outright at all," said John. "Done by some of the best professionals in the business."

"Really? Who is that?"

"My mother. Trust me, these are perfect."

"Good God," Jesup said, staring, looking defeated. "There will be an awful hell to pay if Laughing Boy ever discovers it."

"There will be an awful hell to pay if any harm ever comes to her. You tell Laughing Boy MacCuaig we will raid every slave pen he has. That I will personally slit the throat of every Creek child in Florida, and this war will continue," said John, full of fury. "And I will make this personal for you to. If I must go to Virginia, I will."

"How dare you threaten my family? I should have you shot right now."

"Yet you think you can threaten mine with impunity," John said.

Long seconds passed. I expected them to leap on each other with knives, or the very air to explode from the white-hot anger that practically glowed off the men.

"I'll do it," Jesup finally sighed, staring John hard in the eye. "If that will bring this war to an end."

"Then do so," said John. "He paid for their freedom with his life."

"Very well," said Jesup.

***

I walked with John to Wild Cat's camp. We said little. John walked with the weight of another man on his back.

"We cannot go further on this journey with you, brother," said John to Wild Cat, tears streaming down his face. "I must save my family. My fire is gone. My heart is heavy. My soul is sick. All the blood we shed is wasted. Our people can mourn no more. They are empty. Try not to hold a hardness in your heart for me for too long, brother."

"Hooah. We have fought a good fight. I do not hold any ill will," said Wild Cat. "This is the land of my father, where he has died and shed blood, the land of my mother, and all my people's ancestors before me. Your father is not of this land, and your mother's people were brought here in chains. It is not the same. You must think of your children."

"Thank you, brother," said John.

"I hope you can find a land that someday your people can call their own," said Wild Cat.

The next day John and Alligator surrendered, riding Army horses and dressed in their finest clothes, gorgets and feathers. A procession of five hundred people walked behind. Two hundred were Estelusti warriors. We were the last of the Black Seminole as fighters in Florida.

About the Author

Roy V. Gaston is a native of Athens, Ohio and a graduate of Ohio University. He now resides in Columbus, Ohio. He began writing after finishing his career as a unit supervisor in Ohio's Department of Rehabilitation and Correction.

Gaston writes historically based novels about 19th Century America, focusing on the American West and the American Civil War.

His novel *Beyond the Goodnight Trail* won the 2021 Western Fictioneers Peacemaker Award for Best First Novel and was the 2021 Spur Award finalist.

His favorite genres are historical fiction, noir, hard boiled, Southern Gothic, and Westerns. He is a fan of Harry Turtledove, Clint, the Duke, Harry Flashman, Hitch and Cole, Gus and Woodrow, Hap and Leonard, Spenser and Hawk, Marty and Rusty, Gravedigger and Coffin Ed, Statler and Waldorf, Buck and Roy, Willie and Waylon, and Conspiracy Theories.

Coming Soon!

ROY V. GASTON'S

THE TRAIL OF YELLOW WOLF
PETE HORSE SERIES

Forced from his Florida home to the Western Territories during the Trail of Tears, Pete Horse has begun a family. However, the same enemies that pursued the Estelusti during the Seminole War still terrorize and try to enslave them.

A vicious raid sends Pete on a quest to return his kidnapped people and seek personal, bloody revenge on the men responsible, Chebona Bula MacCuaig, the Creek slaver, and Yellow Wolf, the renegade Comanche chief.

The trail of the marauders takes Pete into wild and lawless Texas, where his trail crosses that of Jack Hays, Texas Ranger captain, and his company of Bigfoot Wallace, Sam Walker, Ben McCulloch, Creed Taylor, and many others…

For more information
visit: www.SpeakingVolumes.us

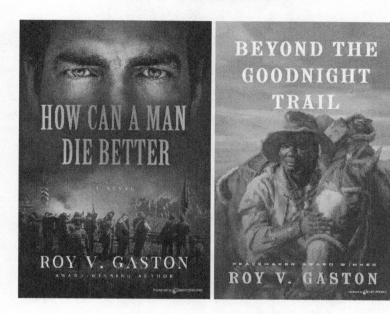

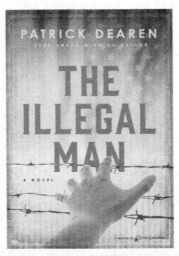
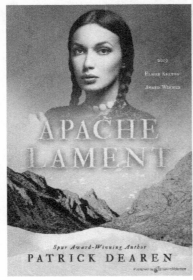
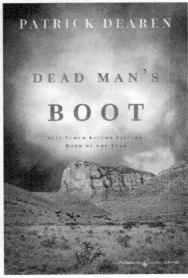

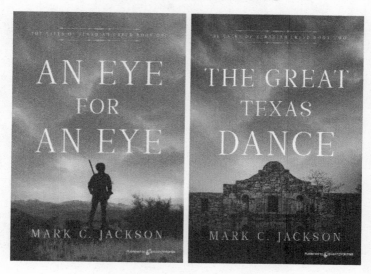

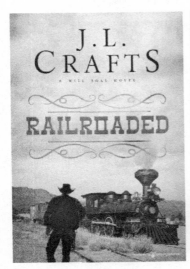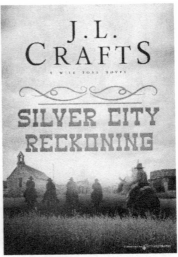

Made in the USA
Coppell, TX
19 September 2023

21703846R00184